I0748414

GHOST ECONOMY

By
Millard Crow

MODERN LOVERS PUBLISHING

The “Ghost Economy”, broadly defined, is the hidden cost associated with the stock and re-sale of used products. These costs are rarely measured by businesses, despite the overwhelming impact to their bottom line.

▲

{1}

{THE ANATOMY OF POLYGONS}

A vertex is the smallest point in three-dimensional space. Curves, lines, edges, and polygons cannot exist without a set of vertices to plot them out. They are the structure of structure. They exist without form but forms cannot exist without them. Though it's possible to create 3D models without the need to edit each polygon's individual vertices, the difference between fine vertex manipulation and quicker, more broad modeling techniques is the same difference between a painter that flicks acrylic on a night-primed canvas and one that grips a wet brush to map out each point of nocturnal light with careful precision. The results might be the same—a starry artwork in the chosen medium—but the choices made along the way determine the energy of the painting's atmosphere, the plausibility of its world, and the type of crowd it will gather around the canvas.

If, of course, the painting summons anyone at all.

{}

MAY 2015, SADDLETOWNE, 9:12 A.M.

Dust floated through the cuts of sunlight from blinds rarely opened. The man behind the counter squinted at the expiration date on Reese Gagnon's driver's license. His old eyes blurred between the smooth faced photo and the stubbly man-child in front of him. Hub caps and newspaper clippings of the attendant's tournament-winning bass catch in the 1970's lined the wall and haloed his mullet in chrome and faded print.

"This is expired, boy," the attendant's thick mustache obscured the small movement of his lips as he mumbled. The photo of his younger self pinned to the cork-board stared over his shoulder at Reese with equal indignation. Even the 95-pound bass, held in the attendant's past-hands, glared at the customer.

Reese brushed his blonde hair, fluffed and wild from a night of sleeplessness, behind his ear. He scratched at the stubble as it brushed on his knuckles, as aware of its strange contrast on his baby-face as the attendant was. "No, it expires later this month. Not yet."

They shared scrutiny. Swaddled in baggy blue sweat pants and a tank top thinned from age, Reese sunk in his ill-fitting clothes, and shrunk under the man's gaze.

"Dude," he popped the knuckles of his right hand on his hip, "I'm *moving*. I'm not gonna go to the DMV here in Saddletowne when—"

"I'm givin' ya guff," the attendant tossed Reese's license. It spun like a propeller blade and smacked against his chest. Reese's reactions, dulled by the morning hours, were far from enough to catch it. "Lemme go get the keys for your trailer. Truck's filled up right now. You're responsible for gas, so you can either fill up before you get to Dundolk or pay the difference when you arrive."

Reese only spent money on necessary things. This moving-rental company may not have been the highest rated in the state, but after an online discount, the only other cost aside from gas was a little awkward conversation with an old man. In a world where he could afford little, Reese could at least afford that.

{}

MAY 2015, SADDLETOWNE, 11:32 A.M.

The metal steps at the ends of Reese's apartment rattled violently no matter how much weight was applied to them. In the cedar-soaked hot air of Saddletowne, Reese was thankful that this was the last time he'd have to listen to the clang of rubber-on-steel—sound carried easily through the thin walls of the complex.

There was little in the way of heavy furniture to move into the bed of the trailer. Reese's whole life folded neatly into boxes—had he not lived on the fourth floor, and if his four roommates had helped him move out, he might have already been on the road, traveling down the long stretch of cedar-framed highways towards Dundolk.

"That's the last one," Ryan, the only roommate willing to help Reese move, grunted as he dropped a box of acrylic paints into the bed. He wiped a bead of sweat away from his dark skin. Both boys were skinny-fat, affable shut-ins that were only barely aware of each others existence for the year or so Ryan lived there. He was the last to move in and the last one to find out about Reese leaving. To say anyone in that apartment was close would be a lie—the only ties they shared were proximity, rent, and occasionally, an opinion on a video game.

"Awesome," Reese pulled down the metal trailer door till it slammed shut. "Thanks, man. I appreciate it."

Ryan sucked in his lips. He watched Reese round the corner of the truck, and clenched his fist.

"I'm sorry," he said.

Reese turned back around, his hand buried in his pocket. His keys rattled, tangled in the fold of his worn leather wallet.

"For what?"

"For..." Ryan waved his hands at his waist, "...this. This sucks."

"It's fine," Reese pulled a weak smile on his face, so slight that shadows failed to find his dimples, "I'm not exactly breaking anyone's heart by leaving."

They both looked up to the fourth floor of their apartment building. Ryan did so with a glance, and Reese with an eye-roll.

“I started watching your show!” Ryan spat the words out, eager to make them heard before Reese left, “I wish I had known how much time you spent on it.”

Reese blinked. In the whole time he lived there, he never heard a remark, positive or negative, about his work. He wasn’t sure why Ryan felt the need to say something, and now, of all times.

“Oh. Well, thanks,” Reese untangled his keys and unlocked the driver side door.

Ryan’s eyes lidded in thought, then he shook his head. He talked as if words could reverse the inevitable tide, “Is it really enough? Are you sure you can just... up and move like this? Just on the money from your show?”

“I’ll be fine,” Reese used the last bits of his coffee buzz to pull his cheeks back into a smile, the most he could offer for the longest conversation he had ever had with a roommate. “I have a plan. Not a great one, mind you. But, you know. You gotta take risks sometimes.”

Reese gripped the steel handle and pulled himself into the truck. He considered how silly it must’ve looked to Ryan to watch him lift his leg to his chest, to have to exert so much just to get inside a vehicle. He remembered, as he always inevitability did, that America wasn’t sized for his height, especially not its trucks. The world never has and never would fit him, and that’s fine. This step would neither be the first, nor last, reminder in his life of this fact. It was just a step, and that’s all they ever will be.

“I’ll see ya,” Ryan lifted his hand. He wanted to bring it higher into a full wave, but could only muster a single swipe at his abdomen before uncertainty weighed it down, as if he didn’t want to appear too upset at Reese’s leaving, or show too much regret at the opportunities he missed to get to know him better.

"Yeah," Reese frowned. They both knew he never would, or could, come back to Saddletowne. "See ya."

{}

MAY 2019, DUNDOLK, 5:27 P.M.

With his clean cherub face aglow in the panels of his two laptops, Reese Gagnon worked on the same 3D model for nearly three-and-a-half hours. His amber eyes, which twitched with micro-decisions in time with mouse-clicks, were colored by the swirl of artificial blues glowing from his devices. These violet waves were the only source of light to be found in the storage space, save the peeking sliver from the hallway light underneath the shutters. They terminated into the darkness of ripped cardboard box lids, hampers, and worn clothes.

Technically, it was 3.4 hours of work, if one counted the 17 minute breaks he took every 52 minutes. This was a formula for efficient work he read in a source half-remembered, one of which he wasn't sure the validity of, but still appreciated the mental focus his memory's interpretation of someone else's math seemed to keep him in. It allowed breaks long enough to stretch the legs, work sessions short enough to keep his imagination elastic. To be in a quiet place and piece together bits of digital dots till it clumped into the shape of the cartoons he saw in his mind was nearly all he wanted in life.

Despite the daily devotion to his craft, however, Reese's work was not good. "Good" in the strictest sense of execution and polish, at least; in the areas of expertise most 3D modelers would spend years fine tuning or studying, Reese either satisfied himself with superficial knowledge or intentional ignorance. A small part of this amateurism was a by-product of the fact he was self-taught. If he chose to be honest with himself, he would admit most of the weakest qualities of his creations stemmed from his own impatience. Deep within him was a vision that wouldn't wait for practice and research. He slapped digital bones and polygons together with a boorish disregard for alignment or elegance. He needed to see his work realized, and with every second wasted, he grew hungrier—not for sustenance, but for satisfaction.

3.4 hours, it's worth noting, is a drop in the bucket of what would qualify as "professional" work in the 3D modeling world. Reese knew this, and knew his work was far from professional. Though he was routinely embarrassed by his selfishness, he nonetheless owned it: his world was his, and that's all that mattered.

His life was spent behind the metal shutters of a storage unit, surrounded by scant personal belongings: bean bag chairs, baggy clothes, cardboard boxes, and plastic bins with odds and ends of all manner of color and craftiness. This was an unwise and wildly illegal life decision, and yet, he had grown to feel it was the safest place for him. He lived like a turtle, his most vulnerable parts drawn within. The turtle did this for four years, buoyed by the luck of his discovery of a storage unit he could blend into the shadows of, and the mild success of the only life skill he had any confidence in.

Reese clicked "save" and ripped the USB drive out of the laptop. He didn't check to see if it reached 100%. He jammed it into the slot of laptop #2, and threw the new creature into a test environment.

The model was a vulture-wizard of an unnatural orb shape, swaddled in poorly textured purple robes. Reese clicked on its blunt beak and dragged it around. Its dead, red-and-white eyes deformed as it wobbled across the test-light source, its brown-and-white chubby feathers blobbed around, and its star-patterned robes pulled away at strange angles that never quite matched its folds or placements.

Reese giggled a giggle tinted with pity most typically reserved for a dog that whined for pets, or for a toddler that tried to walk, and tumbled instead. "I love them. Oh my god, I love them. Their name is...

their name is..." he popped his knuckles, "their name is Wimbly. I think. Yeah."

An alarm went off on laptop #1. Another 52 minutes lost behind shutters.

Reese fished a past-generation cell-phone out of his pocket and began to look through listings of local eateries. Whenever he finished a model, he liked to reward himself with something nice: a meal, a game, a toy, anything to trick his brain into accepting the work he had done was worth the effort. More often than not, this meant Reese would go and eat at a restaurant and bury himself into the back cushions of a corner booth, bury his up-turned nose in the maillard smell of a fresh scorched burger, and fill his small mouth cheek-to-cheek with french fries.

But Reese wasn't hungry. Whether it was the march of time catching up with his work-life balance or his horrendous diet slowing his blood, Reese felt a certain drowsiness from his mid-day work. This wouldn't do: the creation of 3D models was only part of his job. He needed a jolt to get him ready for the real work later that night.

Reese changed the settings on his app (which, due to its out-of-date-model moved as slowly as he did) and looked up local coffee shops. He threw his finger like a dart and pulled up the address to Jolly Molly's Coffee Shop.

{2}

{CAFFEINATED ZEROS}

One could drive by Jolly Molly's Coffee Shop and never realize it. It was tucked away in the small corner of a miserable strip mall made of speckled brick, and only accessible from a side road obstructed by trees, unless one was willing to navigate the poorly plotted parking lot that served as a concrete moat for anyone that dared traverse its sharp turns. This terrible location made it one of the cheaper places to set up shop in Dundolk and at any other era in history would condemn it to failure regardless of how good its wares were.

Internet reviews built up goodwill for "the little coffee shop that could," and the owner, 28-year old Molly Bambi, leaned into her budding e-reputation. She created internet-only deals, sought promotional work with local venues and artists, rented out her space for concerts, and anything else that would get the name of her shop out into the world. Four years later, it proved to be a winning formula—Molly's little shop not only survived, it thrived. Customers were willing to suffer its accessibility issues for her passionate, caffeinated brews and close connection with the community.

Molly was the sole owner—she managed to start her business thanks to both the money she saved up from two concurrent jobs and an *incredibly* generous donation from her parents, a doctor and tenured teacher power couple. Even with the luck and love of her parents' support, the coffee shop wouldn't have survived without another pair of slip-resistant shoes behind the counter.

Her longtime friend, Jalen Eze, was her first and only employee. She thanked every religion's idea of god for him: Jalen hit 6'6" early in his high school days and as the years took him from teenager to adult, he filled out his lanky form with natural muscle torn from the pages of fantasy. He was an athlete, a work horse, a gym rat, and a kid that grew into the evenly proportioned, chiseled visage of the ideal man. If she propped Jalen at the counter and asked him to do nothing else but smile, he'd still boost her sales. She used him like a weapon. His smooth taupe skin and wide smile and eyebrows upturned in a permanent expression of soft concern were deployed against lines of customers as often and as ruthlessly as possible. The wildly askew female-to-male ratio of the clientele in the first few months of the "Jolly Molly" experiment was not a coincidence, but a product of this staffing decision, Molly concluded.

And Jalen knew why he stood behind the register, too.

Theirs was not a parasitic relationship. The two met in geometry class; black kids with parallel lines for lives stuck in the adolescent void of hormones and institutionalized existential dread known as 'high school.' At first, they bonded over small things: pop songs, weird comedians, their amazement that Mr. Garland never got Jalen's last name right over the course of an entire semester. (Though pronounced *Eh-zz*, he would always, no matter how often Jalen corrected him, pronounce it *Ee-zee*.) They hung out during lunch and breaks and after school and on weekends.

Molly fully understood the solid foundation of their friendship when she started to date a fellow classmate, Corey. Jalen's treatment of her did not change once they started dating, not a hint of jealously could be found in their new conversations, no lines were crossed, no feelings were betrayed. A month later, it was Jalen who punched Corey in the mouth when her (now former) boyfriend tried to force himself on her in the backroom of a house party. She knew she was safe in Jalen's orbit, but it wasn't until their senior year that she found out why.

On a dark night in an empty coffee shop on a sleepy Sunday, Jalen came out to her. He expressed the pain of passing through his entire life knowing exactly what he was and not knowing how he could tell anyone without losing them. She slapped his arm. "You're not gonna get rid of me that easily." They hugged, and cried, and built each other up. From that day onward, those parallel lines guided each other.

After their graduation, Jalen and Molly had a tendency to work at the same places at the same time, from fast food to call centers to coffee shops. When Molly opened her own cafe, Jalen happily followed along. In a world where his skin color and sexual orientation put him at risk of social isolation and unemployment, the safety of a steady job alongside his best friend was the stability he was sure he needed. Years went by, and he became comfortable in the routine of his life and fulfillment of his needs. On a particular summer afternoon, however, in a dry Dundolk heat that drove up blended coffee sales, his needs and wants came into argument.

At the end of a rush of moms and IT professionals on the prowl for one last jolt of bean juice before highway traffic became a queue, Reese Gagnon entered Jolly Molly's and stepped to the counter just as Jalen emerged from the kitchen. With the menu to the side of the glass pastry display, Reese found himself distracted by a list of gimmicky drinks and their descriptions. They moved, customer and employee, through the motions of their roles, aware of each other without eye contact.

Green Piccolo? Reese rubbed the side of his face in thought. *And it's description is just 'Piccolo Latte, but from Namek.' There's at least one nerd here. Looks like I chose the right place.*

"Let me know when you're ready," Jalen said as he placed a red pen into a half-full cup of coffee beans. The pen stayed upright in the mound of beans, like a sword stabbed into the earth.

"Sure! Sorry," Reese mulled over the menu-tower. "I won't take long."

The customer's voice caught Jalen off guard. Reese spoke light and low, with a soft bass. Jalen peered over the menu—it was normal for him to watch a customer's face and camp out with his palms on the counter until they looked towards him. It wasn't normal, however, for the rhythm of his breath to idle from what he saw.

Reese combed a stray clump of lime-coloured dyed hair back into his wheat-blonde part and revealed that the skin of his forehead, almost marshmallow from its aversion to light, had the faintest dew of sweat from the summer heat. The singular bead trickled past his deep set amber eyes, round the soft shape of his cheek, down the valley of his throat as he swallowed, and disappeared behind the thin collar of his faded t-shirt. Jalen saw the shirt's elaborate design and fonts, a world of pink and green colors that advertised what was *probably* a band. His eyes weren't burdened with the task of reading, though; they studied architecture, the structure of folds draped from Reese's petite frame, the assembly of the slight tilt in the slight curves of his slight hips that held up his complete lack of ambiguity over other people's ideas of masculinity. Jalen traced that poised silhouette into his memory.

"Okay, Sorry! I'm not sure I see it here, but I think I know what..."

Reese looked up from the menu. The trip opened his sleepy eyes wide.

Jalen towered over the counter, register, and most creatures of the earth. As if his height weren't enough to hold the eyes hostage, he wore red-and-silver dyed locs tied into a neat bun behind his head that lifted him that much closer to heaven. As if the crafted spheres of his deltoids that struggled to stay in his uniform's sleeves weren't enough to pin Reese down, his hands, large and sculpted from rigorous use, drew with gentle patience across the glossy countertop to remind him of their presence. As if his full lips weren't enough to hypnotize Reese in place, they parted, a cracked window to his glossy-white teeth, and exhaled a breeze that carried with it the faintest permission to continue the male gaze.

When their eyes met, they knew, instinctively, that they had let themselves wander.

"...I want." Reese's statement started with innocent consumerist intent and finished with meaning the free market could not regulate. Jalen's upturned eyebrows rose with curiosity.

"Let's hear it," he said.

"Sorry. This might annoy you."

"I doubt it."

One of Reese's sneakers squeaked as his foot pivoted inward.

"I don't think I remember the name..." Reese's eyes averted from Jalen and parked at the register's digital display. It told him he currently owed zero dollars to the store, and he thought that zero was also the chance he had of getting to admire Jalen's face and form for any longer amount of time without coming off like a creep. "It's, uh... I saw a picture on your site. I think it's a scoop of ice cream that climbed in a cup and took an espresso-shower..."

Jalen squinted, tilted his head, and suppressed a smirk as the cartoonish description animated in his mind.

"That's an affogato. Molly named it the 'Ah Gotchu,' and it uses mint-chocolate ice cream," Jalen smiled and shook his head, "You don't have to call it that, though. We've got vanilla, too, if you'd like. That's how it's normally served."

"Affogato," Reese repeated. He wagged his fingers towards the floor as if he typed the word into his mind, "*but-I-won't-forgett-o*."

Both men lowered their heads to hide embarrassing smiles. Their cheek muscles betrayed them. Reese combed back the lime-strands, and only then understood that he had been given a choice.

"Ah! Surprise me," he paid.

Jalen pushed his tongue briefly into his cheek. "Gimmie a second," he floated away to the kitchen, which left Reese alone at the counter.

By this point, the usual rush hour patrons had left to join the conga line of cars on the highway. Reese studied the odd trinkets on the wall, pop vinyl albums, wrestling posters, and a high school fencing trophy in the shape of a gold foil. Below the trophy, in a corner booth far in the back, was "Jolly" Molly herself. She kept her head down and wrote on a clipboard, her smooth, black straightened hair tied into a ponytail. Her pen scrawled at a workman's pace; Reese deduced that this was the manager, and reminded himself that he was in public.

Even if there's only one other person here, I shouldn't press anymore, he thought. *It doesn't matter how handsome he is. He's at work. Don't bother people at work, Reese. Besides, I could be misreading him. He could just be* really *nice, and* really *not-gay. There's a hundred thousand ways this can go wrong. It doesn't have to be anything more than him being a sweet, sweet man.*

Jalen returned with his hands latched to the sides of a saucer. Biceps and traps of a bruiser's size, and here they were, employed to scoot a dainty cup to a dainty lad. Reese took the cup handle and saucer with much clumsier grace.

Drizzled in caramel syrup and shaved chocolate, a scoop of vanilla ice cream sat in the cup and held the smallest, most polished silver spoon in Dundolk. None of its toppings were in the picture Reese remembered from online, and the heat from the espresso had already started to melt the ingredients and thicken into a slurry. When Reese looked up from the saucer, Jalen made direct eye contact with him, and his smile showed a hint of his teeth. He looked proud of what he had made.

"Thank you, it looks awesome," Reese, rosy-cheeked, took the saucer and slunk to a window seat.

Jalen attended to some light but necessary counter cleaning, simple tasks that kept him within view. And in that view, one he found himself addicted to, Reese was porcelain, and he shimmered with the fading summer light that streaked through the window.

Okay, okay, Reese thought as he burned with indecision. Every sip was sweet beyond its individual ingredients, and the heat of the espresso raised his body temperature and wound his mind. *That had to have been flirting. I'm... awful at picking up stuff like this. So if I felt it... it probably would've been obvious to anyone else.*

Reese heard the rumble of small wheels as they rolled over tile. He looked up to see Jalen in the midst of mopping the far end of the restaurant. He swore he could sense Jalen's gaze, but each time he looked up to catch it, the coffee clerk's vision was locked to the floor, elusive, agile, clever.

Oh, god. There's no way. There's no way! He's way too hot to be flirting with me, Reese shook. *What the fuck is wrong with me?*

Near the end of his drink, Reese lifted the cup and heard a crinkle. He realized that there was a small sheet of paper stuck to the bottom. His left hand removed the scrap and, though it had been slightly warped from collected moisture, its contents were quite clear.

In red-ink, he found a phone number and a short sentence: *The next one's on me.*

Reese fumbled the cup handle, and it clanked against his plate and silverware.

This is really happening, his eyes dilated.

Reese's fingers drummed across the table with a pace that could have started a fire. He checked the time on his phone, huffed through his nose, took one last look at Jalen, and bolted out the door. The electronic chime failed to keep up with him, and Jalen was disappointed to find no new phone numbers appeared in his text messages.

{3}

{THUNDER VULTURE SKELETON KNIGHT}

About an hour later, Jolly Molly's two employees began their routine closing procedures. Jalen had set his phone on the chrome lid of a drop-in freezer, and from its small speaker oozed the glaze of Frank Ocean's music into the empty restaurant atmosphere. His phone buzzed as he wrapped the yellow plastic tabs of a full trash bag, and he could make out the shape of a text-message notification over Frank Ocean's face before it retreated into the menus.

Jalen read the text as he dragged trash out to the dumpster:

Sorry for the wait. I didn't want to text and drive, it read. *Also, I'm a coward.*

He snorted.

And I wanted to think about how to respond. Never had the coffee guy hit on me before.

Jalen tossed the trash-bag into the metal mouth and continued to thumb through the messages. "Oh, there's... a couple of these."

My name is Reese. I'll cut to the chase. You're handsome as hell, built like a boxer, and the affogato was great. I remembered.

"Like a boxer, huh?" Jalen clicked his tongue. The simile wasn't far from wrong. He strolled away from the dumpster and back through the kitchen door.

"I wondered why I couldn't hear Lonny anymore," Molly flipped through some receipts on a clipboard when she breezed past Jalen.

I don't know anything else about you. I want to change that. But it wouldn't be fair of me to ask you out without being honest. If this is serious...

Jalen wrinkled his brow. "Hey, Molly."

Molly peaked out from around the corner. "What's up?"

Jalen brought both hands to his phone and traced the messages with his finger. "Come here. That customer texted me back."

"The guy you flirted with *on the clock*?" Molly snickered. Her slip-resistant shoes shuffled towards Jalen. "Didn't know you had a thing for doughy white boys."

"I mean, I guess I don't, normally," Jalen's nervous laugh shook his head to the side as if Molly hit him in the jaw. Over the years, she had borne witness to the men Jalen had dated, men of impressive size and masculinity. She had noted to him more than once that every new catch was bigger, thicker, more muscular than the last, and in each relationship, Jalen seemed to spend an inverse amount of time with them, to the point where he seemed destined for one-night stands. "But he... I dunno. He just described his drink to me without knowing its name. Most roundabout description he could've given me."

"That stuff irritates you, doesn't it?"

"Yeah, but..." Jalen leaned on the counter and let his eyes roll across the kitchen tile. "I knew what he wanted. He smiled like I gave him a compliment," he glanced back to the text messages.

If this isn't a prank, you should watch this at around 7, if you can. It'll be there if you have to miss it. You're at work. I understand.

"He sent me some weird link. It's a video. Wait, no, it's a stream. It's about to go live."

Molly craned her head around Jalen's bicep and peeked at his phone. She scrunched her face in disapproval when she realized the stream was on a popular gaming site.

"He's a gamer," she poked him in the ribs. "Abandon ship. He can't please you."

"You're wrong for that," Jalen laughed and twisted away from the jabs. He swam through his apps to see Reese's final text:

This is who I am.

Jalen stared at those five isolated words, a lightning rod of clarity in the middle of a nervous text storm.

"Well," Molly shrugged, "It's almost 7. No one's here. We're about to close. Let's watch him embarrass himself on the internet."

Jalen propped his phone up on the register and idled in Reese's stream chat room as he left to wipe down lobby booths.

{}

Reese downed an entire bottle of water in one continuous gulp, cleared his airway with a loud exhale, and sat down in his computer chair. The green screen was positioned correctly, his box-lights were aligned, his microphone levels were perfect, and he was scared as hell.

"If he's there..." Reese gripped the cool black mouse a little harder than normal, "...he's there. I won't be any different."

He clicked.

"Here we go."

{}

A trumpet blared through Jalen's speaker. The sudden brass stab alarmed both coffee employees.

"What the fuck?" Molly laughed. "It's so *loud*."

Jalen stepped over the counter with a swing of his legs, like a tall wrestler over the top rope of a ring. Molly smacked him with a towel she kept tied around her apron.

"Don't do that," she took as serious a tone as she could manage with her best friend, "you're gonna clean the counter again. Walk around like a normal person next time."

Reese's stream started with a title card of dense drawings, cartoon creatures of all manner of distorted shape and form. They were detailed enough with crosshatch line and pores to appear unnerving despite their simplified shapes, and bright and diverse enough in palette to clash and contrast into a pool of assaulting color. Buried somewhere in the mush of creatures was the logo of the show: *SKELEVENTURE*. The letters squirmed and pulsed.

"Damn," Jalen blinked. "He made all that?"

The neon cartoons exploded in a visceral mess of blue and green guts. Their goo splashed onto the virtual screen and melted down to reveal Reese, lit in black-light, his white skin blue, his blonde-and-green hair fluorescent in the center of the digital chaos. Animated stars shot behind him on the fake-sky he existed in.

"Hello, chat-" Reese's low-tone was amplified by his close proximity to the microphone. The bass of his voice was drawn out in post-processing echoes, and made him sound far more sinister than he ever could have managed in real life. A sample of a syrupy acoustic guitar strummed, and with it, a message appeared on the stream that read:

GhoulishGeorge156 donated $5!
"HI DADDY"

An animated toaster with glowing eyes bounced above the message, and it spat out 3D dollar signs in celebration.

"Shh!" Reese's eyes lit up and he clawed at the computer mouse. "I mean, thank you, but I haven't done anything yet! Behave!"

"That was fast," Jalen boggled.

"I know no one is callin' this scrawny thing a 'Daddy,'" Molly seemed offended at the donation. "Lemme see somethin'..."

She took Jalen's phone, attacked with her fingertip through menus, and retched at what she saw. "Oh my god."

"What's up?" Jalen asked.

She showed Jalen the stream's viewer count: 200 people were tuned in. The number rapidly climbed by another 10-15 people every few seconds. Jalen covered his mouth.

“Okay, sorry, but I gotta mute notifications for a little bit,” Reese dodged bouncing messages for all manner of donations and subscriptions. “Thank you guys, I’ll read em’ all aloud, but I have to show you something first. I’ve got my serious voice and everything. As you know, we left off when Sir Mortimer got zapped by a thunderbolt.”

A skeleton-faced knight with a mustache was brought into frame. Sir Mortimer the skeleton was covered in cartoon scuffs and ashes that puffed off his stubby body. The chat filled with messages of joy at the knight’s appearance, and sorrow at his electric fate.

“I wanted to reveal the thunder-tossin’ thug today. I could have done this in the story itself, but I know a lot of you follow along for the behind-the-scenes wonk, so here they are! Let me present to you... Wimbly!”

Dragged by mouse pointer, a bi-pedal vulture of child-like proportions appeared on the stream. Its limbs and frame wobbled like gelatin.

“I didn’t have time to give them bones,” Reese echo-giggled while he dragged Wimbly around the screen. His self-deprecation tinted his amusement. “They have no *bones*, chat. Look at this absolute lack of bones. Who did this?” He jerked the floppy vulture mage up and down with each word.

TyrantTyrant donated $1!
"WHO TOOK THE BONES?????"

“Great question!” Reese threw his hands in the air. “We gotta find ‘em.”

“I am getting a contact high from this,” Molly rubbed the temples of her forehead. “This is *really* annoying.”

She expected to look at Jalen and see an expression that shared her sentiment, but his mouth was hidden behind the mitt of his hand. His eyes, unblinking, were bolted to the stream; they micro-adjusted with each new detail within the frame. She couldn't tell if he heard her.

"So! Let's talk about bones," Reese plopped Wimbly down, and its form—beak, hat, feathers and all—congealed into a digital lump on the video player window. "'Bones are the basis for animation in 3D rigs. You don't necessarily have to have bones for animating stuff in 3D and this was probably avoidable. My... lazy... process in this particular program makes anything that doesn't use bones behave like cloth, which looks fine for cartoon hats and stuff but not for, you know, whole bodies. No one's ever accused me of doing things right, I guess. Wimbly's weird movement is just the result of the program's attempt to interpret this bad model I made."

"It's a puppet show," Jalen whispered.

Molly raised her eyebrows. "What?"

"He makes puppet shows with 3D models."

"So now you know how Wimbly got so floppy," Reese stroked some keys and pulled himself out of the shot. "For any of you aspiring animators out there, let this be a lesson: give bones to your friends. Or, not, I guess, because boneless Wimbly gave me an idea. Mistakes are only mistakes if you can't give them a reason for existence."

"And he interacts with the chat at the same time," Jalen shifted. "It's silly, but I would've never thought he was this charismatic in person. He's put work into this."

"That he didn't finish," Molly pointed out.

Reese wiggled Sir Mortimer, the mustached skeleton, around by the mouse-pointer. Charred bits shook off his form and his cleaned, bony face smiled with big cartoon sparkles. The skeleton-hero had a permanent smile, of course, one no amount of thunderbolts could ever wipe-off.

"It's cute," Jalen tapped his chin.

Molly clicked her tongue against the roof of her mouth in disagreement.

"So why *did* Wimbly strike Sir Mortimer?" Reese's disembodied voice asked, swaddled in echoes and bass.

"Well I'm glad you like it," Molly said.

"Because they need..." Reese inhaled.

"You can finish watching it later after we lockup," Molly grabbed Jalen's phone.

"BONES!" Reese laughed maniacally as stock thunder shook the speakers. He threw the floppy vulture across the screen at Sir Mortimer. The two 3D models collided with the force of squeaky toy hammers.

Jalen tried to snatch his phone back. Molly closed the app.

"Aw, come on," Jalen pouted.

"He said there's an archive of it, right?" Molly handed it back to her employee. "You can flirt with the dough-nerd on your own time. Come on, we're almost finished."

Jalen frowned and resumed the last of his closing duties. Between the stacking and clacking of plates and cups, he found a moment when Molly was out of sight, and used it to open the stream again. He lowered the sound to a whisper and made a donation:

XCoffeeDropX donated $10!
"Bones don't mix with coffee!"

Reese, in the middle of serious, deep-throated narration, stumbled when he read the message. "Maybe not," he said with a softness and relief the post-processing couldn't mask, "but I bet I can work the two topics into the same conversation."

Jalen's shoulders drew inwards with his smile. He slipped the phone back into his pocket.

{4}

{THE ART OF SELLING}

Matteo Bianchi took a swig of water. He liked to suck on the swirled tip of polyethylene to the point that the plastic walls of the bottle would crinkle in submission. He did this to get his class's attention, and to break the lethargy that naturally sets in with physical and mental stress.

"To close out today, I'm gonna teach you the flat-back bump," he screwed the white cap back on and tossed the bottle out over the top rope of the wrestling ring. It landed on his large gym bag and nestled into the nylon.

He sauntered into the center of the ring. Suddenly, as if a ghost socked him in the jaw, he rocked backwards, his legs in the air as he crumbled onto the mat. He remained there for long enough to give the impression that he was stunned, then sprung back to life; his legs helicoptered and whisked him back to his feet with dexterity that defied the intense pain in his 56-year-old hips. A younger version of himself could do this trick without painkillers. He hoped his class, after this lesson, would be able to as well.

"What you want to do when you take a back bump is..." Matteo combed back strands of his thinning black hair, "you want to land on your upper back. You don't want to hit your lower back or your mid-back. The impact needs to be around the shoulders. The real trick is to not timber back. The best way to do this is to jump forward. If you timber, you might get whiplash. Jalen, get over here."

Jalen's gray-and-red topknot poked out from behind a mountain of cameras and computer monitors. This being his fourth year with Matteo's promotion, he was accustomed to sudden summons. Despite this, his head-space was stuffed in the memory of Reese's stream from a few hours prior, and the rest of his mental faculties were dedicated to the organization of promos he filmed with wrestlers from the Dundolk East Federation. When Jalen rose up at the sound of his name, his pursed-lip surprise was genuine.

Four years of being called on made the trot to the ring routine for the coffee-fueled athlete. Once he passed through the ropes, Matteo's nod to Jalen was imperceptible to anyone outside the industry. They locked eyes, then Matteo barreled into Jalen's chest with a forearm clothesline and knocked him down. Afterwards, Matteo leaned on a taped rope and pointed down at Jalen, who remained frozen on the canvas.

"Look at Jalen's form," Matteo guided the eyes of the 15 sweaty, exhausted men and women to stare at the downed barista. "Look at the hand position. You're gonna slap the mat as hard as you can, palms down flat. As you slap, your chin is going to tuck to your chest. You don't want your feet on the floor, you don't want to *even come close* to accidentally landing on your feet, that's an easy way to hit your heel, or your ankle, and break bones. As you fall, throw your feet up in the air. I want you all to look like a cartoon that slipped on a banana peel. This isn't just selling damage from the move, it's safety. Slap harder than you want the first time you do it. This spreads out the impact and reduces the risk of injury. Jalen?"

Jalen kipped back to his feet.

"Again."

Jalen's gazelle-like legs slipped out in front of him and he landed flat on his upper back, curled like a dead bug, palms glued to the canvas. It was the exact same impact he took from Matteo's clothesline, sans any visible attack.

Matteo rubbed the thick stubble on his cheek. "This is probably the most complicated bump we've covered thus far, but it takes bits and pieces of everything else we've looked at. All of these little bits, when pieced together, are an integral part of match storytelling, and they make that fight both believable and as safe as possible. This is important, because your body is not meant to do this naturally. Jalen?"

Jalen rolled forward to his feet.

"If Jalen can make it look like this elderly Italian man can knock down a tall, fit warrior like him," Matteo slapped Jalen's shoulder, "then imagine what you kids can do with it as you improve."

{}

Every week after his shift at Jolly Molly's, Jalen transitioned from coffee to clotheslines. Over the years, the sound of bodies bumping into mats and canvas had become white noise. If it wasn't the sound of Matteo calling his name, he could tune it out. Matteo Bianchi could always cut through the noise.

Mr. Bianchi, who's primary income came from a small car wash, had started the DEF (or Dundolk East Federation—he liked that DEF could be read as short for "Defense") years ago as a way to generate enough of a secondary income to pay off his family's home and to send his son Daniel to college. A younger Matteo wrestled for side money at the type of small-time indie promotions which inspired the DEF's existence. He figured management of a local promotion would be no problem between what he learned from his own business and his knowledge as a former wrestler. He was wrong, in all of the ways a man can be wrong when he applies old logic to new times.

In the age of the internet and in an industry dominated by one worldwide monolithic company, the DEF's local-focused product struggled to attract spectators or interest. Despite Matteo's low expectations, the DEF's first two years failed to turn a profit. Still,

Matteo didn't give up. When he needed money in his youth, wrestling helped him, and he wanted to do the same for those in his employ. Matteo promoted his entertainment like his car-wash and could not figure out why his laser focus on hard work and determination worked for one business and not the other.

Jalen had been referred to Matteo through his friend, a local high school P.E. teacher, as a potential wrestler for the promotion. The recommendation came around the same time he had started to give wrestling lessons to make up for the lost costs of the DEF. Jalen, according to Matteo's friend, was a talented wrestler in his freshman year who got sidelined by a rotator cuff injury. Tall, built, handsome, fresh out of high school, Matteo met with Jalen for a job interview on a humid, dusty evening. Matteo was certain this was a face that could bring in a younger audience, and a body that would cause the wives and girlfriends dragged to his shows to cheer. He looked at Jalen and saw ticket sales.

They were behind the building of Matteo's closed car-wash. Mosquitoes buzzed against parking lot lights that drooped and eavesdropped on their conversation. Red bulbs of the "exit" sign flickered on Jalen's dark skin. He handed the older man a folder. Matteo looked at its contents—diagrams and marketing strategies—then back at Jalen.

"What the fuck is this?" Mr. Bianchi's mustache twitched.

"These are my ideas on how you could up attendance for DEF shows without spending that much money."

"You *do* realize I want you to be a wrestler, right?"

"Yeah, but," Jalen's wide chest filled with the electric air between them, "I don't."

Matteo looked Jalen up and down with disdain. It took his eyes a long time to map the wasted potential of his height and musculature.

“So let me get this straight,” Matteo’s eyelid twitched as he lit a cigarette. “You found out your P.E. teacher had an in with a wrestling promoter, you twisted the conversation enough to get him to recommend you to me so you can meet me here, in the dark, behind a small town car wash, to hand me a folder full of charts and essays on how to run my business?”

“Well, not to run your business,” Jalen wasn’t phased by the rising intensity of Matteo’s voice, “just the advertising part.”

Matteo tilted his head. Smoke billowed out his pursed lips.

“You got a degree?”

“No.”

“You got a job at all?”

“Yeah.”

Matteo’s eyes narrowed with thought while he took another drag. “You work nights?”

“No. I work at a friend’s coffee shop, so we’re done by the evening. ”

Matteo took another glance down at the paragraphs of formatted propositions in front of him, slapped the folder shut, and tucked it under his arm. His star-spangled polyester jacket rustled.

“For one month, every Wednesday, you’ll be here working for me on this. I’m gonna pay you $3 an hour under the table. I have a show at the YMCA on the first of next month. If your ideas get me a 10% larger buy-in than usual, I’ll consider hiring you like an actual employee. 50% higher or more and I’ll guarantee a position for you, permanently.”

“Alright. What time?”

Matteo’s cigarette hand shook. The offer he made was intended as a threat; it was a deal so bad Jalen wouldn’t accept it unless he was either that desperate for money, or he believed that much in what he wanted to do. He craned his head to look up at the gladiator in front of him, and was taken in by his soft features, the gentle curve of seriousness and calm around his eyebrows, a thought-burdened face pasted on a carved mantle.

"Just let me know when you're free," Matteo said. They shook hands.

Jalen filmed promos with DEF wrestlers and uploaded them to the internet, and encouraged the talent to be as weird and wild as possible. He made Matteo do radio and TV commercials for his new wrestling school, even if it stretched the definition of "school" since lessons were done in a ring he constructed in his backyard. He partnered with local bands and name dropped the DEF to coffee patrons. Jalen's strategy doubled attendance at the next show, and he became Matteo's right hand man, and his apprentice. Jalen seemed content with that.

Matteo wasn't.

{}

"So, it's that time," Mr. Bianchi plopped into a rolling chair and glided over to Jalen's cubicle of computers. In Matteo's gym—the DEF was successful enough to purchase a dedicated gym for the school last year. Jalen had commandeered a corner as his own office, and in it sat: three monitors, two tables, a waste basket, a white board, and a locked filing cabinet with his cameras. Matteo offered for Jalen to work in his office, but Jalen preferred to work in the gym. This suited Mr. Bianchi fine, since it allowed him to call on Jalen at any time he needed.

"Our yearly ritual," Jalen's gaze didn't break from the monitor. He cut and spliced clips of a burly luchador screaming into a camera.

"You have taken every class I have, and you have a real scholastic wrestling background, and you've come up with some of the gimmicks on the current roster," Matteo frowned. Within the first year of Jalen's employment, Matteo incorporated him into the wrestling school lessons as an attempt to stir something within him. Jalen took any bump any amount of times Matteo needed him to. This never tricked Jalen into pursuit of a ring-role, though.

"Speaking of gimmicks," Jalen straightened his back. He pushed himself towards another monitor and brought up a spreadsheet. "Where's Sir Pierre? This guy hasn't recorded a new promo in a while, but you have him booked on the next show. Do I need to call him?"

"And this is where you deflect," Matteo leaned his elbows on the table.

Jalen leaned back in his chair. "Yeah, but, I mean, I'm serious. I do need him to record a promo if he's going to be on the card."

Matteo matched Jalen's posture and tossed back into his own swivel chair, the gentle glide of his body bumped the leathery back into the wall. He fished out a cigarette and stuck it to his bottom lip. "I'm not going to pry too hard into why you won't get in a ring for me. I'm not keen on being a broken record."

"That'll make this the shortest version of our battle we've ever had," Jalen laughed. He let the tips of his sneakers push his own chair into the wall to meet Matteo.

"You're not gonna get any younger, Jalen. It's not like you're not in shape, and it's not like you don't love the business," Matteo puffed the smoke of his frustration. "I can't believe you're satisfied behind a desk, and behind this desk, in particular. You outgrew my outlaw show a long time ago. You have to grow someday. You have to move up, and the only way you'll do that is if you take control—"

"I'm doing fine," Jalen pushed the limits of his smile. His voice was low, barely above the hum of the computer's fans. "You need to stop worrying about me."

"Alright," the DEF's owner sighed and forced himself up with slow enough patience to placate his hip bones, which were still angry at his flat-back bump earlier. As he rounded the corner of Jalen's desk, he pivoted. "I'll call Sir Pierre and get him in here. I'll get it sorted out."

"Soon, hopefully," Jalen scratched behind his ear. "Need it up in a week, at best."

"Alright, alright, *boss*," Mr. Bianchi sneered and slapped the side of the table. Jalen smirked.

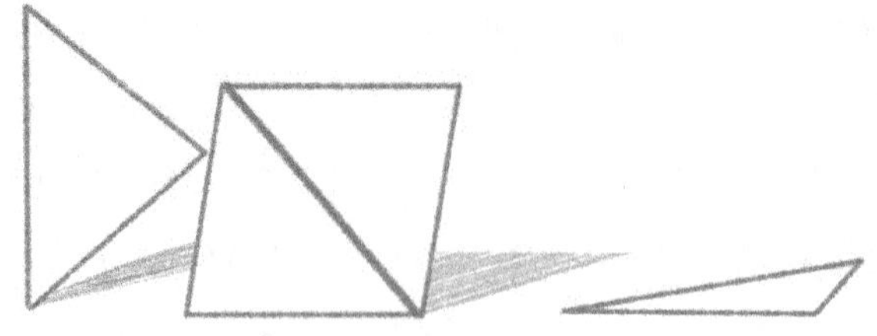

{5}

{THIS PARTICULAR MENU}

For someone with no real home, it was a dangerous life decision for Reese to run his puppet stream out of Store-It's facilities. The risk of getting caught could mean the end of the project he based his life around, both monetarily and emotionally.

Every decision he made had to have a cover that complied with the rules of his unit. He wasn't "doing work" because you're not allowed to work out of a storage unit; that's what office spaces are for. Instead, he was "storing art," which justified his frequent transportation of colorful props and green screens, or "taking inventory," which justified the need of his laptops and the (technically) correct description of himself as an online business. The lean on art also allowed him to have a space with climate control—after all, you wouldn't want to damage an oil painting with excessive heat. He didn't paint in oil, of course. He didn't paint at all. But he might. Someday.

Reese knew he wasn't the first person to ever dream of taking advantage of a storage unit's cheap rent, and did an academic amount of research to learn from other people's mistakes to protect himself. He learned the routes and times of security's golf cart patrols, and scheduled his streams around them. He spent as much time as he could outside of the unit. His days drifted between free Wi-Fi spots in the city. He rarely ate in the unit, and instead treated grocery stores like restaurants. He always showered at the cheapest gym in town, and when he returned "home" to rest, he folded his small frame into a sleeping bag that could disappear under his work table. Reese was a ghost that haunted no one but himself.

Tonight, he haunted himself with thoughts of Jalen while he squirmed his way into the small crevice reserved for his sleeping bag. On the back of his eyelids he saw Jalen's face, handsome and carved and out of reach, yet still pointed in one direction, towards...

"Me," Reese whispered in disbelief as he zipped the nylon over his face.

That Jalen seemed neither turned off by Reese's frame or voice or mannerisms, nor was he scared away by his art, the centerpiece of the strangest parts of his mind put on display for the world to consume, seemed too good to be true. Reese wasn't cowardly enough to turn tail—he knew he had to make another stop to Jolly Molly's and follow up. But he had never been in this position before, on the precipice of a new connection outside of the context of his work. Sleep eventually came to him, but through great difficulty—his mind buzzed with chemical processes of worry and excitement far beyond the capabilities of coffee.

{}

The whirr of the security golf cart shook the shutter of his unit. Reese's eyes bolted open in routine response—this patrol was the first one of a new day. He inhaled, stretched with pain and release as the upper part of his spine popped in-between squeezed shoulder blades. He then made the most terrifying decision he had made in years: he was going to alter his daily routine.

He changed into his standby casual clothes—whatever band t-shirt and jeans he could fish out in the near darkness of his unit—slung his backpack over his shoulder, and quietly slipped out the door. With his phone he ordered a ride-share to meet him at the entrance of the street, far enough away from Store-It to be out of sight of security, and close enough he could walk to it without a coat of summer sweat.

Reese's typical daily drift was centered on a specific set of roads downtown that allowed him to maximize work-and-walk time. This new path laid before him was not quite so convenient: his feet met much longer stretches of road, with more meaningful destinations. At a big-box grocer, he picked up the cheapest cologne he could afford. At a clothing store, he bought new shoes to replace the smudged, torn sneakers that had accompanied him for years. In a restaurant bathroom, he plucked a hair too close to the middle of his brow he'd never noticed before, and prayed that no one else ever noticed it, either. While he buried himself in the corner of a small diner, the sculpture process of his 3D modeling swelled his chest with pride and purpose.

Finally, during the after-rush hours, his journey brought him back to the entrance of Jolly Molly's Coffee Shop.

{}

The earthy aroma of coffee, the varnish of jazz-rap over the speakers, the glisten of chrome surfaces, the whole world parted for Reese and guided him to the register. Jalen watched his stride with a smile.

I'm gonna do it, Reese thought to himself. *I'm gonna ask him out.*

His new sneakers, pristine red-and-white, tapped with his hesitant steps.

I'm not scared, he lied. He reached the counter, and lost himself in Jalen's almond eyes and quizzical expression, *Just do it. Say, "Hey, I'm glad you could stop by the stream. I was wondering if you were doing anything after work?" Use your dumb mouth to make your dumb sounds.*

But, no words came. Gravity welled in his heels and toes, as if his new shoes wanted to betray him and pull him out of the cafe and fling him straight into oncoming traffic.

No, no, no, no, Reese panicked, *I didn't come all this way to clam up. I'm here. I bought new shoes. I cleaned myself up. Oh god. It was never gonna be that simple, was it? I'm so dumb, I'm so-*

"I'm glad you came back," Jalen said. "I think you're right. Let's talk coffee and bones."

"I'd have to think," Reese auto-piloted, "you're probably pretty used to coffee. It feels weird to ask you to 'have a coffee sometime.'"

"How about pizza?"

"No one has ever said 'no' to pizza before," Reese operated on fumes. Adrenaline carried his words out of his mouth despite his mind's protest. "No one I *trust* at least."

Jalen smirked. "Pizza it is, then. Where do you want to go?"

"Oh, uh," Reese bobbled, "I hate to admit this, but I don't know too many places off the top of my head-"

Why didn't I look up date-spots before I came out?! Reese screamed in his mind. *What is WRONG with me?*

"Well, I personally love Pizzapolis over on 6th street. I'm busy tonight after work, but I'm off tomorrow. How's 1 p.m. sound? Pizza and chattin'. Maybe we can roam 6th street afterwards if you've got the time."

"Sounds great!" Reese felt his brain slip and slide around in his head. He spent his whole day in preparation, and he was the one swept away, instead.

"Great," Jalen said. "So that's tomorrow. What can I get you today?"

Reese blanked. "I'm sorry?"

"Well, this is a coffee shop. I assume you wanted something to drink," Jalen rested his forearms on the counter and leaned down. He brought his face close to Reese's and whispered, "Truth be told, I'm not on this particular menu, and Molly will yell at me if I don't sell you something. If you came all this way just to see me, though, then that's adorable as fuck."

Reese's voice cracked. "Affogato. That's the name, right?"

Jalen grinned, rolled his broad shoulders, and tapped in the order. "You got it."

Jalen withdrew to make his specialty. Reese looked at the register's digital display. It read zero, the percent chance he previously thought he had of going out with this titan. Now, it was the cost of his drink. It was the amount of doubt he had in Jalen's interests. It was the amount of fear he should've had all along. It was the most positive zero he'd ever seen in his life.

Reese's coffee crush emerged. Clutched between Jalen's mitts was a small saucer that contained the day's freestyle: chocolate ice cream, whipped cream, espresso, and an almond biscotti overly eager to absorb the liquid.

"Oh, this is too much," Reese held a pale hand over his flushed face.

Jalen laughed. "I'm not gonna get in trouble. Just go enjoy it."

"Yes, he will," Molly yelled from the back.

"I'm paying for it," Jalen yelled back.

"No, he won't," Molly loudly corrected herself.

"Molly's my best friend," Jalen pushed the cup into Reese's hands. "If you can handle some light sarcasm, you can handle her. She *does* want me to keep flirting on the clock to a minimum, though. You go enjoy this, enjoy your night, and I'll text you the Pizzapolis address for tomorrow, okay?"

The aroma of the chocolate and coffee's dance smothered around Reese's reddened cheeks. "I look forward to it."

Reese took the cup away from the register. Jalen reached into his pocket to pull out his wallet and pay for the order, and noticed the register read the cost of the item as $0. Jalen didn't know how to perform a manual override—only Molly did—so he stared at the number with confusion.

"Huh," he muttered to himself, "I guess she did that while I was in the back. Weird..."

Reese buried himself near the window of Jolly Molly's. The evening light dimmed over the saucer. He wondered if there was a drink any sweeter than the one pressed to his lips.

His phone buzzed. He blasted through his lock screen in anticipation of the pizza parlor's address, but was surprised to see the notification was from his business email. It was an offer, a contract for work, a rare opportunity of monetarily beneficial collaboration.

Reese's drink soured. His stomach churned when he pored over details and jargon. The taste in his mouth, so sweet and dreamy, corroded into reality. This was always Reese's reaction to commissions, collaborations, "professional" work that offered so little and so much at the same time.

Mercifully, he was near the end of his drink anyway, so he finished the last few sips out of politeness. It wasn't Jalen's fault, after all, that the taste was knocked out of his mouth.

It's mine, Reese inhaled, closed his eyes, and deleted the email. He knew where the icon was on his phone without looking. *It's my world. I can't make yours. Only mine.*

After he finished his drink, he looked around the restaurant. Jalen sprayed cleaner on tables and pushed his biceps into each long, slow swirl across the surface. Molly stood behind him with a clipboard. He caught Jalen's eyes drifting over to him, and Reese waved his fingertips sheepishly before he slipped out.

...how on Earth is he in it?

{6}

{PROMOS AND VIDEOS}

"Two days in a row, huh?" Sean ran a fine-toothed comb through his greased-back hair. "He's paying you overtime, I hope."

Jalen and Sean were in a side hallway of DEF's gym that struggled to maintain electricity. These nooks and the rooms they hooked to were rarely used for anything other than storage for a simple reason: unless it was during the day or you had a portable light, you probably couldn't navigate the path on your own due to its darkness.

"I'm practically becoming a regular," Jalen muttered as he glued his vision to the rubber eye-cup of the camera's viewfinder. He tweaked knobs and buttons. Sean's roman nose and sweaty pores came into focus. The chiseled heel smirked in the camera frame.

"I'm sorry I had to make you come in again. I got wrapped up in work. You know how it is."

"Yeah, yeah," Jalen adjusted his makeshift par-can light, which ran off a portable battery he dragged into the hallway. "Don't think about that. Think about this promo."

"I'm ready when you are," Sean practiced scrunching his face in disdain.

Jalen looked back into the viewfinder one more time. Sir Pierre, the sadistic aristocrat "heel"—or villain—of the DEF, was framed ominously with a light from below, greened by the natural darkness of the hallway. In frame, it took on the presence of an abandoned hospital, or an alleyway, or the nondescript void of darkness that all villains seem to drift to in their most sinister moments.

Jalen pointed. Sean morphed into the heel this environment was made for. He tilted his head down; shadows twisted round the bridge of his nose and crushed brow, and framed his sneer.

"You broke my jaw, Silver Beetle," Sir Pierre spit down the barrel of the lens. "You broke my perfect face and took me out of action for a month! That's money out of my wallet, that's protection for my family, that's security for my future, all gone because... what, I beat you by count out?" By design, Sir Pierre neglected to mention his illegal use of a steel chair to knock the Silver Beetle out in their last brawl. (Jalen made a mental note to add footage of the chair-shot in this exact point of the speech.) The two had discussed the promo prior to filming; Sean rarely wrote anything down, but he knew what bullet points he wanted to hit. Jalen moved in at the mention of the 'count out.'

"Well don't worry, because you don't have to worry about a 10-second count anymore," Sir Pierre snarled. "You won't have to worry about a pin-fall count, or about your paycheck, your job security, or wrestling ever again. In two weeks, I'm ending your career. I will *break* you. And as they cobble the remainder of your bones onto a stretcher and usher you out of the ring, you're gonna learn why I'm..."

Sir Pierre inhaled. The wall of meat that made up his pecs glistened in the hint of Jalen's makeshift light, and swelled as he filled his nostrils with dramatic air. On release, he opened his eyes and stared hard into the camera,

"*...superior.*"

"Awesome," Jalen cut the recording. "I can splice footage from the last match you guys had, and the jaw photos."

In reality, Sean had taken time off when his wife's mother died. The broken jaw grudge match was an attempt to construct a meaningful storyline around Sir Pierre's absence during his family's time of grief. They had staged a photoshoot a month ago of Sir Pierre's bandaged, fake-bloodied face in a hospital gown. Jalen wished he had time to come up with something a little more interesting than a 'you hurt my pretty, narcissistic face' plot-line for two of the company's better wrestlers.

He also wasn't quite sure if he wanted to use photos of broken jaw x-rays in the final product, and worried whether it'd make the promo come off as cheesy to his audience. Two important lessons he had learned over the years helped him whenever the fear of being too on-the-nose crept into his script: pro-wrestling survived because of the elastic boundaries in its storytelling, and more often than not, the bolder ideas drew more views to their videos regardless of whether they were "good" or not. He didn't have time to second guess himself. If it didn't work, the DEF was the perfect place to try an idea, see whether it failed or not, and then learn from the process and move on.

But it's not like I'll ever be anywhere else, Jalen thought as he pushed the door open for Sean. The gym light saturated their skin and Sean's royal purple spandex. *I'm just a guy in the back.*

"See ya," Sean saluted with a single finger from his brow, a subtle motion of nonchalance out of character for his alter-ego, Sir Pierre. "Can't wait to see it."

Jalen nodded as he pushed through the doorway. He watched Sean cross the gym mats and disappear behind the doors to the showers. He admired the work Sean put into his body like an ornithologist appreciates a bird's bright plumage. It was a moment of hot-blooded attraction, the kind he always felt a brief pang of around the men that broke themselves to reach the top of the strange, man-made mountain of masculinity. As it always did, it faded the moment Sean turned the corner. It faded when he needed to start a promo. It faded when they needed to construct a story. It faded when they needed to do anything that took creativity, work, or oxygen. Jalen was used to the fade. His eyes drifted across the mats and to the corner of the room his computers sat in. He crunched the number of hours he'd realistically need to finish the video, and prepared himself for a long night.

As he crossed the threshold of the gym, a full water bottle flew past his face, landed with an echo-thud on a yoga mat, and sloshed along the floor. Jalen stopped in his tracks and looked in the direction it came from.

A Hispanic man stood in the main entrance way of the gym. His cut shoulders and biceps, tattooed on his right side with the phases of the moon, were out of proportion with his neglected forearms and flabby stomach. Shadows fell harsh down on his face from the yellow light above the door, and aged his jaunt cheek bones beyond their 20 years. His bleached blonde hair was shaved at the sides in an attempt to hide the natural black the rest of the men of his family proudly wore. He adjusted his stained, ribbed tank top and pulled up his ripped jeans.

"You missed," Jalen said.

"On purpose," Daniel sneered. He walked past Jalen and picked up the water bottle. "Why are you still here?"

Matteo's son, Daniel Bianchi, hadn't been seen in the gym for three months. He wasn't on the current card, but if he's back in the gym at all, then he certainly would be on the next one. Daniel was a 'jobber,' a faceless talent whose role was to show up, take a few bumps, lose, and collect a paycheck. Daniel only ever cared about the last part, and only learned enough from his father to get it.

"I have work to do," Jalen latched his eyes back to his computer-corner and hoped they would pull him across the room fast enough to escape a conversation with the Bianchi-child. "I'll be over at my desk. Let me know if you need anything."

"Does my dad know you're here? Why are you here when he's not?"

Jalen didn't answer. Daniel knew he had a key. Daniel knew what he did for the DEF. *He just wants to fight with me*, Jalen thought, *like usual.*

On cue, it took but a few feet before Jalen felt the claw of Daniel's hand sink into his shoulder. Reflexively, Jalen spun and seized Daniel's wrist, and tugged him hard enough to throw the smaller man off-balance. Daniel stalled the fall with erratic footwork and slung spit in Jalen's direction as he spun around.

"Fuck you!" Daniel said as he regained his footing.

Jalen blinked with measured patience. "Yeah, I get it. Was there... like, anything else you wanted to say to me, or can I go back to work?"

Daniel wiped away spit from his chin with his forearm. "I saw you talking to my dad the other day."

Jalen frowned. Much like Matteo's regular attempts to recruit Jalen, his son had a routine of his own—to try and scare Jalen out of the DEF. "Right. That's pretty normal."

"About wrestling. Don't act dumb."

"Yeah, so you heard the part where I declined. *Again.*"

"I know you still think about getting in the ring," Daniel growled as he plodded towards Jalen. "I want to remind you it's *real* easy for someone to get injured in a ring. Happens all the time. It takes only a little bit of poor communication and BOOM! A faggot gets dropped on his head because he wasn't prepared for the right move. Broken neck, career over."

Jalen stepped up to Daniel and looked down. Frustration slashed across his face like a Pollock painting.

"You're right," he nodded, his tied back locs bobbed with the sarcastic motion, "your in-ring work *is* sloppy enough that no one wold be quite sure if it was a botch or malice. There's a small problem with this theory of yours, though; you seem to think, were I to step into the ring with you, that you would be allowed to get any plausible offense on me. I am a foot taller than you, and twice as strong. Not even your own father is going to book you into a situation where you get to do *anything* to me. I'm not a wrestler, I don't plan on being one, and *your dumb-ass* is not the reason why."

Daniel hawk-stared, clenched his fist, then ground his teeth. Jalen towered over him, a mountain he couldn't scale. Daniel's eyes trailed downward through the pores of Jalen's blue mesh tank. He swallowed.

"I'm gonna be around *a lot* more often," Daniel whispered. He combed his bottle-blonde hair back into its slick wave. "I've decided to be a regular. That means I might have to talk to you, unfortunately. Do me a favor and make me look good in your gay-ass videos nobody watches." He pushed past Jalen's shoulder and stormed towards the exit.

"If no one watches them," Jalen smirked and made sure his voice was loud enough for Daniel to hear, "then it doesn't matter what I make you look like, right?"

Daniel lifted a middle finger without turning around. The raised digit was the last part of his anatomy to disappear behind the double-doors under the flickering 'exit' sign.

{7}

{HE LIKES THE SKELETON}

Reese watched himself in the barber's mirror as shears snipped around his head. He made a concentrated effort to look neither concerned nor scared as shreds of blonde-and-green hair fell around his shoulders for the first time in months. If he hadn't kept the dollop of lime, one could assume the new, conservative length was for a job interview.

"Thank you," he paid the woman behind the counter, but looked past her into his reflection and tried to comprehend his new, clean geometry. "It looks great."

The opinion he voiced was a half-truth. He didn't know a damn thing about hair. The tuft of green was from a bottle, spurred by a random night of courage and curiosity. This haircut was for a date, an event of unique rarity in his life. In both instances, he hoped the result looked right in someone else's eyes because he was too ignorant on matters of personal upkeep to know on his own.

Reese Gagnon is going on a date, he stared in the rear view mirror of his ride-share towards a used clothing store. He wondered, *Is this real life? Is this what normal people do? Freak out about how bad they look and try to fix everything at the last minute?*

"I have no idea what I'm doing," he muttered to the mirror at the men's clearance rack. He buttoned up a short-sleeve collared shirt of many hues. The reflection offered no fashion advice, but the 75%-off clearance discount made a strong enough argument to fish out his wallet.

When he stepped out of the ride-share and his new shoes ground into the pavement of 6th street, apprehension held his hands. It spun him around and made sure he could see every street corner. His displacement in downtown and the new visibility it brought him weighed in his chest.

When he gripped the light pole for balance, he caught sight of Jalen rounding a far street corner. The coffee-clerk's bright locs bounced on his tank-top strapped shoulders with each carefree step. His fists were buried in the pockets of black-and-white plaid shorts. Once he caught sight of Reese, a hand launched into the air in an energetic wave.

Jalen crossed the road and scooped Reese up in an effortless hug that lifted the puppeteer off his feet. Reese's eyes bulged, and he froze much in the same way a hognose snake feigns death when attacked. This date had been underway for roughly five seconds and he was already over stimulated.

Jalen sat him back down.

"Man. You dolled yourself up for pizza, huh?" Jalen smiled and poked at the epaulette on the shoulder of Reese's shirt.

"Maybe I overdressed," Reese stared at a blank piece of pavement and was sure he was made of the same substance, hard and absorbing all the heat of the sun, "sorry."

"No, don't apologize. I like it, it's cute," Jalen wrapped an arm around Reese's shoulder and pulled him. Reese, still surprised at Jalen's hands-on nature, didn't realize he was in the way of oncoming pedestrian traffic. A large man, puffed with blood pressure and a furrowed brow underneath a baseball cap, scowled at the two as he walked past. Jalen continued to talk as if he didn't notice or care. "Just... don't get sauce on it. That'd be a shame."

The two walked like this down 6th street, past bar windows fronted with stuffed vultures and band photos, and hot sauce shops with cowboy hats and plastic cacti. It didn't take many steps for Jalen to realize Reese's gait was only in pace with his own because Jalen pulled him along. He felt the hesitance in Reese's body heat, in the way his shoulder never quite settled into Jalen's arm.

"You're uncomfortable," Jalen removed his arm and tried to mask the worry in his voice, and it came out as disappointment instead. He winced at himself and back-tracked, "Sorry. I'm physical by nature. I'll reel it in. First date, I understand."

Reese sucked in his lips. "It's fine, I'm just..."

He stopped and looked back down the street. The man was gone by now, but Reese still saw his angered look. He saw it on everyone's face, whether it was really there or not didn't seem to matter to his mind.

"Worried," he said. "PDA and all. I don't want us to get in trouble."

Jalen looked over Reese and realized it was the first date he had been on where he had to angle his head so far down. He leaned down and whispered: "I'm 6'6", jacked, and black. Anyone that messes with us was probably always going to. I've dealt with it before, and I can handle it."

Reese's lungs sucked all the oxygen around him and stored it in his chest and refused to let it go. "Right," he said. He thought that wasn't a sufficient enough of a response, and added, "Well, I think those are all good reasons for you to be physical."

Jalen's upturned eyebrows reached towards the sky. "Do you, now?"

Reese's cheeks exploded in red. He made eye contact but said nothing. A light laugh escaped Jalen, and he raised his arm. Reese leaned in to the flank, wrapped once more in a shawl of muscle. They walked together, their pace in a new, comfortable sync. Street lights conveniently changed for them whenever they arrived at a crossing.

{}

Pizzapolis was not aimed at the demographic Reese was a part of. Marble and polished wood intersected each other at asymmetrical angles along a vaulted ceiling, arranged with a delicate, intentional chaos that carried over into the diagonal flooring and mirror surfaced booths. The heavy hand of an interior designer shone through sparse metal decorations and hung basil plants. Between the interior and the menu, Reese had the sudden fear he wasn't just out of Jalen's league—he might not be able to afford his way of life at all. When Jalen offered to pay, Reese gave his best effort to not feel guilty or seem overly eager to accept. He was certain he managed to come off as both.

Once the waiter deposited the pizza to their booth with a dancer's grace, Reese stared down at an amount of embellishments far beyond what he was used to. Pepper Jack and fontina cheeses were costumed in pepperoni, capicola and onions. Dusted with chili flakes, jalapeños, and peppadew peppers, the tomato pie had a contrast of avocado ranch speckled across the cheesy canvas like an impressionist painting. Beautiful from afar, overwhelming in detail up close.

"You said you like hot stuff, right?" Jalen drew a slice. "It was either this or the ghost pepper one."

"Y-yeah, it's just..." Reese studied the clash of light green against red pizza sauce. Steam danced from the avocado oil brushed crust and across his face, "...gorgeous. I've never described a pizza like that before. This place is a lot nicer than where I usually go. And by go, I mean 'delivery.'"

"Tastes good, too," Jalen smiled. "Dig in."

Reese's face flushed from the heat of the pizza. "So."

Jalen lifted his brows, cheese stretched from bite to slice. "Mmm?"

"Words," Reese lifted the slice and balanced it on fingertips. "I should probably use them."

Jalen blinked and severed the cheese-line. "Mmm."

"I should probably ask something," Reese continued to stare at the slice, the one he didn't pay for, the one he didn't feel entitled to, purchased by a man, almost a stranger, he never thought would have interest in him. A world of questions swirled around his head and every single one of them felt wrong to ask.

'Why me? What'd you see in me?,' he thought, before he parried himself. *Wow, way to sound like a narcissist and chronically depressed at the same time. That's impressive, I'm sure he'll love negativity on the first date.*

'So, do you just work in the coffee shop?' Rude much, Reese? I dunno, do you 'just' live in a storage facility?

'You're hot, but I want to know more about you.' Well, you're shallow, and he'll want to know less *about you if you say that.*

Reese shook the thoughts away, then slowly spoke.

"So. Uh. Tell me about yourself. What do you like? You've seen my weirdest side already, so I feel a little tapped out on things to surprise you with," he wrangled the words out of his mouth, then filled it with too large of a bite of pizza. His eyes watered.

Jalen smiled and looked to the ceiling in thought.

"Well, let's see. I love city crawling, if that makes sense. One of the reasons I know this area well is just because Molly and I would cruise around on weekends during high school. And, well, after high school too. I used to go to a few clubs regularly. I like Pop. That new Frank Ocean is killin' me. Grew up watching wrestling and *Ninja Turtles*. Now, I'm old and watch wrestling and *Ninja Turtles*."

"You're the most buff *Turtles* fan I think I've met."

Jalen laughed. "Well, I'm eating pizza right now. Probably not the smartest move if I want to keep that title, but it's on brand, so..." he raised up another slice, "what can I do?"

"I remember liking that too, growing up," Reese rubbed his face. "I think *Mystery Science Theater* is what stuck with me the most. I guess that's obvious, puppets and all. Even if they're digital..."

"They're great puppets, too. I liked the skeleton. His name was Sir Mortimer, right?"

Reese blushed and fought back the ever-present need to contest compliments.

"Thank you," he pulled a smile from his resistant lips. "It's all I really do, and there's still a lot I don't know, but... well. Making models is fun. I have fun." Reese chomped into pizza to mute himself.

"Now, I'll ask a question," Jalen laced his fingers, "are you out to your friends and family?"

What the fuck, Reese thought as he coughed a chili flake out of his mouth. In any other situation he might have changed the subject from such a serious question, but when he looked up and saw Jalen's face—beautiful brown eyes shaped by an upturned brow permanently etched in interested concern—Reese found it impossible to consider it as anything but genuine curiosity from a well-meaning man.

"I, uh," Reese sniffed, "let's say I've come out to Schrödinger's friends."

Jalen tilted his head for a moment. "You're out to all of them, *and* none of them?"

Reese couldn't help but smile. His hands and eyes wandered across the table as he parsed the moment. "I'm glad you got that. Yeah, I, um, I'm a shut-in. All I do is work on stuff for the show, pretty much. Most of my interactions are online, and most of *those* interactions are work related. It's a full time gig for me. As for family... well. That's a little harder to talk about. I don't want to ruin a first date with that. I like you—and this pizza—a little too much to drag family into it."

"That's cool. I respect that."

Reese was bowled over by the simple way Jalen navigated Reese's admission.

“However,” Jalen held a palm up, “I feel I should be up front. I want to be *part* of someone’s life, not an *accessory* to it.”

Reese listened, and nodded. “Me too.”

They finished their pizza, then sat in brief silence, neither ready for the date to end.

“Wanna walk around the street a bit?” Jalen asked. “Get rid of a few of those pizza calories?”

“Absolutely,” Reese nodded eagerly as he slid out of the booth.

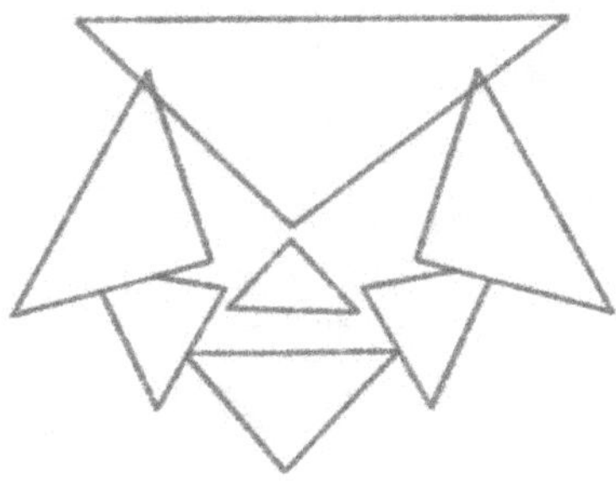

{8}

In the darkness of the storage unit, one of Reese's laptops turned on without input or reason. A save progress dialogue box that had been frozen in background processes climbed to the front from behind Reese's 3D programs.

```
Saving

Saving and compressing data… 99% complete.

Please wait.    Cancel
```

The laptop beeped and hummed. The progress bar flickered.

Saving^{g}

<u>Saving</u> and c$_{om}$pressing data… 99% com_pl__ete

P$_{p}$lease wait.   <u>C</u>an<u>cel</u>

The laptop shook violently, then powered down. The gears of its inner workings whined to silence, and the smell of sulphur leaked out of a USB port.

{9}

{PLEASE BE MINDFUL OF OTHERS WHEN JOGGING}

Reese and Jalen wandered down 6th street, the main hub of downtown Dundolk. They weaved between busy, rosebush dotted sidewalks, shoppers jacketed in plastic bags, electric scooters and their drunken operators. They talked cartoons and men and movies and the divide of their musical taste. Reese struggled to explain his love of Klaus Nomi to Jalen and left the incorrect impression he was a fan of opera, but that was fine—anything, even a misunderstanding, was worth it if it meant he heard one more moment of gentle, guttural punctuation at the end of Jalen's questions, or soft clicks of the tongue, or his slow inhale, a swell of the chest that telegraphed a thoughtful response. Reese wanted to listen. Reese wanted to look up at this beautiful ebony tower and get swallowed up by his amber spotlights and grow deaf from the siren of his light lullaby.

But then, Jalen pivoted the questions back towards him.

"So, what's Sir Mortimer's ultimate goal?" he asked.

In the middle of a sporting goods store Reese would never go into on his own, the spell was broken. The world's saturation dampened. It was with painful clarity he knew where he was, who he was, and who he was talking to.

"W-what?" Reese blinked with a slight slur, like one does when they awaken from a dream.

"I started watching some of the old episodes," Jalen said. He casually scoped the price tags of different brands of ab rollers. "I didn't go crazy and watch all of it or anything, I just peeked at a few episodes. I see he's a knight and he's going on all these adventures, but what is he fighting *for*? I figured there's something he wants to do in the end, right?"

Reese stared down the empty aisle and looked for the right answer on the shelf. It wasn't among cans of tennis balls and jump ropes, so he just said, "Oh."

"If it's spoilers," Jalen said, "you don't have to answer. It's cool. I was just curious."

"You..." Reese rubbed his face, "you went back and watched old streams? *Why*?"

Jalen put the box back on the shelf. "Because I'm a fan. It's not that unusual, is it?"

Reese stuffed his hands in his pockets. He mapped the conversation out in his mind, and searched for an exit. "I'm just... surprised. And flattered. Thank you. I hope they were alright. I never considered you'd find old episodes of me screwing around interesting."

"Well, I did," Jalen settled on the brand of ab roller, and barreled back to his inquiry. "So. Sir Mortimer. What does he want?"

Reese sucked on his teeth.

"Truth be told, my focus has always been more towards improvisation and interaction," he tapped his fingertips together, and his eyes darted around the shadowed aisle. To voice his intentions to another person was foreign territory, and he felt he got more lost with each new word. "That's all. Besides, I mean, if I give him an ending, that's an end to me making adventures for him."

Jalen shrugged. "Ah. Well, I'm hoping to see him happy in the end, I guess. Skele-boy goes through a lot."

Reese stared at Jalen's neon shoelaces, and counted the intersections. "I never thought about it that way."

Jalen smiled and juggled the boxed ab roller between his hands. "Come on."

He had picked up on a few of Reese's tics over the course of the date. The most obvious one was the one he did during his Mortimer explanation: he popped his knuckles when nervous. Reese had already released the tension from his fingers, but he continued to press down on each digit in succession while idle in the check out line. They had no more pops of satisfaction to offer him.

The two made their way back towards Pizzapolis. The sun started to lay down and Reese realized he was drained, emotionally and physically. He felt his eyelids strain under the weight of the day.

"Did you have a good time?" Jalen clicked the intersection's push-to-walk button.

"Absolutely," Reese's eyes shot open. There was a war on his face, cheek muscles battled with energy reserves to show happiness he knew he felt within, but was too tired to express.

Jalen didn't have this problem, and grinned. "Good. I did too. Do you want to do this again next week? Maybe we can try burgers next time."

"Anywhere you want to go, I do too," Reese realized that sounded a little desperate. "Well, within reason. Let's keep it in the state."

"No burger joints 300 miles away," Jalen said, "I think I can manage that. Do you need a ride home?"

Jalen's question muted the beep of the crosswalk and the engines of passing cars.

I would save a lot of money if he took me home, one part of his mind thought.

You cannot, under any circumstance, let him see that you live in a fucking storage unit. You fucking beggar, the other side screamed at himself. *He just paid for your food. He's hot. He has a real job. He's kind. He's gentle. You will never meet someone better than him that has interest in you. How can you even consider ruining your chances with him because you can save a couple of dollars? You're scum. You don't deserve him.*

His inner rebuttal to his own anger-panic was weaker in mental-volume. *Maybe you should just be honest with him about your situation.*

"Did'ja hear me?" Jalen poked Reese's arm. Sound returned to the world.

"Oh! I, uh," Reese stammered. "I'm fine-"

Suddenly, Jalen grabbed Reese around the waist and pressed him hard against his body. His vision darkened into the valley of Jalen's chest. A millisecond later, Reese felt the brush of cloth and body heat, and heard the pant of a runner's breath. Once nestled into Jalen, he heard the scuffle of shoes, concrete and rubber roughhousing.

"Watch where you're going," Jalen sneered at someone. Reese, much as he hated to, peeled his face away from the safety of Jalen's torso and turned to see what happened.

A man in running shorts and a sweat-band turned his head towards the two. He neither slowed or altered his gait as he brushed past, and only glanced when Jalen spoke. If Jalen hadn't moved Reese, the jogger surely would have barreled through him.

The jogger's bearded blank stare twisted into confusion, then panic. At first, Reese thought the jogger was gawking, an open revulsion of Jalen's protective arms around him. But he saw the direction of his eyes in that fleeting moment; they looked beyond the couple. Behind them. *Above* them.

Reese turned. Only the tops of city trees and sparse clouds framed them, mirrored apartment buildings, bars with neon helvetica logos and rough names of memorable simplicity. Joint. Bitter River. Almond

Bar. They were not the sort of places one typically glances at in wonder or astonishment, only to flee in the opposite direction.

By the time Reese looked back to the jogger, he had cleared the intersection and bolted down towards 7th. Reese heard the grind of his sneaker-sprint on the other side of the road, and could see the bare flesh of his shoulders weave in and out of annoyed pedestrians.

"Some people are assholes," Jalen narrowed his eyes, then held Reese by the shoulders. "You alright, Reese?"

Reese shook his head free of the strange encounter. "I'm fine. Thank you. I can't believe I didn't hear him. But, uh...I heard you. I don't need a ride. I do need you to keep in touch, though, okay? Today was the most fun I've had in a long time and it's 100% because of you. If you feel the same way, that is."

Jalen suppressed a laugh. He was accustomed to one night stands through apps and musing on who'd be top and bottom only to discover bedroom incompatibility would signal the abrupt end to his bar-date. This was the first time he had a night with a man that felt like friendship before anything else happened between them. This was new, and its own way, fascinating.

"I'll do some thinking on the best burg-"

Reese pulled on the front of Jalen's tank-top. The tall man bent over with no resistance, though his face was frozen mid syllable. Reese propped himself up on his tip-toes and kissed Jalen's cheek, his soft lips left a light, honest impression Jalen felt spread across the entirety of his face.

"...er," Jalen was stunned. It was much more forward than he expected Reese was capable of.

"Call or text, whatever is fine," Reese's face took the hue of cotton candy, "as long as I get to see you again."

Jalen hinged his hips and returned the peck to Reese's forehead.

"For sure."

They went opposite directions on foot, but they were on the same path.

{}

CanIGetUhhh donated $10!
"yo the new wimbles model is sick"

"Wimbles," Reese laughed. "I made a mistake with Wimbly, clearly. I should've called them Wimbles. Alright, chat, you're allowed to say 'Wimbles' if you want."

Reese returned to his stream with a renewed passion. Armed with the knowledge that Jalen's eyes might be out there, and that his enjoyment of Reese's work was authentic, Reese pushed himself with new inspiration.

He used that inspiration to clean up the Wimbly model. He clarified textures, fixed improper physics, and redesigned the thunderbolt-tossing villain to have a more sinister presence. The bags under its red-and-white eyes were more noticeable, its formerly squishy beak now sharpened with cruel intent, and its purple-starred robes changed to blood red with gold trim. Reese still refused to put a proper skeleton in it, though. *That's canon, after all,* he told himself. *Besides, I think it's cute that this weird monster gets all floppy when I drag them. I like the way it looks even more now, in fact.*

TonytheTaco donated $1!
"wombles is the new star confirmed"

"Thanks man," Reese grabbed the mouse with authority, and darkened his tone. "But 'Wombles?' That's right out. You're going to jail."

He made the Wimbly e-puppet raise its hands. It shot thunderbolts at the donation message, which exploded in cartoon-pieces.

"*Never* call me Wombles," Reese wiggled the Wimbly puppet and rasped in his best sinister voice-over.

JefftheGameGuy donated $1!
"What laptop do you use?"

Reese depressed the mouse button. The Wimbly puppet went limp.

"Thanks! Believe it or not, this is the same laptop that I've had for years," Reese said. "My dad got it for me for my birthday and I've always carted it around since. I did eventually get a second one for work purposes—and that's thanks to you guys, by the way—but I still primarily operate from this one both for familiarity and sentimental reasons. I keep upgrading parts on the inside of it, but someday I need to just replace the whole thing. It's *very* old."

Reese looked across the rows of keys, their caps faded from use. It didn't feel like enough of an answer. It was, in the most technical sense, the correct one, but it isn't the one he would've wanted to hear if he asked someone he respected about their work.

"All of you listening right now," he leaned forward with a seriousness rarely exhibited on camera, "if you learn nothing else from me or this stream, I want you to learn this: don't worry about having the latest and greatest thing. If you have something you want to do, do it! Build yourself up first. Your tool is not as important as your effort."

{}

After the stream concluded, Reese thanked his viewers and powered down the laptop. Normally, this is when Reese would break down his setup, hide his laptops, disassemble his green screen and desk. But instead, he slid into the recess of his seat, folded his arms across his front, closed his eyes, and smiled.

His phone buzzed on his desk.

Reese squirmed himself back to proper alignment and snatched the phone. Earlier that morning, Jalen had sent him a text to thank him for a wonderful first date, and offered him burger options for the next. Reese assumed that what awaited him on his phone screen was a follow-up on burger-confirmation, or just a general message about the stream. Reese didn't care what it was; he just wanted to hear from Jalen again.

There *was* a text message, but it wasn't from Jalen. It was from an unknown number, and the message was blank. Reese restarted the phone to see if it was a glitch, but the text remained, empty and meaningless. He considered a response, but since he didn't know it was possible to send blank messages in the first place, he just turned the phone off in disappointment. Years of scam callers and debt collectors had numbed him.

"I hope he gets to see what I did tonight," he slumped back into his chair.

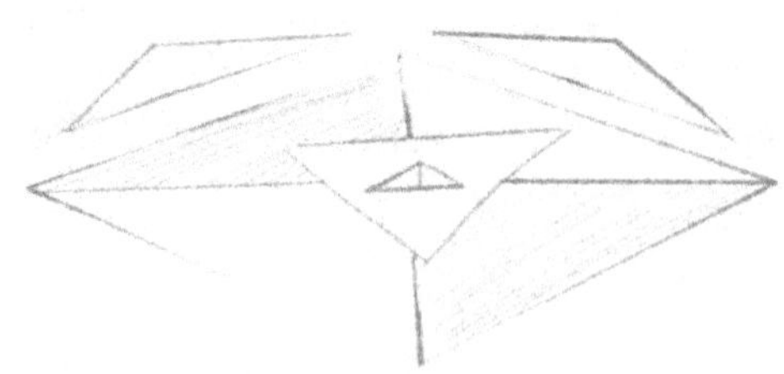

{10}

{OLD PHOTOS}

Daniel Bianchi hated wrestling.

After his final rep, he exhaled a growl of release and dropped the barbells. One of the cast-iron weights bounced and moved just enough in its mid-air wobble to land on his right toe.

"FUCKING!" he tumbled and hopped and threw the towel draped around his neck at the mirrors, "FUCK!"

Daniel hated working out, too.

But he loved his big biceps. Biceps were the most important part of a man. They were mounds of strength, and symbols of discipline. If you don't have biceps, you're not a man in Daniel's eyes, you're a beta, a cuck, a cunt. Whatever he thought would piss you off, that's what you became. If you reacted, if you got mad, if you took issue with mere words, then you were weaker than him in both mind and body, and it was in your reaction that he found his own validation. You had emotional problems you needed to deal with, whereas he could've taken it. You were something less than his biceps, less than his idea of what made a man a man. You hadn't earned your strength.

Not everyone who had biceps earned his respect, though. He hated that wrestlers often had large biceps. They didn't deserve them.

He found the pain of tearing his arms with curls the most rewarding workout he could tolerate, and it was, with great regularity, the only form of exercise he would do. It wasn't that he was ignorant of lifts, nor was it that he lacked care for the health of the rest of his body. Biceps were noble and honest.

He hated that spandex was the most common form of gear in wrestling. The rest of that bullshit, abs and pecs and calves and colorful trunks, that was all aesthetic. He wasn't a painting. He wasn't some limp-wristed ballerina there only to perform in tights for the stage of the world. He was a *man,* he was *real,* he was *normal,* he was *alive.* Anytime he saw a wrestler in spandex tights, he couldn't stop looking at them. He couldn't stop his thoughts about how stupid they looked. No one goes around in public like that, in neon colors and tassels and bright logos and exposed skin! All the time, his mind was latched to thoughts of spandex. He'd never wear it, not for anyone. No. Why, if he never saw spandex again, that'd be just great.

Daniel shook off the pain and limped to his tossed towel. He removed his shoe and looked at the toe, which had started to bruise. With his leg propped on the weight bench, he let his body droop onto his knee.

He hated that wrestlers often succeeded not by their strength or technique, but by charisma. Personality, in his eyes, should never be one's only selling point, even in the artificial world of wrestling.

The wrestling world fooled him once before. He won't be fooled again.

There was a rap at the entrance of the gym. Daniel arched his back into the straightest, most confident posture he could, and attempted to disguise his brief moment of fragility as a transitional movement. He started to put his sock and shoe back on.

"Just dropped a weight on my toe, like a fucking moron," he said. "Just wanted to make sure it didn't bruise. It didn't. I'm fine. Doesn't even hurt. Not at all."

He looked over his shoulder. It was his father, Matteo, who leaned in the doorway with his arms folded, his mustached face frozen. It betrayed no emotion or reaction to anything Daniel said, which pissed Daniel off more.

Daniel Bianchi hated wrestling. Matteo Bianchi is *why* he hated wrestling.

The earliest picture of his father he could remember was a black-and-white photograph of Matteo in the ring. In the photo, a young Matteo drove a clubbing forearm to the side of some masked wrestler's head. He didn't ask why Matteo's mustache was curled and twisted to comical effect, or why his trunks were covered in the Mexican flag when everyone in his family was from Italy. None of that mattered to the young Daniel. This 5 year-old only saw his father, under the spotlight and surrounded by the raised arms of a frenzied crowd, battering an opponent to win a championship belt. He saw his father, frozen in time, as a hero and a warrior.

Neither were true.

"Have you put me on the next card, yet?" Daniel averted his gaze and stared at the wall. His voice flat-lined to cold dissonance; Matteo didn't deserve to hear inflection.

"If you need money," Matteo returned the quiet, stern tone back towards his son, "it'd be easier and safer to just ask for help. And you'd probably get more. You know the pay ain't great in the indies."

Daniel knew the DEF was founded to put him through college.

"Everything I plan to do in my life," the younger Bianchi looked at his father's reflection in the mirror, "I plan to work for."

And even if he didn't know, at this point he would reject the money, anyway. It would have been tainted by the artifice of the man he hated the most.

Daniel only showed up to the DEF to use it for his own advantage. He considered it Matteo's plaything. The whole company, hell, the whole *business* of wrestling was just one big sham for his childish father to play pretend-fight and scrape up a few dollars from idiots that will clap for anything. Daniel was smarter than that. He didn't need to have a passion for the business to gain from it. He could just show up, take a bump, get some bucks, and save it to put towards lessons to become a real fighter, like the ones he saw in MMA.

"Yeah, well, you've been gone for a while, and you damn near killed yourself last time you were in the ring because you tucked your chin during the wrong bump," Matteo said. "You're not getting back in my ring until you prove you can take a bump properly and listen to the person in the ring with you."

Daniel turned around. His eyes were wide, his brow fell in jagged anger.

"Well what the fuck do you want me to do?" Daniel said. "It's not my fault the guy called the wrong audible—"

"He didn't call the wrong audible. I was there. I'm there at every event."

The two stared at each other. Matteo was the first to blink. He sighed and pushed himself off of the door frame, and looked down at the floor.

"Show up to the next few practices as if you're one of the students. Do the drills. Take the bumps properly. If you can do those, I'll let you job again. You're not doing anything other than taking quick, simple losses until you prove to me you give a shit."

Daniel took the long walk to the door and still managed to push against his father's shoulder as he walked out.

"I'll pass your stupid tests, no problem," he said. "Anyone can."

As Daniel exited the DEF building, his phone vibrated. It was a blank text from a blocked number. His nostrils flared and he smashed his thumbs into the digital keyboard:

Unless you got something for me, fuck off.

He chewed his tongue with thought, then added:

And make your number public, you spineless bitch.

{11}

{REESE'S BIRDHOUSE}

MAY 2006, SADDLETOWN, 1:22 P.M.

Adam Gagnon pulled close the front of his gray trench coat, a pointless endeavor in the face of the persistent gusts. The poplin had long ago lost its buttons and if he had the time to learn how to sew, he wouldn't have to constantly tug at the flaps. As a single dad with an all-consuming steel mill job and a son and a dog and mortgage, he rarely had any time for himself, or the state of his dress.

And then there was his wife! He *had* to check in with her, no matter what, and doing so always cost him 30-40 minutes. He walked past the black steel gates, down the carefully arranged rows of black marble and stone. In the first few years he had to read the names, but recently, he had walked this path so often that he was sure he could name the blades of grass, familiar as he was with the layout.

He reached her gravestone and let the plastic-wrapped bouquet drop from his vein-outlined right hand. It crumpled like a wad of paper on the weathered, ant-covered stone, cheap and ceremonial.

"Hey," he lowered to a squat as he scratched at his blonde, curly beard. His knees popped and he felt the awkward push of age on the outside of his ankles. He gave in to the protest of his legs and sat down in the dirt. "Hope you're doing well up there."

He listened to the wind, to the croaks of boat-tailed grackles, to the shifting of shy leaves among the oak. He wanted that calm, natural ambiance to serve as a surrogate for a response, but he knew that Evelyn Smith Gagnon, were she above ground, would not be so subtle. It was one of the reasons he loved her, and no grave could ever be large or bright enough to compare to his memory of her.

"I showed Reese how to build a birdhouse," he scanned the letters of his wife's name back and forth, having memorized the grooves of their relief, and noticed where a crack had started to form on the first 'G' of their shared name. "I thought it'd be nice to show him how something gets made. You know, how it's possible to make something from nothing."

Adam watched the white lilies in the bouquet shudder in the breeze. The invisible hand of nature ripped petals away, ashamed of their fragility in such a solemn moment.

"Because he's gonna have to do that, probably," Adam's eyes fell to the light dirt. "Mortgage sure was a lot easier to handle with you around. Everything was, really."

He curled his wrist to his side and popped the knuckles of his right hand along the edge of his hip-bone. It was a nervous tick that had grown in frequency since Evelyn's departure.

"I'm not sure he enjoyed the manual labor, but bless his heart, he tried," Adam laughed. "I don't think he saw how the pieces were gonna fit together. And even once we had assembled it, I could tell he was disappointed. The roof was a little crooked."

Adam never prayed aloud when he was in church. It never seemed necessary because despite the debt and the long hours at work, he was content. He lived in the world exactly the way one should, with a calm and happy family in a small home with a tidy yard and a few well trimmed bushes and a shed, and he did it without ever lying or cheating his way there.

"But then he painted it. And..." Adam tilted his head until he felt the pop of relief in his neck, "...he just lost himself. Absolutely engrossed in it. I kind of figured that would happen when we were shopping for paint. He wanted to take all the color sample books home with us. If I can get him to like the building part as much as painting, then maybe this can turn into a hobby."

When Evelyn died, though, it wasn't enough for his words to just bounce in his head where only God could hear them. Evelyn always listened. Talking to her was natural, and normal, and he wasn't going to stop just because her body did.

"...I really want him to have a hobby. I want him to have *something*."

Any long term plans the couple had, be it for themselves or their son, were instantly wiped out by the funeral costs. Adam thought the cost of Evelyn's life was something that couldn't be numerated—until the bills came in.

"He almost hurt himself when trying to hammer a nail. Kid swings like he's new to having limbs," he rubbed a finger over the end of a thread that used to hold a black button. "Don't worry, though. He's fine. I'll keep him safe, even if it puts me next to you."

Adam rose to his feet. He looked up and noticed, for the first time since arriving at the graveyard, the gathering of gray clouds as they encroached on the horizon, uncharacteristically dark against the lively blues of the afternoon.

"He tells me he spends a lot of time at the school library, and in the computer lab. I don't have the money right now, so maybe this is stupid, but... I'm thinking about getting him a computer for his birthday next year."

He pulled his coat closed. Another petal whipped away from the bouquet.

"I don't really know, though," he said. "I don't have a fucking clue what I'm doing, Evelyn."

{12}

{**ANYTHING CAN HAPPEN IN AN ARCADE**}

JUNE 2019, DUNDOLK

Jalen and Reese continued to date once a week. Jalen would suggest a new type of food, they would wander the local area and dizzy themselves with stories, their thoughts, their tastes, their innermost worlds, and the strangest things they could find on store shelves and on park paths. Reese's social stamina improved with each new sushi roll he awkwardly shoveled into his mouth, each french fry he fed to Jalen, and each moment their arms scarfed around each other. They saw sunsets on piers, bowling pins fly through the air, and arcades in serious disrepair.

Jalen frequently paid for Reese's meals despite protests, and an unspoken understanding of their finances settled between the two. Jalen was, after all, a member of Reese's audience; he could see first hand the donations he pulled in, and compared it to how frequently he streamed. Reese, likewise, knew Jalen had a *real* job, the kind of which brought stability he had rarely known. Neither knew the full details of each other's finances yet, but stability can reveal itself in silent ways on the shoulders of a man.

On the fourth date, in a near empty arcade, Reese kissed him on the lips. Anytime Reese considered that someone as beautiful and intelligent and honest as Jalen *had* to be a figment of his imagination, the coffee-clerk's touch would electrify him, his lips shock him back to reality. The energy Jalen's presence bled into him could've lit that piece of shit arcade for the next month on its own.

But it wasn't physicality, kindness, or generosity that had Reese ensnared. Not just. The arcade kiss, the strongest physical moment the two had shared with each other to that point, was not spurred on from flirting or flaunting; it came from a darker place, darker than the flickering consumer relic they stood in.

"Well, it's been a month and you haven't gotten tired of me yet," Jalen recoiled as he died on the third stage of *Gradius*.

"You still haven't told me how you have time to keep in shape *and* get this good at video games," Reese leaned against the broad, rounded edge of the machine. The faded labeling—what was once scatter-shot sky blue and gradients of gold text—indicated that this machine was something called a 'Windy II.' Reese thought he should ask Jalen why the cabinet artwork and title didn't match the game they were playing.

"Eh, if I was good, I woulda beat it," Jalen laughed and swiveled a bit in the ripped up leather barstool. This would've been a good time to mention to Reese that trips to the arcade were a regular part of his youth, but there was a more pressing matter at the front of his mind. He sucked on his bottom lip and leaned back from the machine, "Mind if I hit you with some serious vibes for a second?"

Reese forgot about the Windy II, commandeered a barstool from an unused machine, and sat next to Jalen. "Hit me."

"Remember on our first date, I asked you if you were out?" Jalen rested his hands on his knees and hunched over, his red-and-gray locs fell around his face. "It wasn't just a random question or anything. I was trying to gauge how you felt about... you know. *Public facing* love."

Reese nodded, but said nothing.

"I came out to my parents and it didn't end so well," Jalen said. "So, like. If we get any more serious, I need you to know in advance there's probably no Christmas dinners or anything like that with my family."

Reese nodded. "It's fine. I understand."

Jalen clicked his tongue against the roof of his mouth. "Yeah, well. I don't."

Reese blinked. Jalen waved his hand in the air as he tried to swat away the excess of emotions that began to boil up.

"I came out near the end of high school to them, after Molly encouraged me. She thought it'd be fine because to her, they seemed like good people. And I guess they were up until that point. But, she was wrong. My dad took it the hardest. I don't necessarily think it was blatant seeing-red type of homophobia. It could've been, I guess. It's hard to read him sometimes. He was pissed off because he had a giant son he thought could glide into college sports. He wanted grandkids and a daughter-in-law. I realized prior to coming out to him, if he talked to me at all, it was about whether or not I accomplished "something"—always school or sports related—or if I was seeing a girl. Once it became clear it was neither, he didn't have much else to say to me. I didn't play life the way he wanted it for me, and what I wanted... well, it didn't matter."

Reese hung his head. "Did your mom handle it better?"

Jalen's lips drew in during his pause. "She's more progressive. She's still... *game*, though. Does that make sense? She just... wants to know what jobs the men I've seen have. If they own a house. What type of car they drive. She launched into a spiel one time on how it's not nearly as hard for gay people to adopt as it used to be."

"...I'm sorry, man."

Jalen swiveled back around to face *Gradius*. He remembered his first games were from quarters his parents lent him, never to be paid back. "You don't have to be a great person to have a kid. She means well, but in the end my mom and dad are... competitive to a fault. They built their whole lives around 'winning' some social game and I couldn't see myself in these roles they wanted for me. Maybe I wasn't mature enough. Though, if I'm not by now, I'm not sure I ever will be.

There's a lot of stuff I want in the world, but playing by other people's rules isn't one of them."

Reese swayed in his chair. He didn't want to leave Jalen alone with these soured memories. "Well. I make digital dolls punch each other and yell in silly voices at my computer. You won't be judged for your mental age around me."

"Glad to hear it," Jalen chuckled.

Reese furrowed his brow. "Well. It means a lot to me that you shared that. I suppose it wouldn't be fair if I didn't tell you about my parents."

Jalen tapped buttons with an idle rhythm, then glanced over to Reese without turning his body, "You don't have to tell me anything if—"

"I brushed it off once," Reese looked across the arcade floor, at drink spills and crumpled candy wrappers wedged into forgotten corners, "it's not fair if I don't share it with you, of all people."

Jalen let his ship explode in *Gradius*, and turned fully to Reese. Reese took a deep breath.

"The Gagnon family doesn't have a great track record. My mom died when I was young, so my memories of her are... faded, at best. Turned out she had spots in her lungs and she was too stubborn to go to the emergency room until it was too late. Money and all. She thought it was the flu until she turned blue. Most of my upbringing came from my dad. He was a good man, but he was simple. He knew how to lift things. He knew who pitched what ball games in the 80s. That's it. He worked at a steel mill and watched baseball and slept in church and played with the dog. Dog was named Donatello, by the way. I thought you might like that.

"One day he walked in on me watching porn. I was, like... 15? 16? I can't remember. I think... this happens in most families. I'm sure it's super awkward and scary and probably predicates *a big serious talk*. His reaction was different, and I have to think there's a *big gay* reason as to why.

"First he grabbed the CPU and tried to rip it out of the wall. I think he must've electrocuted himself or something, because he grabbed it by the power supply on the tower, pulled, then dropped it and held his hand in pain. Then he grabbed me and I was scared, but he just... hugged me. He was crying, and looking around with this bizarre expression, like he was seeing everything in the house for the first time. I pulled away from him. I was so confused and angry. Like, I'm looking right at him with the same face I've always had, I'm the same person. None of it felt real. He just looked so absent, wide-eyed and blank. It didn't feel like the way he'd normally react to something. Yeah we, like, went to church and all, but I never got the impression it was anything more than a habit for him, I never thought he'd be the sort of person to react like that. I was wrong.

"Anyways, I left the house. I walked around the neighborhood. I came back real late and the doors were unlocked. For three days, we didn't talk much. He didn't bring it up. We ate in different rooms. I want to believe he was coming to terms with what he saw, but... I'll never know. He had a heart attack at the steel mill and they didn't get to him in time. Didn't even leave me a will. In the end the only things I got from my parents was bad money management, health paranoia, and... my first laptop. He apparently ordered a new one to make up for the PC. It arrived in a box a week later. Last thing I ever got from him. Not a smile, not goodbye, not 'I'm sorry,' just... a laptop. Despite all this, I promise he was a good dad. Everyone falters sometimes, even when they're good people, you know? The hardest part is never knowing if he'd have come around. Maybe he already did, but he was always the sort of guy that bottled stuff up instead of causing conflict. It's the Gagnon way. And..."

Reese gave a light tap with the toe of his shoe at Jalen's sneaker.

"I don't want that to be me. I don't want to do that to you, or anyone else."

Jalen squeezed Reese's shoulder and rubbed the side of his neck with a thumb. They sat silently like that for a few minutes, with Reese leaning his weight into Jalen's supportive palm. It was the first time Reese had told someone about his parents in his adult life, and it was the first painful memory Jalen had heard from Reese. A need welled up inside Jalen, and he realized that nothing inspires honesty more than more honesty.

"I need you to know I've dated a lot of men," Jalen slumped. "There were a few years of my life where I was a little obsessed with hook ups. I was partying a few times a week and working long shifts with Molly the next day. I think I was trying to make up for all the years I spent in the closet, and there was something kind of nice about drinking and fucking my extra money away. It was like a middle finger to the way my empty-headed parents lived. But those guys... I never connected with them. I never could manage to stay in a relationship because they either wanted to keep it on the down low out of fear of their jobs finding out, or their whole lives revolved around partying or cars or cash or... at some point I realized it was the same social game my parents played, just with different details, and I got *real* tired of it."

Reese couldn't quite relate, but he did what he thought was most helpful: he laced his fingers and listened carefully.

"One of the things I like the most about you..." Jalen said, "it's not what I saw at first, but I see it now. You just stick your head down and do your work. It doesn't hurt that you're cute as a button, mind you, but if this was only physical, I might've been the one to ghost you. I'm being honest. I'm not just looking for sex or anything. I don't want you to feel pressured..."

Reese started to realize that Jalen wasn't sharing parental regret. He was sharing the shape of his mind, and how time had molded it.

"I know it's not easy. You're making your own world. I want you to know that if I hold you or hug you or whatever, I'm not trying to embarrass you or make a scene. The world *I* want to make is a world where I can show my love to my guy anywhere I damn want. I can understand why you might—"

Reese pushed Jalen's shoulder enough to sit him up-right.

"...be... uncomfortable..."

Reese swung his leg over and saddled Jalen's lap. The coffee-shop clerk's eyes widened.

"*Are* you uncomfortable?" Jalen asked.

"Pretty often, yeah," Reese whispered, "but I'm getting better."

In 2019, the dried out corpse of an 80s era arcade is a tough place to find romance. When the pink lines of the nearby air hockey table reflected in the moisture of Jalen's almond eyes, Reese was certain it was *there*. Romance was *there* in the shape of Jalen Eze. All the colors of the world, all the lights and cheap laser sounds and pinball levers mushed around them, no louder than a fan, no louder than their breaths. They only saw each other, and then they, too, mushed together, hands and lips and tongues and hips for several minutes. They remained undisturbed; no one really went to arcades anymore.

{}

Reese slurped a caramel cake milkshake concoction as they wandered the Dundolk Mall. As deep as he continued to fall for Jalen, he couldn't help but notice that the coffee-clerk leaned towards caramel in his creations *and* his purchases. *I am definitely gonna get a caramel birthday cake for him, Reese* thought, then bounced down a different mental track,

Fuck, I don't know when his birthday is. Is now a good time to ask that? I suppose we did wear each others faces off back in that arcade. Maybe there's not too many 'too soon' questions anymore... But, fuck. What if his birthday is soon? I can't afford a cake right now...

"What's up?"

Reese jerked back to reality.

"Zoning out is a habit of yours, isn't it?" Jalen laughed.

Early afternoons on a weekday left Dundolk Mall emptier than normal, which gave Reese enough courage to lace his free fingers with Jalen's as they walked. The hand/size difference of the two meant Jalen's hand could cleanly engulf his own, and Reese thought that was fine.

"What you said earlier took a lot of strength," Reese spoke just above a whisper. "Thank you."

"The fact you remember it despite what we did afterwards tells me for sure I made the right choice," Jalen slurped his own caramel milkshake.

Reese blushed and sucked his involuntary smile inwards. A related memory bubbled up to the surface, and wiped the smile away. "Can... I ask you something about it, though?"

Jalen removed his lips from the big green straw. "Shoot."

"This is just a dumb curiosity. You said your dad expected you to play sports. Did you? You..."

"I look like I do."

"Yeah," Reese said sheepishly, and took another milkshake slurp.

"I was a wrestler in high school."

Reese choked on caramel-cake-shake.

"You okay?" Jalen leaned his head back.

"You were a *wrestler*?"

"Yeah...?"

Reese swallowed much larger straw-fulls of milkshake, in hopes that it would cool the heat he could feel on his cheeks.

"Is there something wrong with that?" Jalen laughed.

"There's so many sports in high school you could've done," Reese scoped the empty lanes of the mall and, despite there being no one near them, still leaned in to Jalen's arm and kept his voice low, "and you happened to pick the *hottest one*?"

Jalen's eyebrows lifted, and a long laugh forced its way out of his lungs. The laugh died out, and Reese could feel Jalen's grip on his hand loosen and clam up. The coffee-clerk's lips moved in a way that betrayed an argument in his mind. Eventually, he regained his grip. He looked Reese in the eyes and asked, "Have I... not told you what I do after work?"

The two found the closest bench—an odd dinner-table-sized slab of wood with a small tree directly inserted on one side—and Jalen told him about the DEF. He fumbled with the exact details at first, unsure of Reese's actual stance on "pro" wrestling. As he explained away the league's focus on performance and color and story and do-it-yourself grit, he watched Reese's eyes grow wider, his sips of his caramel cake milkshake grew fewer and farther between.

"I..." Reese waved his hands, and the straw in his near-empty cup rattled around the plastic lid," I cannot believe you didn't advertise this sooner. This is so *cool*!"

"I thought you might be disappointed that I wasn't a wrestler," Jalen looked down and squeaked his sneaker-tip against the glossy tile. "Everyone else is."

Reese went quiet. Jalen looked up and into his face.

"You're thinking about it, aren't you?"

"I mean," Reese blushed, "yes. Of course I am."

Jalen snorted and muted potential sarcastic replies with the last slurps of his shake, which had melted down to its base liquids.

"Not that I'm not completely, absolutely floored by what you've done," Reese said. "I mean, holy shit, you do more than I do. That's advertising and script-writing and planning and coordinating with a team and..."

Jalen felt warmth grow in his cheeks. So often when his involvement in wrestling came up, the assumption was made that he should be in the ring. Jalen knew which side of the camera he wanted to be on. He knew what he enjoyed. He knew what he wanted. He had grown so tired of other people's expectations. As he listened to Reese rattle off the mechanisms of production, he thought to himself, *Finally. Finally, someone sees it.*

"Would you like to see a show?" Jalen interrupted.

"Oh my god. *Yes*. Please."

Jalen nodded. "Cool. Well. I'm gonna tell you right away: it's both nowhere near as impressive as what you're thinking, and still somehow a ton of work. But, yeah! We do have a show coming up. I'd love for you to see it. I guess it's only fair. You showed me yours, so..."

Reese put a finger on Jalen's lip. "*Don't* say it like that."

Jalen gave the lightest kiss to the vanilla digit at his lips. They both smiled without restraint.

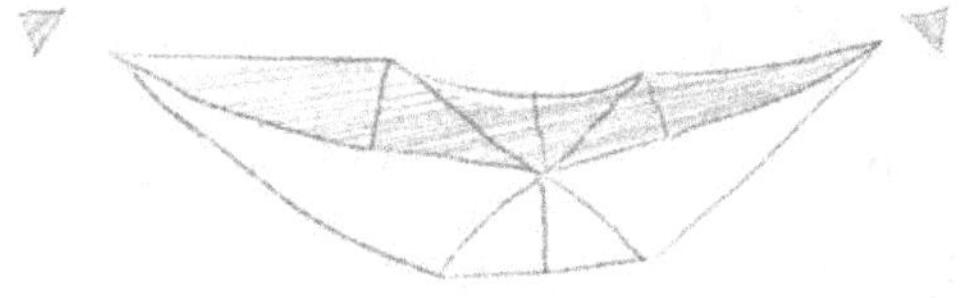

{13}

{ONE STRIKE AND YOU'RE PREGNANT}

Emma Victoria hopped out of the driver's seat of her yellow Ford F-350, a sunshine-steel beast most wouldn't consider for an inner city drive. The only reason she selected this unwieldy vehicle was her real-estate husband, Carter Victoria Jr., had taken the Mercedes-Benz to drop off the youngest kids, Carter Victoria III and Mary Anne Victoria, at judo practice. Her oldest son from her previous marriage, Beau-Alexander Jefferson, had borrowed her SUV for his hiking trip. In her white high heels and long, black-and-blue patterned maxi dress, the spray-tanned owner of Store-It regretted the way her outfit clashed with the truck.

Her heels ground against gravel. She saw no security or customers in the front office parking lot of Store-It. She swiped through some business emails on her phone before she let it drop into her red leather purse. *Someone should always be outside,* she thought with annoyance.

Emma stomped up the short set of wooden stairs and walked into the front office. Soon after she swung open the door, an automatic air-freshener hissed its 10-minute interval spray of the closest chemical approximation of hibiscus-and-papaya. At the receptionist desk she saw the secretary, Mrs. Sarah Green, and one of the security guards, Mrs. Louise Love.

"Mrs. Victoria!" Mrs. Green exclaimed, her magnified eyes bulged beyond the chunky frames. "Now how you doin'?"

"I'm doin' alright, just runnin' some errands, you know," Emma combed her bottle-blonde hair away from her brow-line and revealed her black roots. "If you could do me a favor, Mrs. Green, and print me up the sales report for this month? I know it's a bit early, but I just need it for a meeting I'm going into."

Mrs. Love pursed her lips and tried to slip away.

"Was I interrupting something?" Emma blinked.

"Oh, no, Emma," Louise said. She was a brute-framed woman, but her voice around Emma was more stoic, docile. "My email went down so I came to turn in my security report by hand."

Emma.

Emma Victoria believed when you're someone's superior, they should address you correctly, no matter what. Emma didn't know Mrs. Love well; she was a guard hired two years ago and Emma had heard no complaints from her managers or of the security company *Store-It* contracted out of. As far as Emma knew, there were no strikes against Louise yet as an employee.

Therefore, she hunted. She went into her memory to recall any distinguishing information on Louise. She remembered the last time they met several months ago, Louise was on smoke break.

Emma sniffed the air and only caught the smell of the automatic air freshener. "Did you stop smoking?"

"Yeah!" Louise smiled. "Quit last month."

"Mm-hmm," Emma noticed Louise's bags around her eyes. Clearly she didn't get as much sleep as she used to, and had the suggestion of lower energy levels than she'd expect from a security guard. She also noticed that the woman's shirt didn't quite fit right at the abdomen; A bulge that didn't match with the rest of her body pushed at the buttons of her dark uniform.

If Louise was pregnant, she hadn't told anyone yet in the office. Emma would've heard about it if one of her employees, even a contractor, became pregnant. She stared at Louise's belly and saw the price tag of a temp needed to replace her, and the chaos of scheduling around the time-off she would surely request.

That's the strike she wanted. Louise *had* to be removed before she announced she was expecting. It wasn't affordable to pay a pregnant woman, particularly when other guards could work her hours. Hell, Emma could do a few rounds herself.

I have the free time, she thought. *I don't need to pay someone to walk around if they're just gonna leech off me. She should've had the child and sent them off to college first.*

"Here's the report, Mrs. Victoria," Mrs. Green handed her a set of freshly-printed papers, stapled on the right hand corner how she likes.

"Beautiful. Well, I'm off. Ladies, you have a wonderful evening," Emma nodded as she walked out of the office. She fished her phone out of her purse and started to type up an email to the security contracting company to let them know that she no longer required Louise Love's services. Since they were in an at-will employment state, Emma only needed the approval of her consciousness to fire someone. Her consciousness was quite forgiving of Emma's decisions, and that was a large reason why *Store-It* always found a way to turn a profit.

As Emma typed up the email, a text message shook her phone. She pulled it open and saw it was from an unlisted number, and the message within was blank. She replied to it:

Do not message me again. I will report you to the FTC.

{14}

{QUICKSAND CEILING}

"You told him?" Molly gawked.

"At long last," Jalen said.

Molly killed the switch to the neon "open" sign and stared straight into the fluorescence as it died. The death of the red light revealed the reflection of her cafe; a business that would not exist without Jalen's help. She stood so close to the glass that she could see the pores in her nose. She tried to hold on to the image of herself standing there, at the front of the business she owned, surrounded by dangling lights she hung from rented ladders. In the reflection of night-facing glass, her property was a smear of colors and light, vaguely recognizable as the business she built, but otherwise lost in the noise of other logos in the strip mall outside. When Jalen stood up, she found that he had smeared effortlessly in the reflection of beige brick and dangling lights, and she only picked him out because of his movement.

"You *never* tell them."

"I know."

She turned to Jalen, who, in his automatic nature, had already started to wipe down the tables of the cafe with no need for direction or guidance from her. She noticed a white wire dangle from the drape of his apron. Jalen completed his work procedures with one earbud lodged in. Where he'd normally blast music for both employees, his ears lately had become isolated within the sound of something she knew only *he* enjoyed. Molly needed no hints to guess whose stream played on the other side.

"No, really. I'm surprised," she tossed her baseball cap across the lobby and watched it land on the cash register's digital display. Her long, straightened hair fell in clumps. "I've known you *for-ev-er* and you've never taken anyone you were dating to the DEF. You didn't even tell *me* about it for months."

"I know, right?" Jalen's pearls peeked from his lips as he sprayed down another crumb-and-coffee-stain covered table. "He seemed excited. He's never been to a wrestling show before. He knows what it is but never got into it... I think it's gonna surprise him how much fun-"

"Why *him*, though?"

Her emphasis hit with a certain bitterness. The air soured around Jalen, and he wanted to send the flavor back to its owner. But there she was, his best friend, her head dipped down in a way that carried frustration and disappointment. Her hands on her hips, confusion on her lips, it was a pose he had seen from a loved one before, but not from her.

And it hit a synapse in his memory that he had, until now, left untouched.

{}

"It's great that you get to live your life doing what you love," Jalen plopped a wasabi covered tuna-roll into his mouth, and let the cucumber and rice dance with the sinus-punching heat. "I bet you get to work on games and stuff too, don't you? I'm sure people approach you for work, right?"

It was their third date, and Jalen had picked out a small sushi joint called *Rollin' On Through*. He had enough of an understanding of Japan to know that the food found here wasn't terribly authentic. Western sushi is often crammed full of vegetables never used in the food's home country, and the rice is wrapped on the outside like a hug for its contents. None of this bothered him, of course—the only reason he had that knowledge was because he picked it up accidentally when he researched overseas wrestling promotions. He had never been to Japan, and was unsure if he ever would. He thought he was lucky that Dundolk had a sushi joint at all, Americanized or otherwise. When he learned that Reese had never had sushi before, none of the finer details of authentic cuisine mattered; what was important, he thought, was to get wasabi into that man's mouth.

Reese tried to use chopsticks to pick up an eel-sauce covered sushi roll. Between his poor form and nervous demeanor, it fell repeatedly back to his plate.

"It's not easy," Reese said.

"Oh, you'll get it. Everyone has trouble with chopsticks at first—"

"My work..."

Jalen paused. He looked at Reese, he heard his words, but he didn't quite recognize the expression on the lips that produced them.

"I've never been able to go to college. Average cost of college is $30k, and I eat peanut butter for lunch sometimes. I'll never be able to afford to be trained, so to get where I have, I had to do a whole lot of 'wrong' stuff first. Slowly. You don't get to see the landfill of things I've made and never shown anyone because of how bad they are," Reese pushed the sushi around the perimeter of his plate. "I think I built up a following because I had a weird gimmick no one else was pursuing. I'm probably at the edge of my growth. I'm not good enough of a modeler to make better work. I'm getting older. My gimmick is... *out there.* Everyone that *can* know about my show already knows about it. And I'll never have the money to properly learn this thing I'm suddenly 'known' for."

The armor slipped. Jalen rarely made it far enough with another man to see this moment of vulnerability.

Reese pushed, ever so slightly, the end of the chopstick into the center of the sushi. The contents within bulged out and crumbled the integrity of its rice shell. Right then and there, Reese almost ruined himself and his chances with a man he loved more than he could properly explain. *I don't trust anyone that likes me, and I especially don't trust anyone that likes my work,* Reese almost said. He didn't know why his mind tried so hard to say the worst things it could think of, but he wouldn't let it win. *Not today.*

He lifted the chopsticks over to another sushi roll on his plate and secured it with confidence. He clipped the armor back on.

"But it's fine," Reese dragged a smile to his face. "In the first month of making *SKELEVENTURE*, when I was really pumped on inspiration, I took a night off after days of model making. I had pumped out so many test models, it felt like I was possessed by the act of creation itself. After that week, I was just so spent, man. I couldn't look at the screen anymore, it hurt to have light in my eyes. So I went out at night, I laid down on a hill in a park my dad used to take me to... you're gonna laugh, it's stupid, but I told myself I was willing to give up anything so long as I got to make videos safely. I didn't make that wish because it was easy, right? I'm proud of what I've done. It can be tough, but as long as I remember that I'm working on my own terms, I know I can keep going."

"That's the spirit," Jalen smiled.

{}

Jalen felt the involuntary flex of his eyebrow. He shook his head, covered the table in the blue-mist of cleaner, wiped it with his cloth, then took a seat. He dug out his phone.

"He never answered my question," Jalen said.

Molly blinked. "Huh?"

"It was a while ago, when we went on the sushi date, I asked him..."

"Give me what I want, Sir Mortimer!" Wimbly the vulture-mage wiggled across the screen of Jalen's phone. Its floppy frame froze when Jalen paused the stream, then disappeared as he scrolled through Reese's business information further down the page.

"...I asked him if he did work for other projects," Jalen, though not an artist himself, knew enough about the creative world to know someone who lived on their own in a gig-economy was likely always on the hunt for work. As successful as *SKELEVENTURE* was, Jalen knew it wasn't possible for Reese to live exclusively off of it. He had seen the donations. Reese *had* to have other work. Commissions. A side gig. Weed. *Something*. "I assumed this whole time that he does freelance work as well, but... I can't find anything. I can't find where he's made work for other people on his social media, on his stream... anywhere. The only thing he makes is this show."

Molly slipped into the other side of the booth. She had her own phone out, and after a little bit of digging, she pushed her phone across the smooth, clean surface of the table to face Jalen.

"Did you try looking in the places *he doesn't* have control of?" she asked.

There, on forums outside the jurisdiction of Reese's control, Jalen read:

What ever happened to that collab between *SKELEVENTURE* and Big Box Games?, user "BusinessSuitBear" asked.

Never happened, "RedSoxFan89" wrote.

I have a friend who did contract work for Big Box. *SKELEVENTURE*'s models were unusable. Like, it would've cost Big Box more money and time to fix the issues with what he made than it was worth, "DLCuck" added.

LOL, I guess that's why *SKELEVENTURE* went into hiatus for a month and just straight up doesn't talk about it anymore. Reese is a fucking hack, "TheVideoGameLife" felt vindicated.

I've been saying this forever, I'm glad people finally notice. His shit literally doesn't work outside the context of his stream. There's a reason indie artists are indie, "HentaiHero" shared his insider scoop of the industry.

A text message notification popped up on screen. Molly flicked her fingers out and stole her phone back, clacked her sunshine-yellow nails against the screen, and rolled her eyes. A few moments later, she took a photo of her middle finger and sent it off.

"What was that?" Jalen asked.

"I've been getting these blank texts lately from a blocked number. If it's someone I know, they'll laugh. Hopefully."

Jalen rested his chin on laced fingers. "And if it's someone you don't?"

"Fuck 'em!"

They both snickered. Jalen's snort was hidden in clasped hands, and shortly thereafter, his brow resumed its upturned stance in concern. Molly noticed the change.

"Well, the good news is that this post is from a few years ago," she brushed her hair behind her shoulder. "If this is the first thing that I can find when I search for his show and 'drama,' I guess that's not so bad. But... you've been dating him for a little while now. Shouldn't he be more honest with you?"

"I dunno," Jalen rubbed the back of his neck. "I mean, I haven't told him everything that's ever gone wrong in my life."

"Yeah, but *this* is *out there,*" she waved her phone. "I've watched you ghost or get ghosted by a line of guys in your league and I don't understand why the one guy that *isn't* is the one you're spending time on."

Jalen frowned. "Molly, I love him."

Molly's phone-wielding hand drooped. They stared at each other from across the table. It was in this moment both realized that a pit had formed between them, and they were looking at each other across its width.

"Don't fall in quicksand because you thought it was honey," she sighed. "I don't want you to make the same mistakes I made."

Jalen and Molly remembered the high school party that united them in the first place. It was such a distant memory—so pivotal to the formation of each other as adults and as friends, and yet, Jalen was sure it was a lifetime ago, in someone else's skin.

Jalen rapped the table with his knuckles, and got up and away from it with motivated speed. "...I should get back to work."

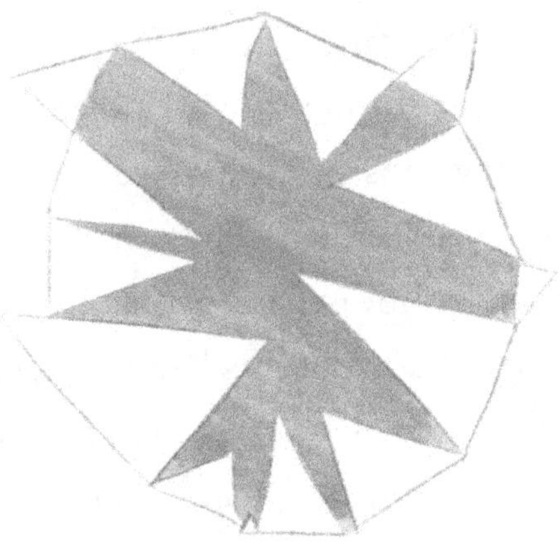

{15}

{REFLEX CONSEQUENCE}

JUNE 2010, SADDLETOWN, 9:22 P.M.

Adam's gray trench coat whipped behind him as he stomped down the muddy path. He gripped the umbrella and tilted it towards the machine-gun rain. It was pointless to try and remain any less wet with the pace he moved, overwhelmed as he was by a frenetic energy that pricked his skin.

"I did a stupid thing today, Evelyn," he wheezed as he rounded the corner. There were no lights to guide him, and the moon was hidden among rude clouds, but Adam needed no help to find Evelyn's grave. He could pick her stone out from any crowd. He found her at her eternal home and ran his fingers over the chipped name-relief, stroking it as he would his wife's arm and face. "I am... ashamed. And embarrassed. And I am sure I have done irreparable damage to our son's view of me."

Raindrops misted his bifocals and dotted the edges of his beard, a forest of unkempt gray and peach-blonde. He spoke through hiccups, lung-jolting sobs and gritted teeth.

"He left the house. I couldn't find him, and I can't really fault him for that. I'm hoping he comes back while I'm here, that way we can both just..." he shook his head, trying to find what could possibly be a proper solution to the problem he created, "...go to sleep."

In the past year, Reese had mowed enough lawns to buy a used computer from a local shop. His new prize was ultimately his new home—if Reese was in the house, Adam knew he'd be sitting at the computer in his room. When the door was open, Adam could see his son working on homework, or looking up facts about beetles, or giggling at the strange abominations he made in a game called *Spore*. When the door was closed, Adam suspected what any father might—that his son was becoming a man, and wrestling with the confusing biology that comes with such inevitability.

"Maybe I have no right to complain to the dead, but I'm a little envious of you at the moment. Goin' off on your vacation to heaven without me and all," he brought his nose to the stone. Images of his confrontation welled up in his mind.

Earlier, Adam caught a sliver of light through Reese's slightly ajar door at the end of the hallway. He approached it slowly so as not to alarm his son. Adam had long prepared for this moment; since he had already given Reese "the talk" a few years ago, and since he was certain he knew what he'd see through the crack, he wanted to use this as an opportunity to explain to Reese the difference between real love, real sex, and the artificiality of pornography. He had planned out this moment in his head a hundred times over, and he was determined with every part of his being to make sure that he was an emotional Sweden, a neutral ground for Reese to come to a normal, proper understanding of the changes in his body.

Adam thought he had surprise-proofed this scenario. He was wrong. When he saw the glimpse of a grainy video of one man pressing his hips into another against a wall with the rhythm of a jackhammer, something inside Adam's mind broke. Years of conditioning that once laid dormant—from the day he was born, to the backhand of his father, through the hazing of school locker rooms, through the rhetoric of television and church, the reinforcement of expectations of men in private and public conversations—every opinion he had ever been fed about a people he had never met in his entire life shot through his body all at once. It filled his leg with electricity, which kicked Reese's door open. It chained his consciousness down, and made him a prisoner in the vehicle of his own body.

Reese quickly closed the porn and pulled the waistband of his gym shorts up, a fluid and practiced motion Adam might've been impressed with had he not been so possessed. Adam screamed but formed no words. He attacked the computer with no plan, no thought, no ideas. He was totally consumed by the need to kill that which turned his son away from normalcy, as if Reese were not present in his own decision making. In that moment of blind rage, Reese did not exist. Adam did not exist. People did not exist, decisions did not exist, right and wrong did not exist. All that existed was the machine, and he had to kill it before it killed his son's future and security.

Adam grabbed the power cable near the base, where rubber met tower. He pulled. The electric shock from the power supply coursed through his body and burnt the inside of his thumb and pointer finger. Blood oozed from the raised skin. His hand blurred in his vision, and his surroundings came into sharp, forced focus. The shoddily assembled pastel-dressed birdhouse from years ago, which broke instantly under the first grackle's inspection, came into clarity as it hung from Reese's ceiling. He saw band posters and stacks of doodle-filled printing paper around the edges of the floor. Reese's homework, finished, was filed shut in a striped binder at his desk. Pencils, pens, ideas scrawled on paper, Adam saw it all! Though none of it was new to him, he saw them all at once, as they were: products of his son's mind and interests.

At the moment Adam regained control of his mind, he fell backwards. He fell out of his head, down through darkness, down through the whirlpool of emotions, down the river of blood that flowed freely from heart to hand, swept away by currents of plasma, drowned in fear, wrapped up by the come-down, submerged, plunged, crushed, then flung back into the void, falling, falling, until gravity slammed him on his ass in the graveyard, head hung in shame in front of Evelyn.

"It doesn't feel very good to have blood right now. To have a heart that pumps out emotion before the brain can think things through. To have bones that prop me up when I am complete shit at supporting the only family I have left."

He popped his knuckles against his side, then curled his bloody-bandaged hand into a fist. The other, which gripped the plastic umbrella handle, shook violently. Rain spilled from the edges of the black nylon.

"What am I supposed to do, Evelyn? They got one of those machines now at the mill that checks your blood pressure. That shit was *exactly* as high as I figured it would be and what the fuck am I gonna do with that information? What has this family ever been able to do when we're told that something's wrong, other than just push through and hope for the best? Why is that all we can do? I hurt in every physical and spiritual place in my body and what has this pain done for me other than take my wife and break my bones and turn my goddamned son gay!?"

Adam froze. Every muscle stopped moving, save those in his lungs, which sucked in air with self-pitying greed. He crouched down and pressed his head against Evelyn's stone skin and sobbed.

"There it is again."

He rocked back, then knocked his head against the stone. He wanted the pain to be penance. The shock rattled between his ears but did nothing to kill the guilt.

"I did it again. I got mad at him without thinking. It's like a fucking reflex, Evelyn."

He swallowed, coughed, and wiped snot on his trench-coat sleeve.

"This is on me. Not you. Not Reese. Not anyone. I just... I want him to have a normal life... a good life. I want to protect him but I don't know *how* because I have no idea *what* kind of life he could end up with, if *this* is who he is. He's still my son and I love him and I am completely fucking unequipped for this."

He pulled his head away from the wet stone. A bolt from the clouds flickered light upon the gravestone, and he noticed a splotch of red on the sharp corner of the "G" in "Gagnon." In synchronicity, a warmth on his forehead throbbed outwards towards Evelyn's final resting place. He raised his fingers up to his forehead, found the sear of a cut, pressed in, then brought his fingers into view. Each digit was dotted with blood. He held his hand out past the perimeter of the umbrella and let the rain wash it away.

"You've been a lot colder lately."

Evelyn's gravestone did not respond. Heaven never felt farther away.

"I feel like you'd laugh at that. I just want to hear someone laugh right now."

Adam's walk back to his car was slow and heavy, but not fruitless in thought. He knew Reese wanted a better machine than the one he settled with, the only one that he could find with the money he earned mowing neighbor's lawns. Adam thought that, though it was absolutely foolish to spend money right now, a laptop would be nice. It could replace Reese's broken computer, and he could use it to make amends, and to have the conversation about pornography he had planned to have all along.

He'd do anything to make amends.

{16}

{FULL HOUSE, EMPTY PARKING LOT}

JULY 2019, DUNDOLK

It was DEF show-night, and it was expected to be its biggest show since the federation's inception. Reese met Jalen at Jolly Molly's Coffee Shop. With the light of the cafe's signs turned off, the wrap of airglow lit the atmosphere in royal purples and tinted Jalen's face in rich tones. Though they were dressed in casual t-shirts and jeans, the stars and caffeine and shared excitement shook the evening with importance. Reese popped his knuckles beyond the point they could make sound, and he squirmed as he climbed into the passenger seat of Jalen's red 1992 Audi S4.

"I promise I'm not trying to be a wet blanket, I'm super pumped you're gonna be there," Jalen said as they coasted down a side street. "I just want to remind you; I'm at work and you're a spectator. Don't feel tied to me if you want to go to the concession stand or get in the crowd. I know crowds aren't your thing, but..."

"Get in the crowd?" Reese tilted his head, "You mean there aren't seats?"

Jalen laughed. "There... *are*, technically, but our show is a lot more personal. You're gonna find people are standing everywhere. Three sides of the ring are open enough for people to slap the mat. Part of the fun of wrestling is cheering, making noise, etc, so it's a little indie trick to keep the crowd involved. The first show I did, I paid a few people to slap the mat and start chants during matches. Haven't had to do that since."

"You aren't worried about someone interfering? Like, what if some asshole grabs a wrestler's leg or something?"

Jalen flashed a tooth in his smirk, and his brow took a sinister shape Reese was unfamiliar with. "Those who fuck with wrestlers typically end up regretting it."

Reese paused, then folded his hands in his lap. "That makes sense."

Jalen pulled the Audi to the back of the DEF gym and, as he did so, Reese pressed his face to the window. Despite their early arrival, the parking lot was near full; young and old alike formed a line outside the building. Banners and posters punched candy-coated color into the world and highlighted the night's attractions in concrete-scraped font. Cartoon stickers of wrestlers like Sir Pierre and Fang Wylin and Silver Beetle covered light poles and entryways and window sills. Rock guitars sizzled from speakers at the entrance.

"I set up a lot of this yesterday, just to save time," Jalen admitted. "It's me and the wrestlers that do set-up and that's about it."

It was the first time Reese got to see the DEF gym. Surrounded by art and inspiration, he felt at once connected to it; he asked questions about every wrestler on every sticker, learned about Sir Pierre's broken jaw at the hands of Silver Beetle, of the transgressions of various heels, and the triumphs of their current champions.

"A while ago, I asked you about Sir Mortimer's goal," Jalen held the door open for Reese.

"I remember..." Reese heard him, but was distracted by the cartoon stickers of wrestlers, and barreled through his thought, "Did you make these?"

"No, I paid a friend of a friend for them. I've always paid attention to what people do as hobbies," Jalen smiled with pride, then sidestepped Reese's misdirection. "Anyways! Sir Mortimer. You said his goals were more on an adventure-to-adventure basis."

Reese's gaze fell from the sticker and puddled to the floor. He was still embarrassed by his admission, as if his answer wasn't good enough, or something to be ashamed of.

"That's not so dissimilar from wrestling," Jalen tugged Reese through the door.

"How so?"

"Well, it's a soap opera, isn't it? There's a loose goal for wrestlers: the championship belt. But the adventure the roster goes through—the matches and drama at each show—that's the most interesting part for the audience. It's not necessarily the achievement of the belt itself."

Jalen led him through a dark hallway. Reese nearly tripped over a stray cable, and Jalen kicked it out of the way, then squeezed his hand.

"Sorry to take you through a weird way," he said. "I wanted to avoid the crowd out front, even if it means we have to walk through the dark. There's something wrong with the breakers. Matteo refuses to fix it since all we use it for is filing cabinets and smoke breaks. Anyways, I just wanted to bring up Sir Mortimer because I thought you might find some inspiration."

"I have!" Reese smiled. "I think... I think I understand a little better why *SKELEVENTURE* didn't send you running away."

Jalen stopped just before they reached the slice of light from the double doors. He turned, bent down, and sucked a kiss out of Reese's lips.

"I've wanted to share this world with someone for a long time," Jalen admitted. "Thanks for wanting to come."

"Thanks for letting me in," Reese beamed. They pushed the doors open together.

{}

Enveloped in arranged spotlights, the wrestling ring's mat, a deep blue with purple trim, carried a deceptive air of prestige despite the paltry budget of the DEF. "Face" wrestlers, good guys in the grandiose narrative of this sport-universe, sat at tables at the front entrance and signed the merchandise of fans in lines barely maintained by the two temp-agency security guards. Jalen's "crew," few as they may be, tested lights and sound systems. Matteo Bianchi loomed over their shoulder with clipboard in hand and a water bottle tucked under his arm.

"Hey boss," Jalen slid behind the desk and tugged Reese along with him, "this is my... plus one." He wanted to say "boyfriend", but thought better of it when he looked between Matteo's blank, wrinkled face and Reese's nervous expression. He wasn't sure who he was softening the introduction for more.

"Hey," Matteo shook Reese's hand with vigor that wobbled Reese's whole arm up and down, "nice to meet you. Don't touch anything."

"I-I won't," Reese laughed nervously, "I couldn't afford to replace any of this if I wanted to."

Matteo's mustache twitched before it was masked by a swig from his water bottle. He shifted and motioned to Jalen, who leaned in. He spoke in a low tone, "Daniel's on the card tonight. He's in a short 2-minute squash."

Jalen's lips thinned. He bolted down his gut reaction and whispered back, "Alright. I'll make sure I have a graphic with his name on it."

"You can have a reaction, you know," Matteo walked to the other side of the desk. The two looked at each other and waited for the other to budge. Matteo, as he often did, submitted, "I just thought I'd give you a heads up. I know my kid's a shithead. But he's been workin' hard and he might..." he fumbled a loose cigarette from the paperboard in his palm, "...actually mean it this time."

Jalen had no interest in being involved in a different family's politics any more than his own. "Okay."

Matteo rapped the table with his knuckles, lit the cigarette in his mouth, and changed the subject. "I'm gonna let the crowd in and have a smoke, we'll be live in 15," he sauntered off into the darkness of DEF's blackened hallway.

And so the flock filtered in, some fanatics, some family, some friends, all readied to submerge their senses in an ocean of sports entertainment. They hung their views of reality on the wall mounted purple silk which, pleated and carefully arranged, shimmered in cascaded lights. The flock drank beer and ate hot dogs. They read card-stock programs and chatted about what winners made more narrative sense. They yelled to quicken the pace of the pump of their blood and encircled the ring to get the closest view.

"I've got cameras around the ceiling and ring," Jalen explained to Reese as he clicked through each of the video outputs on one of his monitors, "and I've even got some cameras in the turnbuckle. It's a low-budget, DIY assembly but I've gotten some incredible shots out of these things."

Though the mechanics of video-making *was* a topic that interested Reese, he found himself distracted: as he watched the crowd filter in, their forms a blur of beards and franchised t-shirts, the details of a faraway face seemed to sharpen with familiarity. The stranger's form twisted through the crowd like liquid, and Reese's eyes ping-ponged with it in an attempt to catch it.

"Wanna see how this stuff works?" Jalen asked.

Reese blinked and shook his head. The person was gone, though his expression, a scowl that seemed to fold into itself, was imprinted on his mind.

"Y-yeah," he rubbed his temple. "I'd love to see."

{}

Daniel Bianchi (or "Danny B." as he was called on the card program) sailed clear across the width of the mat. His eyes bulged, his body rotated like a helicopter blade, he screamed in an octave few could wrangle out of a male intentionally, and he landed face first in the opposite corner.

The crowd applauded.

"Holy shit," Reese stared at the fur-loincloth-adorned Fang Wylin. He was the hairy mountain who torpedoed Daniel's body across the ring. "He threw him like a wad of paper."

Jalen laughed and, with a click, switched camera angles on his monitor. "Yeah. Fang's huge, as tall as I am and twice as wide. He used to be the champion. He's had some time off, so we're building him back up again into a strong monster by feeding him a weak opponent." Daniel pawed helplessly for the ropes the same way one looks for dropped glasses on the floor, and screeched when Fang grabbed his leg and dragged him back to the center of the ring.

As Daniel's body was pulled away, Reese saw the strange face again in the crowd—a furrowed brow, a grimace, a suggestion of anger directed towards him. Just when it seemed like Reese's eyes settled on the visage of venom, it flushed away behind shoulders and bodies. Reese stood up from his chair. The sudden motion pushed the chair backwards, which scraped loudly across the floor behind him.

The crowd raised their hands and roared as Danny B. slapped the mat in submission. Only the bulge of his eyes were visible on his face, as the rest of his expression was covered in the laced, sausage fingers of Fang Wylin as he sat on Daniel's lower back and bent him.

"That's a submission move called a 'Camel Clutch,'" Jalen thought Reese's jump out of his seat was a pop-reaction to the match, its timing so serendipitous it blended in with the crowd's reaction. He chewed on a flirtatious joke in his mind (*You know, I can get on top of ya and show you how it works...*) but never had the chance to deliver it.

"Are the bathrooms that way?" Reese pointed to the double doors he believed the figure bolted through.

Jalen filed the innuendo away for another time. "Oh, yeah. Everything's that way. Go through there, left leads to the outside doors. Go a little past that and you'll find the bathrooms."

"Thanks," Reese exhaled, "I'll be back in a second."

Jalen watched Reese disappear into the crowd. He was so thankful Reese seemed to be having a good time.

{}

Reese ran through the doors. Posters of the wrestlers surrounded him, their faces frozen in growls of warning. Only a lone security worker loitered in the hallway, an overweight man with peppered hair and glasses.

"Excuse me," Reese jogged up to him.

"No running," security said.

"Did someone just come through here?"

"I mean," the older man blinked, "yeah? There's always people going to the bathroom."

Reese wrung his hands in exasperation. "No, like, *right now*. Did someone just run in here in the past few seconds?"

"Just you."

Reese bit his back teeth down.

"Someone went through the entrance just now, though," security shrugged. "I guess they were walkin' kinda fast."

"Thanks," Reese let his annoyance drop out of open palms, and jogged away.

"No running!" security lifted a hand and did nothing more.

Reese blasted through the entrance doors. Their metal clank disturbed a tree of grackles that flew away in squawks. His run stuttered to a halt as he craned his head around the parking lot, so full of cars, so empty of people. He spun around in the night air, which seemed to grow colder as it ran its fingers across his forearm's skin. The lone tree capable of growing near this parking lot rapped a single branch against the side of the gym. The wind kicked up. It knocked in defiance of the man-made intrusion of its roots.

Reese looked down at the pavement and bit his lip. "Go away," he said to the wind. The old night breeze pulled at his shirt in reply, at the liquid film of his eyes. It traced its invisible hands across his jean-clad hips.

"Go away!" he yelled this time, his anger enough to silence even the tree from its attack on the building, "I'm *happy*!"

He pulled at the belt loops on his jeans and stormed back inside. As the metal joints of the door clicked into place, milky drool fell from above the entrance, then landed onto the pavement in scattered dots. When Reese went in, nails scraped across the rooftop and kept pace above him.

{}

During the downtime between Daniel's loss and the start of the next match, Jalen's computer crashed. "God damn it," he slid down the back of his chair and stared into the flat surface of his monitor, as if to will the device back to life.

Jalen's eyes glazed as familiar prompts and error messages whizzed by his screen. It wasn't the first time something like this had happened, so he didn't pay much attention at all to the lines of white-on-black dialogue during the reboot. Buried among usual messages of warnings about safe restarts, he caught a single line at the bottom, in a smaller font, separate from the rest:

PROTECT, the dialogue said.

Jalen leaned forward. Before he had time to fully grasp the command's request, it was gone, replaced by his normal login screen.

Reese plopped down into the seat beside him.

"Welcome back," Jalen said as he logged into his computer, "you haven't missed anything, I'm happy to report. Other than my piece-of-shit computer being, well, exactly that."

Reese leaned over and smooched Jalen on his cheek.

"Well," Reese smiled, "I missed *you*."

After Jalen finished the camera setup, he wrapped his arm around Reese and, together, they enjoyed the rest of the night's festivities. They never noticed any awkward glances, they never heard the anxious scrape of claws across the roof. The crowd, the music, and their hearts were too loud.

{17}

{**RATS**}

Daniel Bianchi, covered in sweat, crumpled to a bench. His limbs hung over the side and he sucked on the tip of his water bottle with force that could have drained the Gulf of Mexico. His breath was shallow, his limbs shook. For a moment, he only perceived the slight hum of the air conditioner, and he was thankful for the low volume and solitude.

A towel landed on his shoulder.

He sprayed a mist of water into the air in surprise, and turned his head to see Sean (or, Sir Pierre) had been in the locker room the whole time. Bent over, Sean stuffed his purple trunks into an open bag, and Daniel's eyes followed the line from bag-zipper to roman nose to sculpted traps and sweat-dolloped biceps. His eyes lingered there against his will. *My god,* he thought, *how did he have the time to get them so big? The* expedition continued to Sir Pierre's bare thigh, and it was then Daniel realized Sean wore only a rough, laboured jockstrap and the scrapes and bruises of a 30-minute, no-disqualification battle with Silver Beetle. Blood trickled down Sean's left calf.

"You did good tonight," Sean said with no trace of the smarmy patronizing his character was known for. "Cleanest bumps I've seen from you."

I've been working hard, Daniel considered his response. The earnest reply climbed up his throat and clawed at his teeth, but with an eyelid twitch he knocked it back down his stomach and remained silent. Talking can lead to a connection. A connection leads to a further spiral down an industry he despised. The last thing he wanted was to get pulled into the whirlpool of sports entertainment and spat out the other side as an empty-husked professional. He was better than that.

He was better than *this,* too, this scraping-by in the indies, but it'd have to do for now.

"We're going to the diner after this to refuel," Sean said. He slid worn denim up his toned thighs and stretched a video game t-shirt over his wide chest. "Wanna come?"

"You're bleeding," Daniel muttered. He melted back down to the bench, wiped his face with the towel, and let his bottle-blonde hair fall over his eyes.

Sean blinked. "What? Where?"

"Your calf."

Sean fished his calf back out of the denim and rested his leg on the bench. This action displayed his blood and jockstrap anew, and Daniel pulled the towel back over his head to obscure his vision.

"Ah shit," Sean hobbled back to his gym bag and treated it with some ointment and bandages. "Must've cut it when I flipped over the top ropes onto Beetle. I knew my leg hit a chair on the way down, but it didn't hurt... well... until now." He slapped a couple of band-aids on the wound, and the sound of hand-to-skin echoed in the gym.

Stop talking, Daniel pressed the towel onto his face to create the darkness he craved, *stop being in here. Stop the slapping sounds, too.*

"Yeah," was all he chose to say.

"Yeah to coming?"

"No!" Daniel was quicker to clarify. His whole body squirmed along the bench. "No, I think... that's probably when you cut yourself."

"Glad you watched my match. This is a new side of you, Daniel."

Oh no, Daniel whimpered in his mind, *you're gonna keep talking.*

"Why do injuries not hurt until you know they're there?" Sean fussed his med-kit back into his bag. "Anyways. Open invite, we'll be leaving in 20 minutes. Beet's driving. It'll be the last time we're in town for a month, we have a few shows in Oklahoma and Kansas we're doing."

Oftentimes, wrestlers on the indie scene have to drive themselves from town to town to raise awareness of their shtick and stay booked. Daniel knew this. He didn't want to drive. Gas is expensive. You have to book hotels. You never break even until your name is big, and who is your name big with? *Not girls,* he thought. *Not hot ones, anyways. Not single ones. If they were nice to look at, they were dragged there by their chud-boyfriends. Or they knew the wrestlers. Big, bulky, biceped wrestlers.* Daniel tried so hard to focus, but Sean, wearing little and dotted in sweat and blood, smiled on the back of his eyelids at him.

"You're so lucky your dad's got a gym you can hang at for free," Sean did a final fine-comb through his hair. "If you keep working, you're gonna be ripped as hell, and a star to boot. It took me forever to get huge because of gym fees. Half my time was flippin' burgers so that I could flip bodies."

Daniel's thoughts were always framed in negatives. He had dislikes, not desires. When faced with Sean's praise, he didn't know what to do or say, so he held his breath and waited.

"Alright," Sean slung his bag over his shoulder. "I'm out. See ya at the diner, dude." He left, and never knew of the silent war Daniel waged with himself.

Once alone, Daniel could breathe again. The rest of his body dangled, motionless and empty. *Maybe some food would be good,* he thought as a bead of sweat escaped the tip of his nose and plopped to the tile below him. *Don't you have to refuel your body with protein and shit after you work out? I don't fuckin' know... shit. I should've gone with them.*

In the dead of dripping showers and flickering lights, he heard a scraping sound.

Daniel turned his head. The scamper of tiny claws against tile came from behind a row of lockers. It certainly wasn't Sean, or a person. It was too small, too panicked.

Did someone let a dog in? he thought. *Do we have rats?*

He heard a thick cough, a staggered sound full of phlegm and grit. A splat smacked against the tile like a mop bucket dumped onto the floor.

Daniel slid his body off the bench and peaked around the corner. A red-and-gray mush puddled underneath the bench. He wasn't sure what this pile of matter was until he inched closer: the body of a rat had been broken and deflated, its head separated from the body by inches, and fragments of its spine dyed in blood dressed the ground around it.

They *had* rats.

Daniel winced, looked away, looked back at it in morbid curiosity, then turned again in regret. He considered cleaning up the mess himself, but thought better of it: if they had a rat problem, then it's something his dad should take care of, after all.

Later that night, Daniel told his father about the dead rat. Matteo appreciated being informed right up till the moment he went into the locker room and found Daniel had left the rat's corpse untouched, and an argument on Daniel's laziness ensued between the two.

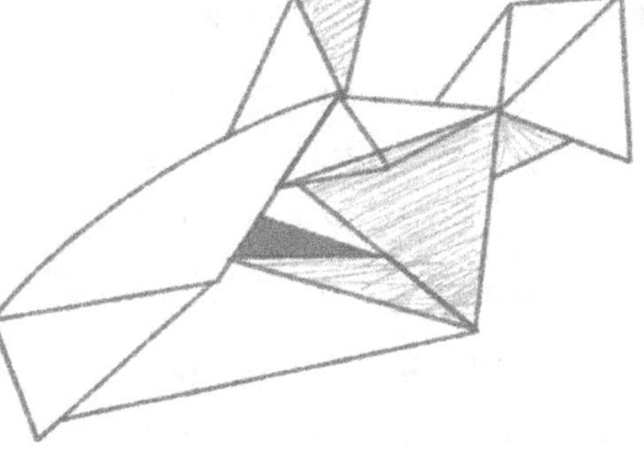

{18}

{THE LONG ROAD TO THE TRUTH}

"So, how was tonight?" Jalen asked as he flicked a black garbage bag open.

Reese had volunteered, along with nearly every wrestler in the DEF, to help clean up after the event. Together, they folded chairs, broke down the ring, and cleaned up discarded food and beer cans and bottles always a foot or so away from the nearest trash can. Reese underhanded a water bottle across a row of chairs. Jalen shifted to catch it in the bag.

"I had a great time," Reese smiled and bent down to fish out more trash.

And how could he not? He'd experienced a public event full of wild noise and an abandonment of the rules of reality. He became one with the crowd, and did it in the safety of his boyfriend's orbit.

My boyfriend, Reese attempted to underline the importance of that phrase in his mind. *Jalen is* my *boyfriend.*

Reese considered he never would have had this mindless joy, this evening of release, without all the awkward dates and embarrassment and risks they had both taken up until that point. He never knew he *could* have this. He never knew he *needed* this. Dating and loving a man from a chance encounter at a coffee shop is the sort of dumb fantasy Reese considered beyond the scope of believability—and his own scope of such things was fairly wide, given his penchant for talking mustached skeletons and bird-wizards. He thought the freedom afforded by being intertwined in the world of someone else's imagination *must* be habit forming. Despite his drained energy levels and despite the hours as they ticked over from double to single digits, he wanted more. He wanted more wrestling shows, more nights out wandering city streets and parks and piers with no concern for the time it would take out of the day, more stars in the sky to push the sun back down over the city and let him have a sliver more of night to appreciate a reality he hadn't known existed.

Jalen snapped a finger.

"You okay?"

Reese blinked and shook his foggy head clear. "Yeah! Never better."

When they piled into Jalen's Audi, they shared a silent understanding of each other's spirits. Reese could see the glow in Jalen's lidded eyes over a successful show, and a sense of relief in the way his cheek muscles relaxed on his face, the way his long body reclined a little further into the driver's seat. Jalen, too, could tell Reese was abuzz. His normally introverted boyfriend chattered in recount of his favorite match-spots between heavy yawns and slow blinks.

Their minds wandered during a quiet, easy ride. Wandering can lead a man to strange places.

I have been going out with this guy for a while now, and we haven't fucked yet, Jalen thought. *Someday we're gonna have to talk about it. It's a nice change of pace from the way other guys have treated me, I guess, but at this point, especially after tonight... is he... afraid to ask me for sex? Is he afraid of sex, period?*

The dotted lines on the mostly empty road began to blur in his vision as he mulled over how he was going to lean into the topic. That train of thought skidded to a halt, however, when they pulled up to a stop sign that, on the trip to the show, had stood in normal duty. Here, it was snapped in half, the red octagon helplessly discarded on the opposite lane. No debris or evidence of a car wreck littered the pavement, and if Jalen didn't know this road so well, he might've missed it altogether.

"Damn, hope this wasn't done by someone going to our show," Jalen muttered as he looked down the darkened streets. "I don't want a drunk asshole hitting the news and putting our name in his mouth."

As they drove past the downed sign, Reese's wandering thoughts took a similar path.

At some point, he's gonna want to come over, he worried, *and he's gonna have to see how I live. I've waited too long to tell him. At this point he's gonna feel hurt I wasn't more open with him, and he has every right to feel that way. Why wasn't I more honest with him, sooner?*

He glanced over at Jalen, who drove with a reclined lean, his wrist draped over the steering wheel. The coffee-clerk caught Reese's glance, twisted his head to give a small grin as warm as freshly-baked cookies, then put his eyes back on the road.

Ah, fuck, Reese's nervous smile more resembled packaged cookies, made with less love and more economic worry, *I can't bring that up tonight. He's on a high from the show. I don't want to ruin the mood.*

He reached into his pocket and pulled out his phone, an unconscious gesture he had developed to escape his thoughts. The moment Reese secured his grip around the device, it vibrated.

Who the fuck is sending me a text at this hour? he thought.

He flipped through apps to read the text.

{ 19 }

bones

{20}

{THE 3D BRAIN}

The single-word message was devoid of rationale. Yet, between the pixels, through the wash of the dim light from his cell phone, Reese felt the coat of violent disdain on the text. He imagined himself on the other side of the blocked number, and stood in the shoes of the type of person that would know him and know how to reach him and text him a single word evocative of structure, the foundation of the main character of his story, and himself. He knew someone like that. Someone who would try to find the shortest, simplest way to make him afraid.

He looked in the rear view mirror but saw no car trail them, and looked around the perimeter but found no antagonist kept pace.

"What's wrong?" Jalen asked. "Did something happen?"

Reese jerked as Jalen's voice fished him from his mind's ocean.

"Can we..." Reese cleared his throat, "...can we go somewhere?"

"Where to? It's a little late, but if you're hungry, I'm sure—"

"Anywhere," he blurted.

Jalen's grip on the steering wheel loosened in surprise.

"Talk to me," he said.

Reese rubbed his lips together. "I don't know if it's the ride-shares I've taken lately or if it's the fact I've been more visible in public... or what," he frowned and stuffed his phone in his pocket. "I've tried to keep a low profile, but I think... I might be getting stalked again."

Jalen leaned back. "Stalked?" he shook his head, and added, "*Again*?"

Reese squeezed his palms together. "Yeah."

"Let's go to the police, and file a report. I'm not gonna let a creeper do something to—"

"No!" Reese shook his head. "I can't do that. I can't."

The veneer of Jalen's patience cracked. "Why the hell not?"

Reese leaned his head against the window, his breath visible on the glass. "I have some stuff I need to tell you."

Jalen gripped the steering wheel a little tighter, and flicked the turn signal on.

"I know where we can go," he said.

{}

Harper Park closed at 10 p.m., but its massive expanses, smooth paths and winding hills made it ideal for the sort of heavy talk that loomed over them. They parked in a cul-de-sac with a damaged guardrail and no houses at the end of the street. Reese hated that a walk in a park with his boyfriend—*that is what he is, dammit*—twisted his innards with worry. He hated that he was at fault for his own feelings even more.

A big, friendly-lettered entrance sign arched above them. Jalen squeezed Reese's hand with reassurance.

"Whenever you're ready," Jalen said.

Reese popped his knuckles with his thumb. He looked around to make sure no one else was in the park.

"When I first started streaming, there was this guy that'd come in my chat named '3DBrain.' He was an early supporter. He donated a lot before anyone else did and... I mean... you can guess based off his name why he liked my work. Before he was a regular in my audience, it was just friends and internet acquaintances that watched me, and I'm not even sure they liked what I was doing. I always remembered him because I didn't know who he was. There was this time on stream I said something like 'I'd do anything to make this my full-time gig' and at the time, when he said something like... 'It'll happen, I'm always here,' it seemed so sweet. It's still hard for me to believe it came from the same person... that..."

Both the streets around Harper Park, and the park itself, were dark in ways that seemed intentionally dangerous. Outside the zoning limits of the capital city, the local conservative government allowed individual communities more freedom on the placement of street lights and signage. If it weren't for the velvet glaze of moonlight, many details of the scenery would be completely swallowed up in darkness. Reese narrowly avoided stepping on a toad, and watched it hop to a moist patch of grass.

"I know my shit is pretty unprofessional, but back then, I was really loose with what I'd talk about. I'd start talking with chat about anything that came up, you know? It was like... half puppet show, half listen-to-Reese-ramble-about-nothing. My roommates at the time were just high school acquaintances, not really friends, that I shared an apartment with because we were all fuckin' broke and splitting costs was the only way any of us could live. They knew I did something on the internet and didn't give a shit what it was as long as I was paying the rent and didn't get in trouble. I felt the same way about them. At the time, I had a car and lived day-to-day between ride-shares and stream revenue. What else was I supposed to do? I couldn't afford to go to college. No family. I flipped burgers for a little bit but it paid less than the ride-shares and the boss changed the schedule like every other day. He expected everyone to be tied to that place at all times, it was on us employees to always come in or call and see if he played roulette with our scheduled shifts. Got sick of that shit real fast. I did the math on the money I earned from there and the toll on my sanity and quit."

The same toad hopped back in front of Reese.

"I'm sorry. I'm rambling. I guess I don't have to relive every detail..." Reese tried to rub the toad's back, which convinced it to flee into the nearby bushes, "*...at you.*"

"It's fine," Jalen rubbed Reese's back. "Take your time."

Reese straightened his poor posture. An audible pop crunched from his neck joints.

"After a while the stream started growing and it just didn't make economic sense to be a ride-share driver since insurance and repairs were so much. I sold my car and went all in on the show. It was risky as hell but the show's donation revenue was *just* close enough to let me break even. It's my dream, right? This was... the only thing that both made me happy *and* felt like I was capable of doing it. I had to chase it, even if I'm not great and it's not exactly stable."

Jalen's eyes drifted towards the darkest blacks in the park: the corners of the restroom, the steel swing set, the dusty wooden fence that separated recreation from neighborhood.

"One time, I came out on stream," Reese stopped walking. "Just like... 'Yeah, I like dudes, period.' I don't even remember what we were talking about. My roommates didn't know I was gay, my stream didn't know, and that particular night, with more people than ever watching me, I just... I felt the need to talk about it well up inside. It felt natural for the moment. I *had* to tell them, I had to show them the most real part of myself. And, you know, for the like... 50 or so people there, the reaction was really positive."

Reese covered his mouth. A slight laugh pushed through his nose.

"Lots of rainbow emojis. I even got some donations just because I said it, which, you know, that's... the fact people gave me money just because I said 'I'm gay' on the internet is a different conversation. I wasn't alone in that room, clearly."

The smirk hidden by his mouth skewed to a grimace as the full memory forced its way in.

"Some comments that I caught in the chat scroll were negative. But it just felt... like... noise. I was too wrapped up in the moment to be affected. That never happens. I didn't even see that one of the negative comments was from 3DBrain. He said 'I didn't know you were a faggot.' I had mods by this point, and they just deleted it and blocked him. I had no clue. If my coming-out wasn't enough to make him angry, I'm sure the fact that my channel had grown to the point where he was lost in the shuffle did."

Jalen rolled his eyes to the sky as the story's inevitable path appeared. "I'm so sorry."

Reese held his hands up in frustration. Years later, he still didn't have the words to explain his disappointment.

"He started to make new accounts, and it was always obvious that it was him. '3DHead', 'BrainsBack', stuff like that. He didn't care. He wanted me to know. He would harass me in chat until a mod blocked him, and he'd come back and would always do something worse. He posted my address. He posted the names of my roommates. He sent mail to our apartment addressed to them that said 'You live with a fag.' It got to be too much, and I decided to quit streaming for a bit. I moved out before my roommates could kick me out. As I was looking around at apartments that I could never afford on my own, I was terrified by the idea of finding new roommates. What if I put myself out there and *he* found out and sabotaged that? I certainly didn't want to put an ad out for a roommate, I've never met the guy in real life, you know? I got scared. I didn't want to do anything other than just... stay in my shell. I thought about what to do, and that's when I had the idea to..."

Reese looked around the park again. He chewed on his bottom lip, cursed himself, then lurched to stand in front of Jalen.

"I live in a storage space."

An interjection welled up behind the surface of Jalen's solemn nod. He swallowed it down.

"I know. I know it's pathetic. I know it's illegal. 'He can't find me if I drop off the grid,' that was the original idea, but I found lots of reasons to love living there outside of that. Way less expensive. I have more freedom since I'm alone. I have to be sneaky to pull it off, but it's mostly worked out. The truth is, being alone most of the time, I haven't had a need to impress anyone with anything other than my work. So... I haven't tried. Until I met you."

He ran his fingers through his blonde-green hair and blinked tears back underneath the lid.

"I came back to streaming after I moved out and the channel kept growing to what it is today. It's like my work got more eyes on it the worse my life outside the stream got. And 3DBrain's harassment in chat got proportionally worse, too. I was invited to some panels at conventions, and that's when it came to a head. It occurred to me that, you know, *this guy*'s donated money to me. I can give the information I have on him to security, all the messages he ever sent, etc. So I did. 3DBrain... his real name was Andrew King. He tried to get in the convention by buying an on-site pass and they searched him and found a knife on him. Who knows if he would've done anything? I'm honestly lucky that he was stupid enough to bring his knife on the premises when he tried to get in, because when I talked to security, they seemed like they didn't take me seriously. He was kicked out and banned, obviously. Last I heard of him."

They passed neatly arranged square bushes. The work that goes into maintaining their shape was strenuous, but it must've been safer than having a stalker, Jalen thought. Everywhere he looked, he saw jobs that Reese could take on—yard work, trash collection, dog-walking—that he wanted to suggest as a means of escape. None of them seemed quite appropriate for right that moment, but that didn't stop every corner of the park from its suggestions.

"When I got involved with the police, it was still relatively close enough to when I lived at the old apartment that I could use that address. I don't feel like I can get away with that now, I don't even know if my old roommates still live there. I think it's been almost four years now. Long enough that it feels like a different life."

Jalen could hear the memory of his mother's snarl telling him to focus his career on something. *Anything*. Stop working dead-end retail and partying with men and start working in IT and politely brown-nose your boss until you get a raise. Somehow she was speaking past Jalen, and at Reese. Her voice got louder, and it tried to scream out of Jalen's mouth. Jalen bit it back.

"Are you sure that it's him texting you?" Jalen asked. "I know he seems like the most likely person, of course, I just want to know... are you *sure*?"

Reese felt a dull pressure in his eyes when he tried to look at his phone screen. The contrast between the depths of night and the blue artificial light of the screen weighed heavy on his retinas, as if the technology itself tried to ward him away. He squinted at the single-word message to see if time had brought clarity to it.

"Once he had my address and personal info he would paste things like... 'Reese', or my roommate's names, then vanish. One time he just typed a restaurant name into chat, and it was a place I had gone to the day before. I think he wanted me to be afraid enough to not stream anymore. So, sending me something cryptic out of the blue is... absolutely his M.O."

They came to a fork in the paved path that split down opposite ends of the park. The sounds of boat-tailed grackles rang in the perimeter of trees. These birds sang their night song to the world, a chorus of beeps that could be mistaken for laser sound effects from a cheap B-movie, shrill inhales and exhales with no concern for any other creature's sleep. It was a scream at, and to, the world. Jalen and Reese stared at the loudest tree in the park, and wordlessly agreed to take the path away from it.

"But... something's off. I don't know what 'bones' means. Sir Mortimer is made of bones, if the intent is to reference the show. But that's obtuse, even for him. There's a part of me that thinks I'm just being paranoid, you know? I've moved hundreds of miles away from where I was. I keep thinking I see someone looking at me in the crowd anywhere we go out, for example. But, it's never him. He's never there."

Jalen looked across the manicured grass, across the line of moonlight that trimmed the metal playground bars. This bizarre story was unloaded on him in the drape of such a normal place, and the contrast seized him. The normalcy of the park whispered to him of opportunities, and now, they spoke in his father's voice. *This wouldn't have happened with a girl,* his dad's voice, gravel and cynical, rumbled in his skull. *Get a job, find a girl, marry her, get a nice house, have my grandkids. It's not fucking science. It's just fucking.*

"I'm sorry. My absolute worst fear..." Reese hid his eyes as he rubbed his brow and temples, "...is scaring you away. I know there's nothing attractive about a past like that, or about living in the squalor I currently do. I love you... more than I thought I was capable of loving people. I didn't want to ruin anything."

Jalen crossed his arms and secured the hem of his shirt, then lifted the fabric over his head. The voices of his parents faded.

Reese watched the reveal of Jalen's carved back, his V-trimmed waist and the deep valley of his muscle-walled spine. Maybe, in a different moment, under a different tint of night, Reese would have been in awe of the sculpture of his body, swooned, aroused. The air was thick with a different emotion, the glaze of uncertainty and vulnerability stuck to Reese's skin.

He saw Jalen's scar.

"I wanted to be a wrestler, and I mean the proper kind. Folk-style, amateur, stuff like that," Jalen turned to face Reese. The scar wrapped around his shoulder, an upside down 'J' that will forever mark his rotator cuff surgery. "I loved the physical challenge in it, the close contact, and the training required to be in shape. I mistook all of that as a love of being competitive. It didn't help any that my parents *really* wanted me to do well. They saw a scholarship and a full bank account and a girlfriend that would surely become a wife in every takedown I did. I forgot that the real reason I liked wrestling at all was because when I was a kid, I saw Booker T on TV. He was a tall black man that set the world on fire just by raising his hands. I didn't know anything about wrestling or competition or performance or being gay, none of that mattered to me. I just felt something powerful when I saw the arena—and the fans—explode around him on TV."

Jalen let the cotton hang from two tired fingers. The stars in the sky danced across the build of his bare shoulders.

"I got injured in one of my first high school wrestling matches. After the surgery they said I'd be out up to six months. If I'm being honest, I think I lost my will to compete before the match even began. The way the crowd cheered was different than what I felt when I was a kid. I obviously knew what I saw on TV was 'fake' by this point, but the way the crowd interacted with the two different events was not something I understood until I was in that moment on the 'real' side. The fun was sucked right out of the whole thing for me. Even though

I'm now legitimately in the business of the type of wrestling I love the most, the desire to be in the ring has been kicked out of me.

"My parents didn't understand pro wrestling or why I liked it. I have this scar to remind myself of how bad of an idea it is to mindlessly do something because other people tell you it's what you should do. I second guess everything I want now because I don't know if it's right for me, or if I'll just get hurt again. I'm lucky that I've found happiness behind the camera, at least."

"Jalen," Reese frowned, "I'm not... I'm not gonna run away from you because of a *scar*."

Jalen slipped the fabric back over his head and tugged it down. "That's what I'm trying to say to you."

Reese's nose scrunched.

"By now, I was hoping we were at a point where you could trust me with anything," Jalen said. "What we're doing isn't that different, you know? We both toil away in video, we piece together hero stories in strange worlds that only a *very particular* audience wants to see. Put all that aside, and consider this: I flirted with you before I knew about the stream, before you got a haircut, before you got new clothes, before you told me *anything*."

Reese struggled to look up from the rocks on the path.

"Yes, I noticed the haircut," Jalen smiled and placed a hand on Reese's shoulder. "Just be real with me. The real you is the most attractive thing about you. Hiding what your dealing with... isn't."

Reese didn't know what to do. He didn't know if he should move forward and hug Jalen, cry, pull away, or protest the validity of hiding such an embarrassing aspect of his life. He wanted to do all those at once, and, burdened by choice, did none of them.

"Anyways, it's not my place to demand what you should and shouldn't do. My parents are king and queen of nagging and it's a pet peeve of mine," Jalen stuffed his hands in his pockets. "But I *am* going to nag a little bit, because I want to be clear. Honesty is the absolute most important thing to me. Yes, I'm a touch annoyed that you hid your living situation from me. I'm way, *way* more annoyed that you're fending for yourself against a situation that's actively hurting your mental state."

"I'm..." Reese sniffed, "...I'm sorry."

"You shouldn't be sorry, that's not what I meant," Jalen shook his head and tried to course correct. "What I mean is... I'm here. And..."

No matter how far away they got from the grackle tree, Jalen could still hear them. He wanted no distractions for himself or for Reese, so he reached down, bent his knees, and hugged Reese hard into his chest. Reese's hearing was muffled from the arms around his temples and he could, for a moment, hear Jalen's heartbeat.

"How about you spend the night with me?"

{21}

{VELVET ON THE CONCRETE}

A young buck ambled through the gray-brown thicket near Store-It. Its antlers were bloodied and vibrant and in stark contrast to its soft pelt. This blood-coating wasn't the result of a fight, but rather of a natural process deer undergo when they grow new antlers. The fuzzy skin of the antlers, called velvet, had begun to rip now they'd reached their full size. This tearing is quite uncomfortable for the young buck, so he found a sturdy tree and began to rub vigorously in an attempt to scrape the velvet away.

The "tree" was, in fact, no tree at all, but an electrical pole. The buck knew not the difference, and even if he did, he certainly would have cared less about it than the discomfort his shedding caused him. He headbutted and left red stripes of blood on the pole and velvet on the concrete. A euphoria overcame the deer as he shed his old skin. A simple mind is easily overwhelmed by simple pleasures.

A burnt, chlorine-like scent skittered its way into his nostrils. There was a soft crackle from nearby. The deer's ears swayed like satellite dishes. His nostrils flared and tried to categorize the unfamiliar smell; it wasn't a rival deer, nor any predator he knew. The buck's eyes had a 310-degree vision that found nothing out of the ordinary in the stillness of the night. He stamped and snorted in confusion.

Alas, a deer knows nothing of plane angles. As it turned its head, it discovered that it was the 50 degrees of vision it lacked that mattered the most. With its white tail flagged up to the night sky, it tried to bound away from the figure behind it. A gnarled claw glommed the deer around his neck, bent it to an angle the deer could never understand, and dragged its carcass away into the thicket.

{22}

{A BEAUTIFUL STORM CAME}

Of course I'd say yes, Reese watched the blur of trees glide past his reflection in the passenger window. Dark clouds had started to creep in along a backdrop of purple diffuse, and colored his mirror image. The kelly-green of the undeveloped land turned black in the distance. *Of course I want to spend a night with him. That's completely normal.*

Apartment buildings and corner stores came into view on the main road. New street corners brought greater clarity to Reese that he would soon be at Jalen's door, in his kitchen, in his bed, in his arms. This awareness should have warmed him, but the cold realization that he still thought of Jalen as a man apart from him, separate but present, made him pop his knuckles with frustration.

No, he's my boyfriend. Call him 'my boyfriend,' Reese thought. *The whole point of that park conversation was to establish trust and prove you're ready for the next stage of a relationship. Don't think 'Oh, of COURSE you'd say 'yes,' you slut.' I'm allowed to have a good night. We've dated for a few months, and...*

Reese looked at Jalen's hands as they clutched seven and five on the steering wheel.

...am I ready? Reese popped his left-hand knuckles with his thumb. The muscles pulled skin forward as he pressed down on his pointer finger, but the crack, and subsequent relief, had already been wrestled from the joint minutes prior. Jalen's Audi chewed away the scenery and left the past behind; all that remained was ahead of them.

Am I ever *going to be ready?*

{}

You can only access the gated Washington Hills Apartments with the proper code for its keypad. When Reese saw the small steel box, he remembered his combat with their setup when he was a driver; his short stature meant he had to climb out of the seat to reach the keypad buttons, often well worn from months of being jammed in by residents. This assumed his customer provided him with the code at all. They usually didn't.

Jalen parked under a covered carport. Specks of yellow light lit up stairwells and white-painted doors. Strategically planted trees and gaudy angel sculptures in the center of roundabouts stood like forced smiles in the soil of suburbia. The petrichor of an impending storm floated into their senses. A small dog yapped at the sound of a mechanical threat outside his window. Reese saw these worlds of apartments as a foreign country; familiar humanity in a land he could never live in.

"Dude's always barkin'," Jalen squeezed Reese's hand. "The world's tiniest dog apparently never sleeps. Luckily, you can't hear him once you're inside."

Reese was compelled to look in the shadows for the shapes of threats—shoulders hunched or grimaces of hate. If the shadow of his stalker existed at all, it blended in with the purple-blacks and failed to follow him. He listened for the crush of sneakers on the acorns littered in the parking lot, but only heard his own. Jalen's thick forearm pulled him through blue hallways. Fans flicked yellowed lights across the ceiling. A leopard moth sat in calm repose on the wall near Jalen's door, remaining still even when their shadows crossed over it. No matter where Reese looked for danger, lifeforms smaller and more fragile than he felt safe between these walls.

Once inside, they slipped their shoes off and placed them on a small rack near the front door. Reese noticed a smooth wooden object on the inside of Jalen's shoes; he realized he had never known anyone that owned a shoe-tree until now. He wasn't even sure he had seen one before, but based off of what he knew about them, he assumed that's what the objects had to be. Up until his attempts to impress Jalen on their first date, Reese had worn the same pair of shoes since high school. Barring total disintegration, he was sure he'd still wear the dirt-stained sneakers if left to his own devices.

Jalen's apartment was a transitional hub in his life. It showed little sign it was lived in; DVDs and CDs were organized on a shelf by genre in the living room. There were no decorations on the walls, drink coasters rested on the kitchen table by themselves, and there was no TV, only his computer, a perpetually powered-on, outdated machine whose fans wheezed with age. No stray pots or pans cluttered the kitchen. The lone glass in the sink stood out far more among its clean environment than the stacks of dishes Reese had grown accustomed to when he last shared an apartment. More accurately, Reese thought, Jalen lived in the world outside his doors, and only visited this apartment when he had to. Given Reese's own transient nature, this was a way of living he understood well.

They stopped in the hallway, and shuffled awkwardly on the carpet. Their stare was quiet and loud, tired and electric.

"So, do you want..."

"Yes," Reese blurted.

Jalen pulled off his shirt and slid his fingers underneath the hem of Reese's. Snap-buttons popped as Jalen pressed tips, then palms, into Reese's stomach and drew upwards. The couch became a clothes-hanger. He hooked his hands under Reese's thighs and destroyed the conceit of gravity. Through the contact of lips, they tasted each other's joy and fear and passion and pain all at once. The wrestler's tongue jabbed, the puppeteer's strung him along. When they ran out of breath and were forced to separate their faces, the line of saliva between them flicked them back together. *You won't get away,* their hormones growled into their anxieties, *I've got you.*

Lightning struck as the two collapsed into Jalen's bed. Reese pressed his palms into the mattress, looked down, and tried to make sense of the reality below him. Rain rattled the window. Jalen's lips, full and wet and parted by his slight pant, were colored dark blue in the low light of the room. His locs splayed and framed him in holy circles. Reese shivered at the sight; he imagined if lavender blossomed around Jalen's head, straight through the bedspread, it would not have been out of place among his natural beauty. Reese kept that image, a marriage of love-drunk imagination and adrenaline, and seared it into himself. It was the last good look he had of Jalen's face for the next several minutes.

Outside, the storm blessed the freedom they enjoyed over each other, and kept its thunder to a respectful rumble. Lightning lit the outline of their disparate body sizes twisted in blue sateen. Reese worshiped Jalen's chest in the way a runner drinks from a water fountain. These same pectorals, weeks ago, took brutal knife-edge chops in a demonstration of correct form for rookie wrestlers; the welt-bearing palms then, and Reese's mouth now, both lit Jalen's eyes to new widths and left him ragged and worn. Though different nerve receptors were involved, they produced the same sweat, the same tense of muscles in the forearm and fist.

Jalen was unprepared for Reese. His normally shy companion, with the hint of permission, became obsequious and mad. He left no domain of Jalen's skin unattended, no soil uncultivated, no land left dry. Jalen might have been shocked at how long Reese spent in worship before he tried to dip his fingers below the waistband, but he was a little too busy, too lost, to understand the passage of time. When Reese eventually did attack the gold button on his rough blue jeans, Jalen's trance finally broke.

Size may seem important on paper, but rarely do men who relish the fantasy of excess length and girth consider its drawbacks. Even though Reese felt the warm growth from Jalen's loins, the unfamiliar and untrained can never truly be prepared for first contact. Reese's pale hands pulled down the fabric. He stared in stunned silence at the obelisk it hid. Fantasy would lead one to believe the reveal would bring any expression other than the flash of fear and math Reese's face wore. Jalen had seen it before; he expected this moment, but despite how many times he had lived it, he never grew used to it. No matter what Reese said afterwards, Jalen knew his lover was locked in a geometrical problem he could not solve. Few people could. This moment was always a downer for him, an intimate incompatibility with the rest of the world. To Jalen's surprise, Reese's expression disappeared between his legs. He arched as he was drawn upwards with Reese's determined ministrations.

Well, good, Jalen's last coherent thought was one of relief. *I guess we can have that conversation some other time*.

Reese could never swallow Jalen to his hilt, the size disparity between his oral cavity and Jalen's length was too great, too cruel. As with most of life's greatest joys, though, the real destination was the journey. Reese pinned the wrestler by his hips and found a rhythm for suction that matched the overburdened swivel of the man below. The throb of rapture rolled in tense waves through Jalen's muscles. He clenched bed sheets in his fist and fought a losing battle to keep his breath in his lungs. His mind regressed back to an earlier time in his species's evolution when there was no vocabulary to profess his love to the world. His cries of passion were swallowed up into the air, into the walls, into Reese's hungry lips and soft palate.

And what flavor! Reese was no passive bystander; control was shared among these two captains. He kept steady pace so his selfish need to taste velvet salt was satiated. Jalen's potency meant Reese rarely turned up for air, and his laboured breaths through his nose warmed the wrestler's pelvis. When he pulled his mouth from middle to tip with a slow and rapacious slurp, it was to check in on the co-pilot's status. With approval, he inhaled, and dived again, over and over until the mission was completed.

{}

Reese toweled his face, spit into the sink, gargled, spit again, then filled up a small plastic cup and drank. Jalen wiped away some splash damage on his abs with a paper towel.

Jalen's bathroom was standard fare, though it showed more signs of human activity than any other part of his apartment. Jalen's many grooming tools sat on a large wooden shelf tower on the sink counter, and despite the many shelves, most of his toiletries were shoved onto the second shelf up. There were many hair care products Reese had never seen before, a combination of oils and shimmering purple hair caps that made it clear that Jalen's long, colorful locs required concentrated effort to maintain. Merely standing in the presence of the tools of such commitment made the small green tuft in Reese's hair appear more desaturated and unkempt to him than ever before.

"I have to admit: I'm a top. I normally prefer to be in control," Jalen said as he gave Reese's neck a peck. "But that was fuckin' great. I sure as hell wasn't going to stop you."

Reese blushed. Compliments were difficult for him to accept, and prior to that night, he had never considered the idea of getting one for a blow job. "Thanks."

"So..." Jalen wrapped his arms around Reese's shoulders and rested his chin on top of his head. The two looked at each other through the mirror's surface.

"So?"

"So what about you? Why don't I return the favor?"

Reese fidgeted with the empty plastic cup in his hands. "Well, this is embarrassing, but I've never gotten a blow-job before. Honestly, I haven't done much in bed. I'm not a virgin, per se, but I'm not experienced, either. I don't know if I'm quite ready for that."

Jalen hugged him a little tighter, a reflex partially made up of pity and surprise. "Could've fooled me. But, it's fine, we can try some other time."

Reese leaned back against the wall of Jalen's body. "I hooked up with one dude through an app a couple of years ago. He was a financial analyst, red goatee, probably would be a bear if he had more pounds on him. He was looking for a conservative guy to settle down with. We gave each other hand jobs in the burger bar bathroom and never talked to each other again. My overwhelming memory of that date was that he talked about the Yankees for 25 minutes and I'm sitting there in my *Mystery Science Theater* t-shirt staring at his red tie wondering how the hell I ended up there."

Jalen wobbled a little with his laughter. "So, currently, the bar sits at 'mediocre handjob in a bathroom.' That's what I got to clear to give you a better night to reflect on."

Reese rubbed his red face. "Yeah, I guess."

Jalen smooched Reese's neck again and pulled him away from the sink. With a flourish he pulled open the cabinets and produced a massive, black-labeled canister of lube with a comically large pump-handle on the top.

Reese's eyes widened. "Jesus. That's a lot of lube, Jalen."

Jalen, with a smirk, held his hand down at his own nether regions, as if it was the only reply needed. Reese looked down, back up to Jalen's face, then away.

"...fair enough," a faint smile pulled at the edge of his lips.

Suddenly, Jalen wrapped a tree-trunk arm around Reese's waist and lifted him up. Reese gasped and clung his limbs around the wrestler's torso for support. He buried his face into Jalen's neck. Jalen felt growth against his abdomen, grinned, hooked the handle of the lube in his other hand, and took him back into the bedroom.

{}

They settled into the headboard. The rain spritzed on the glass. Through their exploration, Jalen learned Reese, when not in control, had a natural inclination to squirm with restless dilemma. As the wrestler's hands roamed, Reese's body would twist and turn, the puppeteer tangled in his own strings, unable to right himself. Eventually, they found peace, with Reese sat on Jalen's upper thigh, cradled against his torso. Jalen stroked him with a slow underhand grip and craned his head down to water Reese's mouth with a pitcher of kisses.

Lost in their love and lust, neither noticed the gradual increase in the intensity of the storm outside the apartment. As Reese neared climax, at the moment his eyes felt clenched tightest, a bright thunderbolt lit the sky, and rattled the walls with a loud boom.

Reese cried out, and jerked in fear and release. His hips shot hard into Jalen's hands, and rifled his love several feet from the bed. Jalen leaned back in surprise.

"Ah... ah, fuck, that was so loud," Reese panted, "and by 'that', I mean both me and that fucking thunder. I think I just had a fear orgasm. What the fuck, is that even possible?"

Jalen laughed as he dabbed and rubbed the fluids from their hands and persons, then climbed off the bed to wipe up the floor. "Apparently. Jesus, Reese. You keep doing that and I won't get my security deposit back."

{}

The two spent lovers collapsed onto each other. Jalen's long body curled like a cat in slumber. When he breathed, his massive chest lifted Reese's head along with it. Reese stared at the clock, a blur of red numbers which bore no control over his afterglow. The lights went up, and down, and back up again with the rhythm of Jalen's breath. He was content to lay and watch it for as long as the endorphins refused to translate those numbers into meaning, or until his eyes finally closed.

The physical act of sex always left Reese with a bittersweet cocktail of emotions. He believed that he suffered from 'PCD,' or post-coital dysphoria. His belief was born of self-diagnosis—Reese had never had the money in his adult life to get health insurance or go to the doctor, and if he did, there were aches and pains in his body more worthy of investigation than his post-cum blues. It was a problem he had dealt with since he first reached sexual maturity, and he had developed a myriad ways to deal with: he'd run, make food, or draw ideas for new cartoons until the feeling went away. As an adult with access to a world of health information on the internet, just having the name of his enemy was enough to get by whenever he masturbated. He could say, "Ah, there's my PCD again," and bury those emotions down in the cellar of known personal problems, where they couldn't reach him.

After a night of exploration with Jalen, he found those familiar tendrils of darkness were further back in the distance of his mind. The way Jalen trailed his finger tips down the small of Reese's back made it easier to deal with the beast that lived there. When they inevitably separated their bodies among the tangled sheets, Jalen faced the same direction Reese laid, his back knuckles brushed against Reese's hand. Enough touch to let him know he was there, soft enough to let him drift to sleep.

{}

Sunlight dribbled in behind partially drawn curtains. Reese had spent so much life waking in sleeping bags in windowless rooms that a single little ray's warmth over his eyelids was enough to flutter them open. His bones thanked him for the one-night vacation in an actual, honest-to-God bed. His blood's traffic started to move. His limbs became real, as did the sensation of Jalen's arm draped over him.

He rolled over, unsatisfied with just a hand; he wanted to see Jalen's face, and have it next to his. Such a romantic dream was not meant to be; the turn of his body in bed woke Jalen up. The wrestler kissed Reese's forehead reflexively and pulled him close.

"Good morning," Jalen mumbled.

Reese had been awake long enough that his default state, mild anxiety, had kicked in. "Did you set an alarm?"

Jalen rolled over and glared at the nightstand clock. He furrowed his brow, as if an angry stare would scare the digital display to roll back thirty minutes.

"Ugh," Jalen groaned, "No, but it's fine. We have time. Barely."

The collective Reese-Jalen unit fought against the bed's gravity and squirmed to their feet.

They vacuumed up bowls of cereal. ("I'm sorry. I hoped to make omelets for you the first time you ever came over," Jalen frowned. Reese had lived off protein bars and fast food in the morning for years. No version of himself was going to complain about frosted flakes.) They showered. ("I'm sorry. I wanted to spend more time here this morning..." Jalen whispered in Reese's ear as he drew a suds-slick hand down his flank. Reese was never going to complain about any length of time in any temperature of water with Jalen.) They both leapt into Jalen's Audi. Mr. Eze was in his cafe uniform, and Mr. Gagnon was still stuck in the clothes from the night before. The scent of a night at the DEF battled Jalen's lemon-scented body wash.

"I'm sorry," Reese tugged at the hem of his shirt.

"For what?"

"For hitting you with a weird freak-out prior to what was otherwise the best night I've had in a long time."

Jalen's mouth pulled at the side of his face, unsure of whether to turn up or down. "What's important is if you feel safe or not. The moment, I mean the *nanosecond* you think you're not in a good place, let's figure something out, okay?"

Reese turned his head. He saw Jalen's cushion-soft smile. Reese smiled back, but wondered if his expression had the same glee that he saw in Jalen's. He wondered if Jalen could see the tension behind the muscles, the slurry of traveling worries. Reese thought to himself, in some bitter morning mixture of pride and pain: *I have fallen in love with the right man for the wrong reasons.*

{}

There was no moment Reese feared more than this. Every corner closer to Store-It filled him with fear and embarrassment. When stoplights took longer than usual to turn from red to green, he begged them to break altogether, as if their failure would cause Jalen to take the day off and take him back to his apartment.

I don't want him to see how I live, or what I am.

The last city block contained barber shops and gas stations with empty lots, bus stops with large advertisements that hadn't been updated in years. They all stood cracked and crumbling on old legs. The grackles were so comfortable with people, they stood at the doors of convenience stores and stared holes into customers in hopes someone would spare any food scrap. Only the grackles came to this part of town by choice, and even they were beggars.

He likes me. Whatever image he has of me, I don't want him to lose it.

Yellow police tape fluttered in the wind.

Ever.

"Is that the turn?" Jalen asked.

Reese looked up. Policemen talked into walkie-talkies with security guards from Store-It. The sidewalk was marked off by orange traffic cones. The owner of the convenience store on the street corner shrugged during an interview with a notepad-armed rookie, his hairy, mottled hands waved wildly in the air.

The Audi passed the intersection. A deer's serrated head, ripped free of its antlers and body, was smashed into the side of an electrical pole, which teetered and sparked as city crew surrounded it with utility trucks and baffled expressions. The buck's body was so crushed and violated by force that, in its spread out state along the branches of trees and the sidewalk, it appeared liquefied, drained of form and life all at once.

Reese retched and covered his mouth. The reaction prompted Jalen to also peer as they rolled past the street.

“Fucking hell,” Jalen regretted turning his head, “that’s one hell of a hit-and-run. Hate to see the car that ran into it, assuming it’s not completely totaled.”

He pulled over into a nearby parking lot. They both sat in silence and processed what they just saw.

“I didn’t see a car involved...” Reese gripped the seat and tried to think of anything other than the dead eyes of a deer permanently fused into wood and metal.

“Well, I don’t want to make decisions for you, but I don’t know if I can wait for them to clear the street. I can drop you off and you can try to walk through all that, or you can hang with me till I’m out,” Jalen brushed his knuckles on Reese’s hand, and hoped that it would soothe his visibly shook boyfriend. “How’s that sound?”

“Y-you have work today, I don’t want to get in the way—”

“Yeah, but that’s fine, right? You’ve hung out at the shop before. I’ll explain to Molly what’s up, she’ll be fine with it. And you’re welcome to come and go whenever you please, of course.”

Say “no,” the deer head growled in Reese’s mind.

“Let’s go,” Reese’s breath shook in its exhale, “I think I can drink a lot of coffee right now, anyways.”

There was an awful lot of red at the street corner, so much so it was easy for them to miss Emma Victoria, who stood in the middle of the fray.

She was dressed in a searing crimson quarter-sleeve tunic and white pumps. She snapped photos on her cell phone and sent them to her husband, an avid hunter, to get his official confirmation that, no, a gun did *not* do this. She knew this wouldn’t help the investigation, but she craved control over all situations in her life, and this monstrosity was so far beyond her understanding of the world that she’d rather appear wrong than let the police officers think she wasn’t an active part of everything that happened around her business. She hovered around the officers and prodded them with questions and orders as if she were on active duty. The notepad-wielding rookie pulled her away and interviewed her, but only so the other police officers wouldn't have to deal with her anymore.

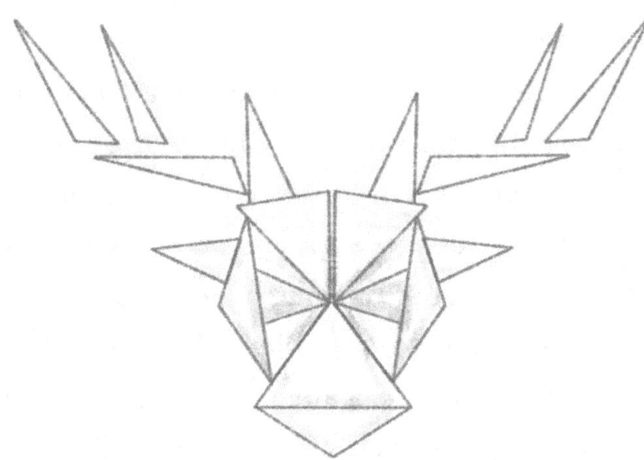

{23}

{WORK BY COMMISSION}

Reese knew Molly was staring at him.

There was a distinct difference in the sensation on his skin between Jalen's glance and Molly's glare. He knew not the science that allowed the hairs on the back of his neck to differentiate the gaze of love and animosity, why they pricked his skin with alternating warmth and cold. He worried more about the meaning behind her glare, rather than its biological explanations. Reese did not know Molly well, and given the preoccupations in his life, was unsure if her glare in his peripheral vision was real or imagined.

Molly had okay'd his presence in the shop, but it was only with the stipulation that he bought something (he did: an affogato) and that he and Jalen kept interaction with each other to a minimum, especially when other customers were in the lobby. This was no problem for Reese, who had an endless supply of creative problems to solve for *SKELEVENTURE*, and certainly no problem for Jalen, who was happy to to keep an eye on Reese after learning of the existence of his stalker, 3DBrain. It was that last part, where Molly could clearly see that a percentage of Jalen's focus was distracted by Reese at all times, that annoyed her the most.

After the afternoon rush, Molly sent Jalen out to get more change from the bank—something the restaurant didn't need—so she'd be alone with Reese. Once Jalen was gone, she introduced herself properly, and cut to the chase:

"Jalen told me what's going on with your apartment entrance," she combed back a clump of straightened jet-black hair and adjusted her ball-cap. Reese was thankful to hear that Jalen obscured his actual living situation in polite conversation.

"Yeah," the images of the deer soured Reese's sweet drink, "it was, uh, gross."

"I know he brought you here so that he wouldn't be late, but I'm glad that he did because I want to talk to you," Molly laced her fingers and leaned on the table's edge. "You see, Jalen's my best friend. We've been friends for years. If you're dating him, I think we should be straightforward with each other: I don't get what you do."

Reese shifted in his seat. "My job?"

"Your cartoons. Puppets. Whatever."

"Yeah. Okay," Reese nodded, though the filler words and downcast eyes made it clear he was unprepared, emotionally or physically, to defend his lifestyle. He hadn't even finished the affogato yet. Still, as all working artists do, he inhaled deeply and turned into his own defense lawyer in the court of justification. "So, my main inspirations are old-time public access shows. Monetarily, it's work by donation. I've been crafting it for years and have a dedicated audience. It gets me by, and that's all I can ask for."

"I'm gonna be real with you," the brim of Molly's cap dipped over her unblinking eyes. "I wanted to make sure you're not some deadbeat trying to leech off of him."

Reese rested his hand on his chin. One of the perks of the single-hermit life he had lived up until this point was avoiding these exact conversations.

"That's fair. I try pretty hard not to be a deadbeat, either," he lifted his coffee cup and raised it with praise, and tried his luck at deescalation, "which is why I'm glad I bought this. You're gonna get me addicted to these."

"I'm assuming you work by commission, too," Molly looked up to the ceiling, as if one of Reese's vulnerabilities just happened to be written there as a reminder.

Reese set the cup down to saucer and took a longer look at her eyes, the motion of her mouth, well-rehearsed and tense. She wasn't about to ask for prices. He realized, *this is an attack*. They were only words; quiet, calm, but the predator makes little noise before it strikes. This was orchestrated to unease him, to cast doubt on his compatibility with Jalen. Molly put him on trial for the crime of a dishonest love and his hobbies were both the evidence and the jury.

He sucked his tongue between his teeth and considered his words carefully: "I have learned to do what I can with what I have. I'm more focused on the show these days, but if the right project comes along, I'll consider it. I have given up a lot just to get where I am, even if that doesn't seem like much on the surface."

Molly's smile scrunched her skin towards her nose. "I'm just paying Jalen back. He protected me from a toxic relationship, so I'd like to do the same for him. If you're really working as often as you say you are, that makes me a little bit more confident in you, I think."

Reese pushed at the handle of his coffee cup. The porcelain-on-porcelain clink served as a distraction from his confused blinks; he didn't know how to explain that work for the stream didn't feel like work for him. It was "work" in the technical sense, yes, but it was also fun. He didn't see how what he did with his stream, or how he did it, was any of her business.

"I don't get your relationship, but I guess I don't have to," Molly slapped her hands on the table and pushed herself to her feet. "If you're good for him, then you're good for me. That's all I wanted to make sure of."

He raised his hand as if he had a point to make, then let it drop to the table, "I guess I'm not invited to the cookout."

"No. Not for a while," she laughed. She adjusted her cap, which she only noticed then had tightened around her head, then walked back behind the service counter. "Maybe you'll get some discounts on coffee though. Especially if you shout out Jolly Molly's on your stream."

A few minutes passed, and the door sang its electronic chime when Jalen came back. He looked to his left and saw the bags of Reese's eyes more clearly in the morning light than he had ever noticed before.

"What's up?" Jalen fumbled blue leather zip-up pouches full of rolled coins.

"I think I need another coffee," Reese said.

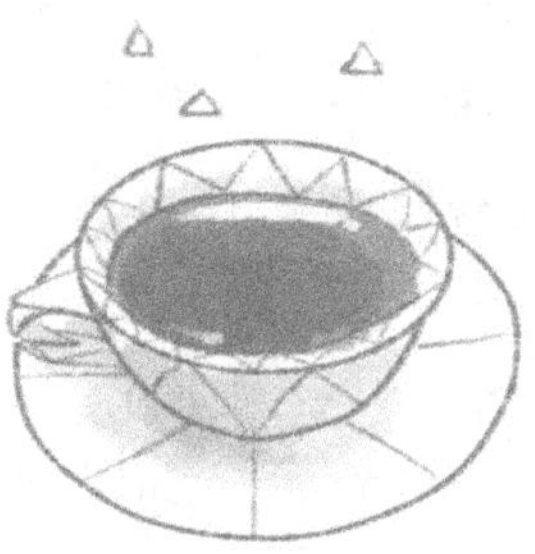

{24}

{TOUGH—TAX}

“How much blood do I have to shit before I’m *ripped*!?” Daniel Bianchi yelled in the bathroom mirror. A drop of sweat jumped from his button nose. He kicked open the door and left a sneaker mark on the gray paint, then went to the DEF’s small kitchen.

He slammed a bag of GUY-TOUGH protein onto the counter. He mixed in three scoops of the fine brown powder with a banana, almond milk, and ice, and ravaged the ingredients together in a blender until it became a mysterious beige goo. He snorted like a frustrated bull as he looked at Satan’s milkshake, closed his eyes, put his small mouth to the rim of the glass, and guzzled.

No amount of mixing could mask the foul taste of protein powder, and especially not in such high dosage. The powder clumped like wet sawdust in the banana-milk. It gave him a new off color mustache on top of the thin black strap he could never seem to grow to the same bushiness as his father’s. Daniel read the protein label as if it were a Bible and hoped the words would answer his prayers.

What the others at DEF didn’t know was, since his last disappearance, he had tried in earnest to get bigger. Nothing seemed to work. He lifted weights five days a week, and ran every day, but he was no closer to what he believed a real man was than when he worked out recreationally. He attended every stupid class Matteo taught. He studied bumps and practiced what he could on his own. He was obsessed with outgrowing his short stature and odd proportions, to prove his own self-sufficiency. Only then could he leave the DEF and leave the freedom he enjoyed from being the owner’s son. He wanted nothing more than to leave behind the reliance on his failure of a father and the failures he employed for their play-fighting.

Play-fighting, mind you, that put some much needed money in Daniel's pocket. Daniel was a man that struggled to keep work; he had been fired from his last pizza delivery job, which, in and of itself, was not unusual for the younger Bianchi, whose antagonistic nature was never fit for the service industry in the first place. The last customer he delivered to had ordered a pizza, ate three slices, then called the store to claim the order was made wrong. Daniel's manager (or as Daniel would forever remember him as, his "massive, boot-licking cocksucker" of a manager) made him drive back with a new pizza for free. When Daniel saw the pie that he'd delivered earlier on the table missing half of the food they claimed was 'completely wrong,' Daniel's spit flew in the air, landed square between the eyes of an Iraq War vet, and ended his pizza career.

As with most things in Daniel's life, it was a story where some details were easy to sympathize with, but his vitriol would isolate him in the end, no matter the circumstance. Or, if you listened to Daniel; in this fucked up world built around the con of the audience, the abuse of workers, and the appeal to base desires, Daniel was the only real man left.

His body's form never did seem to agree with that assessment.

His inability to grow his muscles and trim his skinny-fat gut had driven him to sob alone in his apartment on more than one occasion. On those nights, even the gains he'd made—his shoulders and biceps—seemed small and weak. He wondered if tonight would be one of those nights where he just couldn't take it anymore. His breakdowns routinely happened on his heaviest workout days, but Daniel never correlated the two.

"No," he whispered to himself as he stuffed the protein powder into his book-bag, "I'm *guy-tough*. I'm fine. Everything's fine."

"Well I'm glad to hear it," Matteo said.

Daniel pivoted in place, milk-stained glass in hand. His father closed the door behind himself.

"Whatcha got there?"

Daniel's nostril twitched and he set the glass on the counter. He kept his grip on the base and watched the beige goo pool at the bottom. "Some gross-ass shit I bought off the internet I now regret putting in my mouth."

"That doesn't narrow it down much," Matteo tried to force a smile and hoped that it would color his statement enough that it sounded like a joke. Daniel no-sold his father's humor and washed out the glass in the sink. "You've been working out a lot lately. I'm glad to see family using the facilities. You think you got an exercise bug?"

"No," Daniel said. "No one *likes* working out. They like results. That's what I'm working on."

"I mean, it's 2019. More people like more things than ever before. I'm sure there's people out there crazy about exercise."

"Crazy," Daniel toweled down the glass, "is the right word."

Matteo leaned against the wall. "Well, if you're working towards a goal, you should talk to Sean. He got ripped real fast, I'm sure he could share some tips—"

"I don't like Sean," Daniel cut him off quickly, "so I'd rather not. I got the internet. I'm fine."

Matteo felt the Bianchi eye-twitch start to creep at the corner of his wrinkled lid. He tried to bite back bile, and as he so often had in the past, failed.

"Do you actually like anything?" Matteo fumbled into his polyester jacket and pulled out a cigarette pack.

Daniel's lip quivered.

"I mean, I know what you don't like. You're always quick to tell people *that*. But if you don't like being here, if you don't like wrestling, just... go. The last thing I want—"

"—is me, right?" Daniel spun around. Water dripped from his hands and the rinsed glass.

"—is for you to force yourself into something you don't feel at home in. Come on, Daniel. I'm your *father*—"

"You have been a fucking fraud your whole life," Daniel pointed the wet glass at Matteo. Water flung across the counter. "*My* whole life. *Father* is the last thing you are to me."

"*This* again," Matteo sighed.

"If you don't want me here, fucking fire me. Grow a pair."

"I wanted to tell you I'm impressed with the work you've been doing lately. I didn't come here to fight with you."

"I know. That's because you don't fight anyone for real. You *can't* fight anyone. You never have and you never will, unless it's fucking choreographed."

"I... really thought you were changing. I guess I was wrong."

Daniel studied the tile on the ground. "You asked me what I like. Does it matter? You never gave me a chance to like anything. You were too busy deciding what I'd be for me. *Choreograph*. That's all you do."

"Daniel, the DEF—"

"Mom told me what the DEF was supposed to be."

The deep inhale Matteo took wasn't because he enjoyed the taste of smoke. He needed it. Maria Bianchi was never far from his mind, no matter how many packs of cigarettes he went through in a day. She reappeared out of the lips of his only son, employed as a weapon against him.

"Keep it. I don't want your filthy money unless I earn it," Daniel said. "You'd probably just take it away if I started studying something you don't like, right? What if I started, I don't know, fucking gymnastics, or English Lit or something? You can't stand that shit, right? If I move even slightly outside the lanes, you'd fuckin' lose your mind, wouldn't you? Just like you did when Mom wanted to change jobs."

"That's not true—"

"That's not what mom said."

Matteo sucked hard on the cigarette. It wasn't enough.

"*Daniel*," he said, his head hung, his voice low to the point it became a growl.

"Don't you fuckin' talk to me like I'm still your son, when the only reason you married mom, and the only reason you had me, was for tax benefits," Daniel straightened his back. For the first time ever, he felt like he had escaped a hold Matteo kept on him his whole life. "I'm an employee pushing himself to get back on his feet and move forward. I was born as fucking tax credit, right? I've had 20 years of hearing you say 'Daniel' like that and all I can think of now is what you're hiding from me every time your fake-ass says my name. You can call me an *employee*, or you can *fire me*, but I am not your *fucking dependent*, you absolute *piece-of-shit*."

"Do you think saving money so your son can go to college is an ulterior motive, Daniel?"

Daniel threw his glass into the wall, "How many years did you say shit like that to mom before she finally left you? Or were you always like this?"

Matteo's mustache twitched. "I'm *not like that*."

"Yeah, *sure*," Daniel's hands shook. "Do you not see that the only reason the DEF still exists is because someone else came in and took over most of the work? Do you not see that the best thing in your life, damn near the *only thing* you have anymore aside from that stupid ass car wash, is because you didn't micromanage it into the ground?"

"Of course I do," Matteo squinted. "That's what it means to hire someone, and keep them on."

"And why him? Why not your own son?"

"What the *fuck* Daniel, you have *never* expressed interest in this place beyond quick cash."

"I wasn't interested," Daniel searched for the bitterness in mouth so he could seize it and stick it to the tip of his tongue, "until I realized all the artifice of this wrestling pageantry shit is just another excuse for you to control people. That doesn't explain why you trust him, though. This random jackass from the street gets better treatment from you than—"

The door rattled, as if a great weight were trying to push it open. Matteo opened it and Jalen walked in backwards with a large, heavy box.

"Fucking cinematic-timing ass bitch," Daniel exhaled.

Jalen turned, his face partially obscured by cardboard. "*What*?"

"Glass broke over there," Matteo puffed his cigarette, "watch your step."

Jalen sat the box down on the counter. "Here's the new coffee machine. Shit's way bigger than I thought it would be. I know I said I'd have it set up but I have a rogue boyfriend I gotta jet home. I'll get it up before tomorrow's practice, I promise."

Daniel froze. He looked to Matteo and expected to see his face twisted in disgust or anger or terror, and saw no reaction: the sentence that Jalen just said was apparently only news to the younger Bianchi.

"Wait, you have a boyfriend?" Daniel said, "and you didn't tell me?"

Jalen and Matteo looked at each other, then back to Daniel.

"I have a running list in my head of ways I thought you'd react to this," Jalen folded his hands, "and that sentence was nowhere on there."

Daniel didn't know what to say. He swiveled his head between his father and his father's protege and tried to figure out why neither acted in the ways that he thought they would. How could he be the last in the room to know something like this?

"Anyways, I'm not kidding, I'm pressed for time," Jalen disappeared behind the frame with a wave, "so I'll see ya tomorrow."

"You knew he's gay?" Daniel blubbered.

Matteo tapped his foot and pulled up his jeans. None of his clothes seemed to fit quite right anymore. He watched the door creak slowly on its own; the years of neglect had killed its plumb. "The best promos have hints of reality in them," he walked to the other side of the door, "and that was a real good promo, Daniel. You've improved. If you can cut out the swearing, you'll be ready for video."

Daniel looked at himself in the reflection of the door's glass as it shut. His jaw hung open. Words wanted to crawl out of his mouth, but all that escaped was the gravel of confusion at the back of his throat.

{}

"Guh, I am *so* sorry," Jalen slipped back into the driver's seat and jammed his keys into the ignition.

Reese tapped away at his phone. "Nothin' to be sorry for."

"Daniel was there. It felt like a long time. It always feels like a long time when I see him."

"Who's that?"

"I guess I haven't talked about him," Jalen rubbed the bridge of his nose. He caught Reese up to speed on Daniel, the antagonism and the slurs that he had given Jalen since they had met, and his familial relationship with his boss.

"...oh," Reese felt his small fists clench in his lap. "Well, I'm mad. I'm mad that you have to deal with someone like that."

"Since Matteo knows I've long stopped caring for Daniel's shitty opinion on anything, you know, I just said it: my boyfriend's in the car, I gotta go," Jalen waved a hand off the steering wheel. Reese had grown to predict the flight pattern of Jalen's hands while he talked, but only when he was particularly stressed. They looped like trick airplanes dancing in the sky. "Daniel's reaction was... I mean, look, he's someone I've never had a problem needling. Dude is a natural heel. He calls everything 'fag' or 'stupid' and is such a default-jackass, it's real easy to assume he's probably a homophobe, too. I honestly thought when I said "boyfriend" that maybe he'd say some ignorant ass shit in front of his dad. He didn't... he..."

Jalen slumped and let the air-twirling hand drop back to the wheel.

"It's weird. You see the same scowl on someone for so long that when they feed you any other expression, it feels impossible to know what's happening behind it. It certainly wasn't a smile. But, it wasn't anger either."

"I wish you didn't have to have such a negative force around you, though," Reese rubbed his knuckles on Jalen's shoulder. "I'd find it hard to work around someone like that."

Jalen's smile crept up as he straightened his posture. "It's fine. I knew you were waiting for me."

{25}

{BUG REPORT}

As the gloaming settled above Store-It, Jalen pulled his Audi around the street corner and stopped at the sidewalk's first square. Reese scanned outside the window; aside from specks of blood splatter on concrete, there was no evidence of the buck's horrid fate near the repaired utility pole. Nevertheless, the deer remained with them, its viscera forever a part of its eyewitnesses' memories.

"Hey," Jalen said as Reese fingered the cool steel of the door handle, "will you be alright tonight?"

"Y-yeah," Reese let the handle slip back into place, "thank you for letting me be with you today. I'm sorry that I can't cancel or—"

"Hey, hey, none of that," Jalen shushed him and brought one of his hands to Reese's face. He palm cupped the puppeteer's chin and stroked his cheek with his thumb. "This is your world. You go play and have fun in it. I'll be watching, okay? I love you."

"I love you, too," Reese was surprised to find how effortlessly these words came out. He never knew that he could know such warm normalcy, such routine intimacy, such freedom of sound.

"Call me if you need anything," Jalen said.

Reese raised his shoulders and, with no restraint, stole a kiss. This quick affirmation gave him the same jolt as coffee, and with twice the efficiency. He bounded down the sidewalk with a smile and a wave.

Emma Victoria drove past in her silver Ford F-150. It matched her nails and jacket and the disco-ball ornament hung round the rear-view mirror. Among all that sparkling gray, Reese's more saturated palette of green-blue shorts and a neon orange t-shirt of Sir Mortimer (merchandise that didn't sell quite well enough to justify its existence) stood out in stark contrast. She watched him disappear behind the entrance gate, and blinked her heavy eyelashes like a hawk when it shifts focus.

{}

Reese's show, *SKELEVENTURE*, saw its largest audience to date.

From a performance perspective, this left him with some mixed emotions. The stream stuttered in odd places, and he wasn't sure if this was a byproduct of his connection to the internet or signs of hardware degradation. The character models of Sir Mortimer and Wimbly seemed to hang more than usual when Reese attempted to move them. The drag of his mouse sent their rag-doll physics angular and scatter-shot. At one point, Wimbly's model broke; his vulture head receded inside his body. Reese had a command that resets the models in case of such a catastrophe. He incorporated the error into the performance; Sir Mortimer struck the vulture-mage with his squeaky-sword. Behind the scenes, Reese timed the reset to make Wimbly's body appear as if the sword strike popped his head back out of his body.

"How dare you!" Reese rasped in Wimbly's voice. "How about I put your bone-head in *your* chest, see how you like *that*!"

From a monetary perspective, however, the night was a total success. His glitches and failures played directly into the audience's enjoyment. At one instance, the donation ticker froze in place, then doubled itself on the screen. Reese tried to delete the duplicate ticker and, instead, the text stuck to the rag-doll Wimbly model. Another donation came in, and the donation ticker doubled again, and stuck to the Sir Mortimer model. The screen was a mess of glitched text and floppy models and laughter-tinged donations and Reese's confused micro expressions as he tried to figure out why on earth he couldn't remove the ever duplicating deluge of new objects on his screen.

Theodorestache donated $5!
"just adding to the chaos, don't mind me :)"

"Thanks for the chaos!" Reese laughed, then fake-cried, "now *help me understand what is happening!*"

A few hours in, Reese's emotional levity over the success of his stream statistics ran into firm and unyielding conflict with his creative and technical frustration. The donation tickers froze yet again, and when he tried to fix it, the Sir Mortimer model began to drift towards the top of the screen without input from Reese. He seemed unable to interact with the model, and his reset command had no effect. The mustached skeleton-knight clung to the top like a balloon stuck on a high ceiling.

Pirioitieicit donated $!
"() /<? i][_ [[]] \\V]E ``// [[]]][_][["

"Uh, thanks," Reese squinted at the jumbled message. It disappeared before he could parse the ASCII art. "Sorry, I didn't quite get to read that message, but I saw that it happened! My ticker is acting up and Mortimer's floating and my webcam is starting to move at half its normal speed and, yeah, alright, cool, everything around me *is on fire*." He pulled up a stock flame animation. At least *that* worked.

To his surprise, the donation didn't show up in his alert history.

I've got to submit a bug report, he frowned. *This is too much.*

{}

Jalen watched the stream's end from his phone while eating ramen in his living room. Since the night had been particularly slow at Jolly Molly's, Jalen was allowed to leave work early to drop Reese off. Jalen rarely cooked in his apartment—he simply never had time for it—but as he sat in front of his propped up phone, his face awash in the digital light, he considered how nice it might be to buy a streaming device for his dust-collecting TV. He looked around his living room as he stabbed at seaweed, and twirled his fork in the broth.

I suppose I have to fill these blank walls someday, he thought as he slurped noodles between his lips.

His phone vibrated. A blank text came in. He looked at the message with some puzzlement, and considered only one of three people could be texting him this late at night: Molly, Matteo, or Reese.

Matteo didn't respond. This wasn't unusual—Matteo seemed to have an aversion to his phone, and Jalen didn't think he was much of a texter in the first place.

Nope, wasn't me, Reese texted back, *thanks for checking in, though. Love you.*

As for Molly...

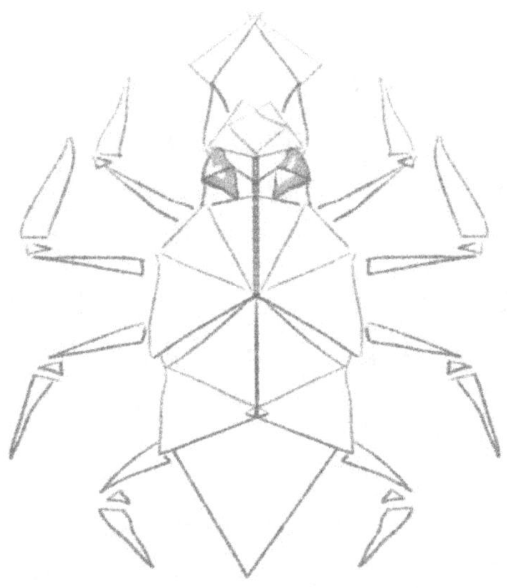

{26}

{SUPER RICH KIDS}

Wasn't me, Molly texted back. *I've been busy closing the store. Alone. By myself. Not a soul to help me at all.*

She looked around the empty cafe. Chairs were turned upside down on tables. The freshly mopped floor glistened, and the counters sparkled from their chemical bath. All of this was done long before she locked the door for the night. She raised the phone and snapped a photo, then sent it to Jalen.

Look at how slammed I was while you were gone, she smiled as she thumbed out her sarcasm, *just absolutely wrecked. I'll never get out of here.*

Molly paced back into the kitchen, set the phone down on a stray chrome counter, and grabbed her clipboard. As she rebounded back towards the kitchen, the phone buzzed audibly against the chrome. It was another text from Jalen, short enough that she could read it from the notification screen.

Didn't you get a blank text message too? the text asked. *A while ago.*

Yeah, never heard back, Molly idly thumbed back a reply and set the phone aside. She preferred to keep distractions away from her during her managerial closing duties—such as counting the till and taking inventory—so if Jalen had any lip for her, he'd just have to wait until she was done.

She pushed back through the kitchen door, clicked her keys into the cashier drawer, and pulled it open. The digital display read out,

`0.k`

and Molly gave a small snort when she noticed the green-lit message. She assumed this was a default display when the register was opened manually. "Why have I never noticed it say that before?" she wondered aloud.

And from there, her mind wandered. She thought about her conversation with Reese as she counted through quarters. He didn't seem so bad to her anymore, since she had a chance to look him in the eye. He had a relatively non-threatening presence, and while she was still worried the little ball of dough was far, far below Jalen's normal standards, she considered maybe that's what Jalen needed.

She moved on to dimes and nickels.

Jalen had stuck with Reese far longer than anyone else in the past—hell, far longer than anyone *she* had dated in *her* past. "Maybe that's what *I* need. A fixer-upper," she punched the nickle count into a calculator. She would have rather Jalen just *not be gay*. But the world's not perfect, and not tailor made to her whims. She understood this, too, and had accepted her life within his friend-zone.

Now she counted pennies, and 20s, and 10s.

Outside of her best friend being perfect for her in every way except for what he wants, Molly had little to complain about in life. Her parents were well off, she was a business owner purely through their pocket books, and when Jalen was up to it, she got to go to as many gay bars and parties as they could physically handle.

She missed the clubs. Ever since Reese started to date Jalen, the wild weekends she shared with Jalen had become memories as opposed to plans. This realization soured her expression. She wondered if they would ever again wander downtown together on weekends, drink mixed Manhattans, applaud drag queens and shout above Robin S's "Show Me Love."

Molly stuck the 10s back in, and reached for the fives.

More and more, it registered she might not ever go out with him again—not unless Reese came along, at least. It didn't take a stretch of the imagination to see how this little white dough ball would become a wet blanket at a bar, and she grew angry at the socially awkward situations that hadn't yet happened between them.

She put the fives back in, punched the count into her calculator, and, by touch alone, reached for the ones. "Wish you fell for a *real man*," Molly muttered.

The register drawer slammed shut.

Her entire body jerked as electric-heat blasted out from the base of her knuckle and up her arm. She looked away from the calculator, across the red-speckled counter, up to the carnelian drip from the sealed mouth of the machine. Blood spurted from where her finger used to be; it covered the keys and stained them crimson. From the loss of one digit, the nerves of her entire right side screamed, and once it fully registered what she had lost, so did she.

She yelled expletives as she ran back into the kitchen. Sweat poured from her body as survival instinct kicked in. "Stop the bleeding, stop the bleeding," she panted. She squeezed at the stump with her left hand and opened the supply closet with the toe of her shoe. She ripped cloth and rubber bands off shelves with her teeth and carried them awkwardly on her chest to the counter. Tears streamed down her face as she hastily assembled a tourniquet. The makeshift bandage-cloth grew red the more she panicked.

"Okay, get the finger," she kicked open the door and ran back to the register. "Keep your hand above your heart. Get the finger, put it in a bag. You got this, Molly. You know what you're doing."

Her uninjured hand fought with her keychain. She stabbed the cashier key in, turned the latch, and ripped the register drawer open. All the bills were stained red. She saw bits of her own skin, and some ripped-away sinew. The finger, however, was gone, absent from within the machine.

"Wh...what?" she shook her head, then dropped to the floor to look under the lip of the counter. There was nothing there, just the lemon-fresh scent of the floor cleaner and the pooling of her own blood. It was possible, she thought, that she kicked the digit away when she ran to the kitchen, though she was also certain that she'd have noticed.

She stood back up and looked at the reddening cloth of her injured hand. She considered how long she'd have to wait for an ambulance, and how expensive the ride would be, even with her health insurance. Her parents were going to give her guff over this regardless, but if she mitigated the cost of the ordeal and showed how strong-willed she was, perhaps they'd continue to support her. The shop's done well, but it won't survive if they pull out. With a digit removed and her own blood escaping her body, Molly's thoughts were frozen on how much this was going to set her, and her cafe, back.

"Fuck, I don't have time for this," she cried. She grabbed her cell phone and keys, ran out, locked up the shop, and drove herself to the emergency room.

{}

Jalen shot up from his bed at 1 a.m. The thudding piano of "Super Rich Kids" by Frank Ocean shook his nightstand. Molly was calling him.

"What's up?" he asked as he wiped sleep from his eyes.

"Jalen, I'm so sorry, I need a huge favor from you," Molly's voice cracked from tears.

"Whoa," he untwisted himself from his sheets. "What happened? Are you okay?"

"I need you to open tomorrow," she sighed. "The fucking register closed on my finger and chopped it off. I don't know how, it just slammed *really* hard on me while I was reaching in. I'm at the hospital.

They sewed me up and I'm getting some pain meds. I haven't slept. I'm a mess. I'm so sorry. I can come back to work on Friday."

Jalen softened his voice to console her. "Of course I'll go in. Don't worry. Take the whole weekend off. Get rest. You know I'm here for you."

"I couldn't find my finger," she sniffled. "So look out for that, too. Probably don't want a customer to find it."

"Probably," he muttered.

Behind his drowsy eyes, he was distracted by many questions: *Where could a whole finger have gone? How much blood am I going to have to clean up when I go in? How could a register even do that in the first place?*

{27}

{CONVEYER BELT}

With the bed sheet pulled taut over his head, Jalen's mind blurred in mental purgatory.

He was neither awake nor asleep. He floated. He floated between states; one state of mind was present in his room, sealed in the sheet with his breath. The diffused lightning of an outside storm peeked through the threads and reached his half-lidded eyes. Every exhale spread warmth over his lips and nose and cheeks.

His other state of mind took that light and heat with it to his dream-world, a non-particular place of non-particular composition, vague and lavender, soft and smudged. There was no ground for him to stand on, yet his feet found footing among clouds, shifting sands, blurs of time and matter. Memories twinkled like starlight in the void. Lungs of the waking-world pulled air in, and the lungs of the dream-world let it go.

In contrast to the dream-world, the warmth of his exhale was particular, and precise, and hard. It was his breath, his *real* breath, the breath trapped in the bed sheet, now manifest in the dreamscape with no change in texture or warmth. Breath so real he could hear its escape, taste his light morning bitterness on his dream-tongue. In the void of artifice, the contrast of his breath's tangibility overwhelmed him, shook his limbs, filled his eyes with tears.

That moisture, he soon realized, burned. He cried light. Bright globs of energy drew from his eyes, and floated away as if sucked out of his tear ducts by some strange magnetism. It, too, was clear and bright and specific—it was the lightning his waking eyes saw outside his window. The light and his breath melded together, stirred in a spark of argument, and morphed into something new, something neither air nor light. It became electric darkness, black and neon, then snaked away through the halls of his starry mind. That which he brought into this world had left his control.

A dark-skinned woman appeared through the lavender clouds of the dream-world, and stood with her back to Jalen. Though he couldn't see her face, the details of her appearance were clear: In her crisp polo and ironed apron and straightened hair and black baseball cap, he recognized Molly, who was ready for a long shift at her cafe. Or perhaps she had just finished, and was ready to exit through the door. Jalen wanted to ask her if she was coming or going, but no words came from his mouth. His limbs bolted him in place—he was an observer, and unable to act upon his own world.

The snake of electric darkness ran to her and struck her hand. Jalen, paralyzed within himself, could only watch as it ripped at her finger, and consumed it in a single bite. To his surprise, she did not scream, she did not cry as she had over the phone about her missing finger. Her form dissolved, and from the foam of her former anatomy, she too became electric darkness. The energy multiplied and chewed at the void of Jalen's dream. Everything it ate, became itself. Soon, it reached Jalen, too.

It chewed him, slashed into him cleanly with teeth of cold and alarm. But the damage was not physical, nor did he feel pain—the separation of his body from his life was punctuated not by feeling but by inevitability, an acceptance that this is just the sort of thing that should happen to someone in the path of such a force. There was a certain serene peace in his spiritual death, one that remained with him until he woke again. He jolted up through the bed sheet as one would break the surface of water when drowning. He gasped for air, horrified by his inability to save his friend, or himself. Cold sweat dotted his skin.

The storm continued, and the patter of rain against the window carried with it a subconscious calm, much like the darkness of his dream, which, eventually, lulled him back to the closest approximation of sleep he could manage.

Jalen fell into this system over and over again. He took air and lightning to the dream-world, watched someone get chewed up by darkness—sometimes he knew them, sometimes he didn't—then he, too, was attacked, and that attack killed him and birthed him back to the waking world. He was a part of the cycle, and it ate him and spat him out, only so that he could later feed it more air, more light, more energy.

Many victims later, a new form appeared through the clouds of crisp and familiar intimacy. Back-turned, the man was small, swaddled in bright clothes too large for his frame. He shuffled nervously, and popped the knuckles of his left hand against his hip bone. Jalen knew that it was Reese. He *knew* him, knew his shape and silhouette and the pores of his flesh. He knew that under those clothes sat patches of light skin that turned rosy with even the slightest grip of his hand, soft and malleable and capable of eliciting sounds of pleasure so high in timber, so low in volume as to be imperceptible without the grace of proximity, without the permission of knowing. Jalen knew him, and wanted to know him again, and know him deeper still. Yet, the fact that none of this, none of the animal love of his body or intellectual love his mind was enough to jolt his legs, his arms to action left Jalen, within the statue of his dream-body, devastated, afraid, and weighed by impotency.

Light drew from Jalen's eyes. His breath was stolen. He tried to suck it back into his lungs, but couldn't. He tried to reach for the lightning, to grab it and shove it back within himself, but his arms would not move. These hard forms danced together in front of Jalen as if to mock his helplessness, and electric darkness formed as it always had before. Jalen tried to yell to Reese, but no sound came. The darkness slithered towards its prey, as it always did before, and will again, and again, and again.

{}

Eventually, his alarm, a cybernetic mesh of 80's synthesizers and guitars he was too languid to recognize, sang him awake. The sun had not yet risen. The rumble of thunder had ceased, but the light patter of rain continued intermittently against the window. Though he felt freed of the dream-wake cycle, he now found himself on the wrong side of it—no longer able to rest, Jalen dragged himself out of bed and through his morning rituals.

While he brushed his teeth, his phone buzzed.

Reese texted him, *Do you need any help?*

Jalen was confused by the question, and he wasn't sure if the confusion was born of his sleeplessness or poor memory. He scrolled up to find he had, between his many dream-wake states, texted Reese what happened to Molly. He was troubled by the fact he had no memory of this, but given the haze of the past few hours, was also unsurprised.

I can't say no to help. I'll have you on register and cleaning, is that okay? Jalen texted.

Anything to help. Just tell me what to do, boss, his phone vibrated cheerfully with a heart emoji.

Jalen was never more thankful for Reese's flexible schedule. No reality existed where Molly would be okay with this, of course, but the extra help seemed worth the risk when he pictured what a typical rush hour looked like at the cafe. Besides, he thought, one could do worse for a co-worker than a loved one.

{28}

{LIGHT BULB}

With all the store's lights off, Jolly Molly's sat against the greenish-gray sky like a cicada's husk on tree bark. Jalen slammed the door of his Audi and hopped over pools of rainwater gathered in the uneven pavement of the parking lot. Despite the coating of rain and the heavy taste of moisture in the air, the cafe itself was dry, bleached, siphoned of life. Jalen thought part of this perception merely came from the dreary overcast clouds, of which he knew would part to bright sunshine within the hour, assuming the forecast was to be believed. But he also worried that the missing saturation was from his own vision, lost somewhere in the sleepless night he had before.

It wasn't long after Jalen entered the cafe that Reese arrived, knocking at the locked glass door. Jalen let him in; the new temp-employee wore ripped jeans and a band-tee so chipped away by wear and time that Jalen could no longer make out what band the bubble letters was supposed to advertise. The only Jolly Molly baseball cap in the store was far too large for Reese; it sat unevenly on his head, and he had to lift the brim every few minutes after it would fall over his eyes. His appearance was not ideal, but Jalen didn't have the energy to nitpick his boyfriend's professional appearance. Besides, as far as he was concerned, as long as Reese smiled and gave out the correct change, he didn't care what he wore.

Reese, as he volunteered he would, cleaned while Jalen took inventory and prepped for opening. He attacked the blood stains with bleach and paper towels and rubber gloves. As he scrubbed, Reese was surprised by his own alertness; it was a fluke he woke up in the middle of the night to see Jalen's text, spurred so by a sudden metallic bump in the ceiling he could not identify. His original plan was to ask for a coffee as soon as he came in. Such plans were dashed when Jalen began to dress him in pseudo-uniform—he stood behind Reese, pulled him flush against his front, kissed his neck, and lassoed the thin white string of his apron across his waist. The brief intimacy served as a sufficient, albeit temporary, caffeine supplement.

Neither of them ever found Molly's finger. It wasn't under any table, any chair, any nook or cranny. There was no smell of decomposition. The blood trails around the register lead to nothing. No flies, no hints. It was as if the register, once it had swallowed her finger whole, then digested bone and meat into some unknown stomach. The digit's disappearance was distressing in its own right, but with the knowledge no customer would or could tear apart the restaurant more than they did, neither employee worried of its discovery.

"Maybe a rat took it?" Reese wondered.

Jalen pulled the small chain on the 'Open' sign. "If we have rats, that would be a different, not better, problem. Don't think I want to tell Molly about either."

{}

Out of an abundance of concern for Reese's safety, Jalen removed the register drawer from its basin and left it underneath the counter, so that there was no reason for his boyfriend to even think about sticking his fingers in harm's way. As for the digital sales system itself, Reese picked up the register with enough ease to function, and his career of smiling in front of an audience despite his mistakes convinced customers he knew what he was doing. The morning and evening rushes came and went. It seemed the gay duo would succeed, against all odds, in a strife-free shift. There was a shared sense of triumph right up until, in the waning hours of business, a lone customer complained to Reese while he mopped.

"Why are you mopping when there's still customers in the lobby?" the man in suit called out from the other side of the empty room. He was alone in the far corner of the cafe, bald and bespectacled, with bushy eyebrows that clumped over the thin rim of his glasses. He wore gray trousers and a collared shirt, pressed and crisped despite the lumpy nature of his body. He startled Reese when he yelled.

"Oh, uh," Reese leaned against the mop. He didn't want to say *Well, my manager told me to!* despite it being the truth. Something about that statement seemed a little more sarcastic than Reese wanted it to be, but he wasn't sure what else to say—or shout from across the room, for that matter. In lieu of the truth, he told the softest lie he could come up with: "there's a little spill, that's all! I'll be done in a moment, sir."

"Also," the man's pin-point eyes narrowed at the hot cup of coffee to his right, which he had set on the corner of his laptop panel, "my Americano is too watery. I want another one."

Reese palpitated with second-hand anxiety at the proximity between laptop and liquid. The observation of the customer's complete disregard for the safety of his own expensive equipment prevented his request from fully registering—but when it did, Reese only had more questions. The main two being: *Didn't Jalen tell me an Americano is made specifically with water? How do I say that without making him angrier?*

Mercifully, Jalen appeared from the push-door. He heard the customer from the kitchen, as anyone would have. He explained how a proper Caffè Americano is made by diluting an espresso with hot water, done so to achieve its specific flavor. As the customer continued to argue with him, Reese grew angrier at his stubbornness. *Why won't he listen to Jalen?* he thought. *Why is he angry that I'm mopping? Why does he yell at the exact same volume no matter how close you stand to him? What is wrong with this guy?*

Reese stopped hearing words. His eyes traced a circle of incremental hatred between the Americano on the laptop, the open leather briefcase, paper strewn across the table, his suit worth more than anything Reese himself had ever owned, his gold watch, the light reflected off his bald head and horn-rimmed glasses, back to the coffee, over and over again a loop of observational irritation and disbelief.

"I want to speak to the manager," the man said.

The reflected light on his head flickered. Reese looked up.

A nearby ceiling bulb interjected its thoughts into the conversation. It erupted in light, shattered, and glass crashed to the floor. All three men jumped in surprise, then froze. Each was paralyzed by uneasiness, unsure of the correct thing to say in reply to the bulb's burst.

The business man collected his papers into his leather briefcase and shook his head. "I'm never coming back *here* again."

All three thought this decision was for the best.

{}

"I can't believe the light bulb exploded," Jalen turned the steering wheel and pushed hard on the gas to beat the red light. "We just got new ones, too."

"At least it happened when it did," Reese laced his fingers and stretched upwards in his reclined passenger seat. "Couldn't have popped around a better customer."

"Yeah," Jalen kept his chuckle within his nose. They pulled to the street corner and Jalen gave a quick kiss to Reese's cheek. "I snuck $100 in a donation on your stream while we were closing. Consider it your paycheck. Thanks for helping me out today. Sorry I have to bolt, I'm already late for DEF."

“I’m glad I was able to help out,” Reese smiled and raised his shoulders. The kiss was light and all too brief, but it’d have to do for tonight; since their “real” work was over, their *real* work began.

{}

When Reese entered his storage unit, the sight of an off-white sludge on the floor wrenched his stomach. It was chunky, the size of his hand, and sat defiantly in the middle of his belongings on the concrete, as if whatever coughed it up wanted to make sure he’d see it. While he cleaned up the mess with paper towels and spray cleaner—it was not lost on him this was the second time that day he had to get down on his knees and clean up an organic mess—he was surprised to find there was no smell at all. He thought for sure the unidentified liquid was cat spew, or some other animal got in and hacked up on the floor. What animal could get in, though, without mark or damage, and vomit such an amount of an odorless material with toothpaste-like consistency?

He considered he should try to find out what the material was, but two things stopped him: one, it was nearly time to start the night’s *SKELEVENTURE*, and two, there was no collection of search terms he could think of that wouldn’t lead him down a series of potentially regrettable images. He instead chose to push the problem aside, and hope to never again encounter such a mess on the floor of his unit, or the creature that left it there.

That night, Reese’s stream began in a most unusual manner. While it was customary for audience members to wait before the stream began, there were far more viewers than normal, and the chat was as active as if Reese had already gone live. Reese, a slave to curiosity, peeked in at their conversations. Clips were shared of his technical failures last week: Sir Mortimer’s body stuck on the ceiling, and the frozen donation ticker that polluted the screen. The glitches captured the imagination of new viewers in ways the more carefully constructed elements of his shows failed to. A bitterness accompanied this realization in his mouth, but he had no trouble swallowing it down—he would rather be loved for his faults than not loved at all.

There were other clips, though; clips from other people's streams were shared just as frequently. Reese checked one out, and was surprised to see his vulture-mage, Wimbly, glitch into view on a random gaming channel he had no affiliation with, then disappeared just as quickly. The viewers wondered if *SKELEVENTURE* had tinkered with the idea of an augmented-reality game, or if these were the roots of future collaborations with other channels.

Another possibility sent heated waves up Reese's fingertips; that his characters were used without his permission, cannibalized for other people's gains. Before his fists curled too tightly, though, he noticed the numbers of pre-show viewers continued to climb, on and on, far beyond the stagnation he had experienced prior to meeting Jalen. He had more viewers waiting for him to go live than he had in his entire audience a few months prior.

"I guess whatever is going on..." Reese rubbed the side of his head, "...is working out for me."

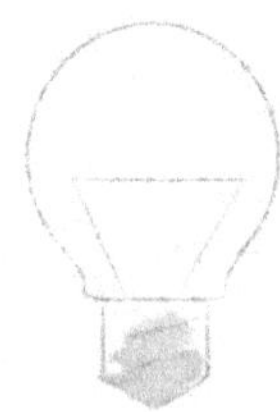

{29}

{LIFE FROM THE EGG}

Despite the confines of his noise-canceling headphones, Jalen seemed hyper-aware of every small movement in the gym, every bulb that struggled to stay lit, every sneaker squeak and ragged breath. His hours of lost sleep collided head first with the triple dose of caffeine in his bloodstream. He was curt with Matteo, and more visibly frustrated by the length of the list of videos he needed to shoot and edit before the next show.

It was a side of vulnerability Matteo rarely saw from his right-hand man, and although he couldn't afford to tell Jalen to take the night off ("I don't know how any of this shit works," Matteo had said this with an incredulous finger pointed at the computers) he still felt sympathy for him. Jalen informed Matteo of what happened to Molly. Matteo knew the burden of sleepless nights and long shifts, and did his best to stay out of Jalen's way.

Someone who didn't know this, however, was Daniel Bianchi.

As the night ended and the crowd of aspiring wrestlers filtered out, Daniel Bianchi hopped up onto Jalen's table. Although Daniel was not one DEF's larger men, his new seat was a sudden enough addition of weight that it caused the monitors to sway on unsure metal legs.

"Not tonight, Daniel," Jalen closed his eyes tight.

It's also likely, even if Daniel did know what Jalen was going through, he'd have bulldozed through to his point anyways.

"I had a real heart-to-heart with Dad today," Daniel let his legs swing above the floor. He wore royal blue short-shorts, much shorter than Jalen ever remembered him in before, the kind which he was certain Daniel would've made fun of anyone else for had they donned them instead.

The "heart-to-heart" he referred to was a terse, mumbled admission of guilt over his outburst the day before. Hardly the emotional outpour Daniel portrayed it as, but Daniel, a slave to the concept of stoic masculinity, believed it was much more than it actually was.

"Daniel, I am *trying* to work," Jalen pointed at the headphones over his ears.

"I got my own key to the place now," Daniel smiled and spun the bronze key-ring around his finger, "like you. I'm gonna be here even more often. It makes sense if I'm going to move up the card that I work out more, right?"

Jalen couldn't deny Daniel's labor had started to pay off. For the first time, Daniel wasn't just a lump with biceps; his upper arms, traps, and forearms all showed the vague mold of cardio and concentrated effort.

"That's great," Jalen tried to keep his attention on the video editor.

"It is!" Daniel laughed. He kicked his leg up, and thought the tone of his exposed thigh was worthy of admiration, even from a rival like Jalen. "I'm getting used to being here. I'm lucky, you know, my dad lets me use the gym for free and all, but I'm making the most of it, right? I've done all this research and shit. I might start working on scripts, too. I'm seeing a new side to wrestling that I'm *really* starting to appreciate. Course, I'll have to talk to you about filming some of my ideas. Unless you want to teach me video editing, then I can do them by myself."

But no matter the work he put into his frame, no matter what his new addiction was, he was still, regrettably, Daniel Bianchi.

Jalen slipped his headphones down around his neck. "I don't care if you work out every day of every second for the rest of your life, Daniel.

I don't care what conversations you have with Matteo, because your family business is not *my* business. Right now, I want to *work*. I want to do *my* work, and do it well. I'm happy you're doing better. All the other vaguely threatening shit you said, however, I'll take seriously when your dad believes in you enough to mention it to me."

Daniel scrunched his face. "What the hell crawled up your ass?"

Jalen, unblinking, grabbed the cups of his headphones and secured them back around his ears.

{}

"Fuck you, Jalen," Daniel huffed as he let the weights drop around him. Cast-iron thumped onto carpet and echoed in the weight room. Those rhythmic bumps, and the heave of Daniel's chest as it sucked for air, was the last evidence of human life in the corridors of the DEF. It was beyond midnight, and even Jalen had gone home after reaching his physical and mental limit of work.

"No one ever fucking listens to me. I tried to be nice to the guy..."

Daniel never made the connection Jalen might not be ready to be nice to someone that had spent so long in direct antagonism towards him. Daniel was not unaware of his antagonism, but had a particular justification for it. His anger and the way it infected his tone was not the cause of his problems, as he viewed it, but rather a response to them. While anger is a justified emotion to the problems one may face in life, he never unraveled the truth that, when held onto long enough, anger is no longer a reaction to, but rather, *is* the problem that breeds its own reactions.

"I wonder if anyone ever *will* listen to me," he whispered as he leaned against the mirrored wall. His voice crack turned this rare honest utterance into a whimper.

Daniel looked up. Pressed against the mirror, he was all that he saw. He watched sweat disappear into the crevice of his defined pecs. He admired himself for the first time in ages in a way that lacked pretense. *I'm really doing it*, he thought. *I'm becoming a man. This is what a man looks like.*

He pushed himself off the glass, took a few steps back, and placed his hands on his hips. He puffed his chest out, and loved the way the straps of his tank top seemed to bulge over the hills of his front. "But I'll be a star on my own terms, and they'll *have* to make videos of *me*, and that's all that matters."

Daniel needed an enemy to defeat, and if it had to be in the farce-world of the DEF, so be it. He'll outperform anyone in his way, he thought. He'll be the man the DEF universe so desperately needs, and he'll move on outside of his father's low expectations, so far beyond any accomplishments he, or Jalen, or anyone else that tried to push him around had obtained that they'll be forced to say, "I should've been nicer to Daniel. I should've noticed what he was capable of."

Maria Bianchi told him she divorced her husband because Matteo only wanted control. She realized they had no romance in their life. Maria was a "thing" for Matteo to own, a box to check, an associate with whom he could collect tax benefits. When Daniel learned the truth of why his family split apart, it took his preexisting hatred for Matteo, all the anger that he had built up for years, and gave it context.

"You can't control me," Daniel snorted. "Both you *and* Jalen can go to hell."

He took a long, slow walk back to the locker room. As he rounded the corner, he dotted his forehead with the soft cotton towel around his neck. This brief obstruction of his sight caused him to step directly into a substance on the ground, slimy and thick. He slipped and stumbled into a locker.

“The hell?” He lifted up his shoe. A red smear marked the toe of his sneaker. He followed the brush stroke of blood his slide made to its source: a raccoon, deflated of form, ripped apart into a mess of red chunks.

Daniel shuddered at the pile of what used to be an animal. “*Again*?”

Something rattled above Daniel. The ceiling panels in the locker room flickered and rumbled, as if something other than the light bulbs lived on the other side. This invisible force shook the glass that contained the fluorescent tubes. Daniel stared into the beveled panel until the light within it died into darkness. The electric crackle of dying light bulbs continued beyond their death, however; the sound traveled across the ceiling, then directly into the locker Daniel’s back leaned against.

The moment Daniel felt the cool steel shake against his back, he lurched forward in fear. He turned to see a gnarled arm punch through the steel and rip the top hinges off. Its muscles bulged with cool, mottled skin which seemed to shift and squirm with restless veins. It pulsed with vague light, not as if it radiated or reflected, but rather, as if it consumed it, as if the existence of light were food for its form. A thin membrane of darkness draped the outline of its pulsing, twitching meat, a byproduct of its particle-wave consumption. It was electric-light with a skin of shadows in constant trade with itself.

“Bones,” it rasped in a voice shattered by electronic distortion and hunger. Its white eyes twinkled in the shadows within the locker, two foul lights which scanned Daniel’s frame and thirsted for what may lay within.

Daniel screamed, kipped up to his feet, and ran like hell. He slipped on the pile of raccoon mush again, which proved fortunate—it was at the same time the creature punched the other hinge off the steel door and hurled it at Daniel, whose body fell in time to avoid the projectile.

He ran through hallways and the kitchen and the corridor and the main event area. When he looked over his shoulder, he saw sparks burst behind him: light bulbs, thermostats, Jalen's computer all erupted. With each pop of electricity, the slow moving shadows of gnarled muscle popped out. Any ground it lost in its pursuit of Daniel, it made up for with a quick jump to a new power source. Daniel, with heavy pants and cries, bolted towards the storage area on the other side of the gym, pushed through the door, and huddled in the shadows.

After he caught his breath and swallowed several times, he realized he wasn't being chased anymore. He put together what he had seen and slowly climbed back to his feet. He looked out the window of the corridor door and realized the creature had ceased motion. It stationed itself directly under a hanging light in the gym.

It *had* to be eight feet tall, as far as Daniel could tell. It was difficult to pinpoint an exact height and width for the creature's form, as it seemed to shift between light and meat and shadow, never content on any one substance, always in an argument with itself. It was a hulking beast, for sure, with each muscle on its tree-trunk-like arms individually capable of crushing his head on their own, much less with the help of the rest of its coiled arm. It seemed impossible to Daniel that such a monstrous thing fit in the locker at all, but as he stared in hypnosis at the matter-roulette the creature habitually played, he concluded he no longer knew what was and wasn't possible. All that was certain was what he could see.

And what he saw, directly underneath a hung light in the DEF gym, was a monster of indiscriminate material, frozen in place. He no longer chased, but observed. His claw arms dragged the floor. The creature stared with white-light eyes that refused to blink; they twitched in anxious wait for Daniel's next move.

"You..." Daniel huffed, "you can't move any further, can you?"

Daniel looked around him, then tripped over a box of paperwork against the wall. He began to laugh—first with nervousness, then with loud, tear-stained triumph.

"You CAN'T MOVE, can you?!" he clutched himself. "Every time I turned, you were poppin' out of something electric. But the electricity died in this part of the building years ago, and my dad was always too much of a cheap-ass to fix it. You're trapped! You're fuckin' trapped, you son of a bitch!"

Daniel slid down the wall and covered his face with his hands. He laughed and cried in hysteria, overcome by his own good luck.

"Holy shit, I can call the police... they can capture you, or kill you, or something... I don't know. I don't care. I'll be known as the first person to meet a supernatural creature! I'm gonna be fuckin' famous because of you, you know that!?"

Daniel climbed to his feet to look at the creature one last time from the safety of the other side of the glass. It was too engulfed in the shadows of its strange matter for Daniel to read an expression. It didn't react to Daniel's threat. As far as he could tell, it didn't understand or rationalize. It was nothing more than an animal, trapped in the cage of its bizarre mobility.

"Fuck you," Daniel said.

With tear-soaked resolve, Daniel gave the electric-warping creature a smile and two defiant middle fingers from the other side of the door. He plodded out the hallway towards the exit and muttered to himself, "I don't need you anymore, Dad... I don't need the DEF anymore..."

Daniel pushed the door open and stepped onto the concrete of the narrow back side of the gym's exterior. He welcomed the moonlight like a warm shower on his head. He held his hands up and exhaled, "I win."

The creature's claw-hand closed over Daniel's head and squeezed.

There was a light pole outside of the hallway's exit. The creature warped to it once Daniel moved down the corridor. Brain-death occurred in a near instant as his skull shattered and pierced inwards, cracked like an egg. Blood splashed from between the creature's fingers and painted the cement. Daniel's arms fell to his side, and his legs no longer supported his weight.

{30}

{LAST SEEN}

Morning shrugged itself awake at Jolly Molly's. Though Molly had returned, she found it difficult to live up to the adjective of her shop's title. The antibiotics she was on drained the bright cafe of tactual energy. She felt nothing, except nothing. She could still flex the knuckles in her palm, and with it, the ghost of her pointer finger remained. She had never been more aware of the absence of something before, and though instructed not to use her left hand, it took all her will power not to tense it, not to reach out towards clipboards and pens and mugs. The finger's presence existed in such profound emptiness that its absence felt more real than any of her surroundings.

"I can't believe you're not taking time off," Jalen shook his head as he restocked napkins and stir-straws. "Girl, you lost a *finger*. Go home."

Molly discovered a new type of guilt after the surgery. She considered, had this happened to Jalen, he would have been financially devastated by the insurance costs alone. It would be more than just a physical loss for him.

"The new register should be arriving tomorrow," she avoided eye contact and kept her eyes glued to the clipboard in her right hand. "I've called the manufacturers of this one and they claim there's no mechanism that closes it automatically. I must've closed it on myself without realizing it, but still, I'd rather be safe than sorry. My parents want me to sue. Of course, we both know that means *they* want to sue. As far as today is concerned... I'll be a little slow on ringing things up, but I can't stand the idea of leaving you here alone, so..."

Jalen buried his gaze in piles of sugar packets and cups of half-n-half. Had Molly not texted him the night before to insist she was coming back in, he would have asked Reese if he was free again. He sucked on his teeth and shuffled in silence for a few minutes as he considered how to address his boss, and his friend, and the person that was lost between the two.

"You don't have to do this," he frowned.

Molly smiled, but it was a smile that turned up at the corner of her mouth despite the tone of her voice. It existed without her permission. "The surgery was surprisingly fast. I mean, to be fair, all they could do was close the wound."

"Molly..."

"Don't worry about me. As long as I stay on the register, I'll be fine. Listen, I'm lucky it happened to me. The bill was wild, even with my insurance. Mom was pissed, but Dad stuck up for me. My biggest worry was they'd stop backing the cafe after I hurt myself, but I guess I've finally impressed my hardest customers."

Molly rarely talked about her parents around Jalen. They both knew she came from money. Jalen thought it was rude to bring up someone else's good fortune, especially since his friendship with her predated his knowledge of their wealth. Conversely, Molly thought it was rude to flaunt her parent's money—after all, she hadn't earned it. That's why she fought so hard to make Jolly Molly's work. She wanted to prove she was independent, that she can earn her own way in the world.

And so, with quiet acceptance of who they were and who their parents were, they simply lived. Jalen knew that, if Molly was bringing this up now, then there was a wound still open, far deeper than her hand.

Molly turned and leaned against the counter. "I spent yesterday thinking about how much worse this would've been for you, since you're on your own, more or less. What if this place was, I dunno, Jolly Jalen's, and you scraped by to make it work, and you were livin' hand to mouth and the profits were only just getting you by and..."

"Molly, it's fine..."

"You'd have to shutter this place the next day, wouldn't you?"

They both went quiet. All the years they'd known each other, and neither were prepared to have this conversation.

"I don't know how Reese does it," Molly said. "I don't think I could live at the edge like that."

Jalen's eyes widened. He chose this time to put up silverware. "Carefully. It's hard."

"The spare hat is missing from the back."

Jalen fumbled a spoon. It clanked loudly on the floor. *Shit,* he thought, *did I forget to get that back from Reese?*

"I was wrong about him," she tapped the counter in front of her and stared out towards the parking lot. "And I think I've been wrong about how to run this place. I always kept it between us because I knew we worked well together and I wanted to keep costs low. But maybe it's time to hire a third or fourth wheel. Just in case something happens, you know? I think it's time I take this as seriously as I can. Like I am living on the edge, even if..."

Jalen picked up the spoon and walked it back to the kitchen. He kept his eyes on the floor, unable to lift them up to meet her. "Yeah, I know."

It wasn't unusual for customers, particularly the gray-haired variety with plenty of free time on their hands, to show up in the parking lot five-to-ten minutes before the store opened. That's why it didn't alarm Molly when two vehicles pulled into her parking lot. It was only once she registered the particular white-and-black stripes, and yellow letters of authority, that she began to worry. Their lights came on, silent and bright, loud without making a sound. One set of police officers emerged from a vehicle, while the shadowy outline of two more laid in wait in the second car. They approached Jolly Molly's, and Molly made sure to greet them before she could find out how serious of a knock they would give the glass of her door.

"You Jolly Molly?" the white police officer said, his thumbs punched into his belt to allow his overhang gut some air.

"I'm Molly," she feigned a smile. "It's still a little early for 'Jolly,' but I think in one more cup I'll get there."

"You have an employee named Jalen Eze?" the second officer said curtly. He was taller, a more fit black man with his hands on his hips and a twitch to his lips. He may have asked a question, but his stone face made it clear he knew the answer.

"I do, he's in the kitchen..."

"We'd like to ask him some questions."

{}

Jalen had sat in the upholstery of the cafe booths many times before, usually on lunch breaks or when the lobby was empty.

"How would you describe your relationship with Daniel Bianchi?"

"Pretty awful," Jalen clasped his hands together. The officers scribbled notes, and Jalen raised an eyebrow. "Did he do something?"

The officers looked at each other, then turned a synchronized stare to Jalen. "Daniel is dead."

"*What*?"

"Daniel was killed behind the DEF at 1 o'clock in the morning," the black officer flipped through his small notebook. "His body was discovered by the convenience store owner across the street when he noticed an awful lot of blood on the side-street near your gym. Based off of reports from other members of the DEF we interviewed, and from security cam footage at the gym and the convenience store, you and Matteo Bianchi were the last people to see Daniel alive. We understand you two are also the only ones that have keys to the building."

Jalen stared at his reflection in the freshly cleaned countertop of the table. "I see."

"You don't seem too rattled by Daniel's death," the white officer observed.

"Daniel spent most of his time around me either antagonizing or belittling me. I'm not happy to hear this happened, but this is the least surprising person you could've come to me and told me had been killed. Besides," Jalen sighed, "I can see where this is going. You think I'm a suspect."

The black officer folded his arms. "We have you exiting the gym at midnight and purchasing two apples from the convenience store. We don't have you on the scene at any other point that night. You drove north on Malcolm Road. Where did you head?"

"Home," Jalen blinked. "It was late. I needed sleep. I had worked all day here prior to going to the DEF. Molly can vouch for that."

"Where do you live?"

"At the Washington Hills Apartments over on Chester Park Ave."

The white officer scrunched his face. "I'd say that's roughly 15 minutes from DEF. How about you, Jalen?"

"Clear traffic? That sounds right."

"Security cam footage from both the DEF and the convenience store went out five minutes before Daniel's death," the black officer leaned in on the table. "Both you and Matteo were long gone by then. Daniel's body looked like a car hit it at 100 mph, which is impossible considering where he was killed. The back part of the building is surrounded by trees, fences, and a dumpster, and there was no property damage outside the gym. The inside of the DEF was wrecked. There's damage in the locker room and hallways. Right now, we have reason to believe either someone, or a group, stayed behind in the gym and waited for everyone else to leave. Matteo told us Daniel didn't get his key until that day, so whoever killed Daniel had to have known he would be there that night long after it was closed."

The faces of everyone Jalen knew at the DEF flew through his mind. None of them looked like killers—not outside the context of a wrestling ring, at least.

"Do you know anyone that would want to kill Daniel, Jalen?" the white officer leaned in as well. Their uniform presence bore down on either side of Jalen. "Someone that would also know how to disable security cam footage?"

"Officers, I'm sorry. I don't know. I don't want to believe anyone at the DEF is capable of such a thing. Also, you probably know this, but, most of the people at DEF are wrestlers. Most of those guys need help ordering food online."

"His body was pulverized," the black officer said. "We figured it was with a sledgehammer, given the nature of the damage inside the gym. Do you know anyone who owns something like that?"

The image of Daniel beaten to the point that his body could no longer be recognized as a living creature struck Jalen. He covered his mouth.

"Most people I know live in apartments, officer," Jalen said. "If any of them had a sledgehammer, I'd want to know why they did, too."

The officers looked at each other and returned to their notebooks. The white officer ripped off a sheet of paper and slid it over to Jalen. "This is our number. Call us if you notice anything at all. As hard as it may seem, we believe Daniel was killed by someone within the DEF, or someone who got in during its open hours and waited. If Daniel wasn't the specific target, then I think it's safe to say others may be in danger, too. We've suggested Matteo shut down the DEF gym until we've had time to interview everyone. We'd also want to stop by your apartment and look around after your shift, if you don't mind."

Jalen folded the paper and stuffed it in his pocket. "Not at all. Anything you need, anytime you need it, let me know."

When the police officers left, Molly instinctively went to Jalen to console him. Sadness wasn't what she found etched into Jalen's face; his back teeth ground, and he stared into the empty space where the police officers had sat.

"I can't believe this shit happened at the DEF..." he growled. His thoughts pieced together the events as they were described to him by the police officer, and at some point they connected on Matteo. He drew his phone out of his pocket to call him and send him his condolences, but before he could dial, he saw that his wrestling boss had sent him texts.

"I'm sure you already know what happened," the text read. "Let's talk as soon as we can."

Jalen let the cell phone drop to the table. He buried his face in his forearms. "I'm glad you didn't take today off, Molly."

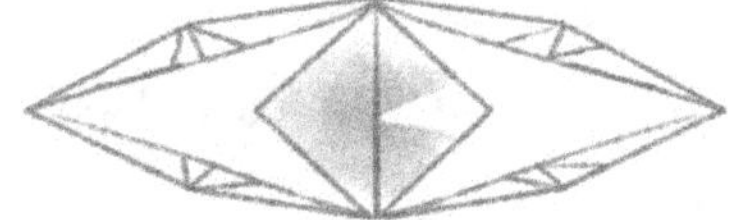 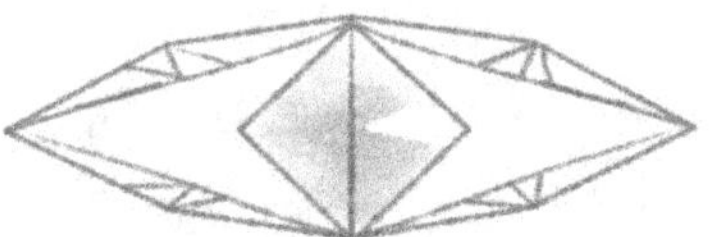

{31}

{MASK OF SMOKE}

Jalen caught sight of Mr. Bianchi in his Audi headlights. He sat in the bed of his open trunk with a cigarette taped to his slack-jawed lip. The DEF owner, and now childless father, stared at the gym through his dark aviators, which reflected the flickering lights of the parking lot. He slumped into the folds of his polyester star-spangled jacket, and the remnants of his black hair blew in the night wind. Jalen wondered if he had been there for hours, motionless, inspecting the walls that he had built.

Jalen got out of his car and sat next to Matteo on the steel door. The two stared at the DEF gym together, but said nothing. Their hands drooped idly at their sides, strong and helpless. Two men breathed for two minutes, the wind whipping at the black trees that framed the dead building. Jalen cleared his throat.

"I'm really sorry, man," Jalen said.

"It's alright," Matteo withdrew the cancer-stick and puffed his release. "The world moves on."

Jalen turned his head. He couldn't help but notice how little Matteo's facial muscles moved; his expression was hung, worn, a tapestry too old and tired to inspire.

"I made backups of my videos the night before," Jalen had no idea how to console someone over the loss of a child, "but I guess that doesn't matter now." He often talked about work as a mechanism to guide a conversation, but in the wake of Daniel's death, Jalen wasn't sure it was appropriate. But what other topic *was*?

"No, it's good," Matteo took a drag. "We're still going to perform."

Jalen sat up. The sudden weight shift squeaked the hinges of the truck's bay door. "Are you... *serious*? Matteo. Your son just died. Take some time off."

"I gotta pay for the funeral somehow."

Jalen was stunned to see no particular shift on Matteo's face. He studied the wrinkles and diffuse light across his boss's leathery skin and tried to map out what had gone wrong underneath it. Matteo passed the cigarette between hands and tapped it against the truck door. The wind carried the ash away.

"The car wash, and the DEF, both only barely pay for themselves," Matteo said. "I never told you; I sold the house last year and moved into an apartment. It was the only way to keep both businesses going. There's this economics term... 'elasticity.' It's pretty much what you think it is. Something like... 'a measurement of quantitative change in a product in response to something else.' I butchered the definition for my own sake, of course. I look at it as one's ability to adjust financially when a revenue stream goes up or down. Maybe that's why I'm on the edge now, huh? I took something from a system I don't understand and tried to apply it to something it wasn't meant for. No wonder I ended up the way I am. Square pegs and round holes."

Matteo removed his aviators, as if he only just now recognized the drape of night had fallen across the sky.

"Daniel was...definitely a Bianchi. He was a real idiot when he got angry, and smart as hell when he acted on his pettiness. Not tremendously good character traits, but you saw the growth he had... before..."

His lip quivered. His voice broke. The creak of the dam began to give. The blockage was located in the exact memory of Daniel's gradual improvement in the ring and in his physical health.

"...the police suggested that, if it wasn't anyone in the DEF that killed him, perhaps Daniel was killed over a drug deal, or an unpaid debt. I don't believe them. My son was a lot of things, but one thing he wasn't was the sort of person that would hide a vice, especially if he thought it'd piss someone off. In his senior year he took my cigarettes and planned to smoke one in front of me. He thought if I saw my son smoke, it would make me stop. I walked in and we looked at each other square in the eyes while he lit up, then he had the worst coughing fit after one puff. Daniel didn't have the charisma to get into anything gang related and there's no way he'd keep an illicit substance down even if he wanted to, much less obtain it."

*Don't get involved in another family's busines*s, Jalen used to think. But he felt glued to the steel seat, as if straps had wrapped around his thighs to keep him in place.

"It didn't matter to me if the only reason he was getting better in the ring was to give me the middle finger. I was just happy to see a semblance of passion in his life. I lost mine a long time ago. All the DEF ever was was an attempt to make the best life for him. Now, all I can do is use it to give him the best resting place. And... that," Matteo looked up, and for the first time that night, made eye-contact with Jalen, "is where I'd like to ask you a favor."

Jalen raised an eyebrow. "Yeah, anything, man. What can I do?"

"I want you to wrestle at the next show."

Jalen's top lip disappeared in a grimace.

"Daniel was going to job out in another squash match, and honestly, I'm hurting for people I can trust to take bumps," Matteo continued. "I need this next show to be a hit. I know you're capable of working again. No longer than 10 minutes. You can get offense if you want, as long as Sir Pierre goes over."

Jalen swayed in discomfort. "I don't know..."

Matteo rubbed the bridge of his nose, looked at the cigarette, and flicked it away onto the concrete. "Jalen. You can't beat systems. Look at me. Look at what happened to me, and to my son, because we tried to 'do things our way.' Every minute you live outside of structured society, you create a debt. It'll work it's tendrils into your life and it'll take it back, it'll take back all that you owe, every minute of compliance you've denied it. Systems are older than you, and they've faced attacks from smarter, stronger, more affluent men. There's no magical way to get ahead in the world without taking part in them."

Jalen bristled. These were the words of his own family. They came out of a different man's mouth, with a different skin color, a different profession, a different upbringing. And yet, they were the same. *Get a real job. Work your way up. Settle down.* Jalen had ran so far away and they still found him in the place he called home, in the world he had created. The very building of his freedom, the DEF, stood before him defiled by the demands of other people's expectations.

"If I hurt someone... or hell, if I just hurt myself, I have to live with that for the rest of my life."

"That's why I'm putting you with Sean. You know he works safely," Matteo leaned back and folded his arms. "You can't beat the system, but you can manipulate it. You can work in the systems of the world to your benefit, rather than against it. My son is dead, Jalen. He's not coming back. You're too good of a person to step up in his place because you'd probably think *I'd* think you're taking advantage of his death. I'm here to tell you this is *exactly* the type of thing you need to do for your sanity's sake. For your happiness's sake. If an opportunity comes up, you take it so that you can *survive*. I'm not naive. I know how much you love wrestling, and I know that coffee job is a means to an end, even if you aren't honest with yourself on what that end is. If you can't take control of this moment opened up to you by this otherwise awful, horrible planet while you're still young and healthy, you may never get another chance. You didn't come to me because you wanted to hold a camera."

Jalen closed his eyes and rocked. Images of his favorite wrestler, Booker T, filled his mind. He could smell his father's burgers; salts and juices and brown sugar charred on an open flame. He heard the sound of weekends past, the fizz of a soda, the fuzzy reception on the TV, the laughter of his father at what he saw on the screen. Laughter that Jalen, at one time, mistook as shared joy, but grew to learn it was mockery, it was contempt for the farce he only watched because his young son watched, and would one day surely grow out of.

"Besides," Matteo reached into his jacket pockets and withdrew his nearly empty packet of cigarettes, "it's a little extra cash in your pocket. It's not like I'm not gonna pay ya."

Jalen tilted his head. As Matteo said those words to him, there was a small, electric spark in his lower back. It crawled up inside him, through his stomach, up his esophagus. The fears of his past and the fears of his future reached the back of his throat, and sparked along his tongue.

"Can I wear a mask?" Jalen's lips moved without conscious effort. He spoke slowly and in a low tone, as if he spoke a language he had studied but not used, "Can I be anonymous? Like, can I get a luchador outfit or something?"

Matteo blinked. "You want to make a fully-designed outfit for a one-time jobbing gig? Jalen, I'm sorry, I'm scraping pennies as is for this show. If you want all new ring-gear..."

"No, I can cover the gear," Jalen rubbed his palm into his face. The normal color of his voice had returned to him. The blend of tones was subtle, so subtle that Matteo missed it completely, "I want to do something special. And listen, I think it'll get Sean's character over, too.

If he needs a sympathetic good guy to slap around so a room full of kids and adults alike will hate him, I got one."

Nothing that Jalen had said in that momentary loss of control was particularly unusual, nor out of character. He thought for a moment that whatever inner will nudged him to consider wrestling again did so for good reasons. Wrestling *will* help Matteo. Wrestling *will* help himself. These are good things. *Step forward, Jalen.*

Matteo popped his neck. "Can you put it together in two weeks?"

Jalen looked up into the starry sky, far above the darkened gym. In wrestling, it isn't enough to just be good at the physical sport: you also need to be able to perform, and a critical component of that is the design of a character. Fortunately for Jalen, Reese had done that work for him.

"Absolutely."

{32}

{IT'S TIME FOR A COMMERCIAL BREAK}

Reese Gagnon believed there are few advantages to being a short man in modern America. The world towered over him. The top grocery shelves were forever out of his reach, and he was the most likely person to get bumped into rounding an end cap. Despite these vertical problems, there was a hidden perk; in the crushing economy of the late '10s, Reese could breathe easy when the receipt printed from the self-checkout. To rip the paper free from the machine and see a total well below the median purchase of his gender and age demographic felt like a triumph, but only in that moment, and never when it came time to eat the apples or snack bars his spare change went to.

He waited at the store entrance for his ride-share to arrive, set his bag of bare essentials at his feet, and zipped up his hoodie. Fall waltzed in and gave the city a chilly shoulder rub that loosened the leaves. The air was damp in perpetuity, a humid veil that hung over the roads regardless of whether or not it rained. When the car pulled up in front of him, Reese could see the drift of moisture in the headlights. The shadows of the car's interior, combined with the smear of headlights, obscured the driver's face, his form, any identifying details other than his tepid grip on the wheel. A mush of features and impatience, the driver could have been anyone from anywhere at any time.

Reese looked at the app to double check the driver's face. He was a tan man with institutionalized half-smile against a blank background. The figure in the car had longer hair and glasses, but if Reese squinted, it was close enough to the picture to ease his worries. He slid into the backseat; the driver asked him to confirm the destination.

“Yeah,” Reese said, used to the routine, “we’re going to Store-It.”

With that, they drove. Reese’s eyes glazed over as he leaned against the window. The lights of bars he’d never go into on his own blurred to thin streaks. They passed him by. The radio played inoffensive jazz until it cut to commercial. For whatever reason, the commercial was twice as loud as the music. It demanded to be heard:

“Did you break your bones at your job and your boss tried to keep you from filing with your insurance? *Mine* did!” the disembodied lawyer sang. “He was wrong, and so is yours! Let’s fix those bones and get you to court! I’m Josephus Ortega, YOUR personal injury lawyer—”

The driver hunted for a different forgettable jazz station. “Sorry, can’t stand those ads.”

It was the first time the driver spoke since they left the grocery store. His clarity and presence snapped Reese’s attention towards the radio knob, then to rear-view mirror. For a brief moment, as Reese stared at the driver’s reflection, he thought he saw Andrew King’s face. 3DBrain. His mind always looked for it, and here, in the throes of alertness, it found it.

In the next split second, the driver’s face morphed. The driver was Molly, Daniel, any person who had ever threatened him or his loved ones flashed through the reflection. Reese’s fears, his paranoia made him relive all his worst nightmares at once. The driver’s turn of the knob shuffled the stations of his mind, a wave of memories and emotions long buried, now forced into broadcast.

Reese choked down the flood in the back of his mouth. “No, it’s fine,” he stammered. “I can’t either.”

He closed his eyes and hated his mind’s insistence on hooking itself to the past for the rest of the drive home. The faces of his fears stayed on the back of his eyelids, and gradually faded with mediation.

Eventually, the car lurched to a stop. Reese's sneakers touched the sidewalk in front of Store-It. He tipped the driver, whose face, after enough time, had returned to neutral alignment. The car disappeared onto the main road. Reese turned to the storage complex and whispered to a past hell-bent on invasion of his present: "Go *away*. I am *happy.*"

Reese punched his access code into the main entrance of Store-It. The gains from his shopping trip were arranged within the confines of his outfit: apples in his pocket, snack bars slipped into his waistband, travel-size toothpaste in his jean's front pockets and a single roll of toilet paper on the inside of the zipper fabric in the hoodie, held up by his pocketed hands. As long as he always kept at least one hand pocketed, he could hold it there inconspicuously; it looked like a paunch which made him appear more well-fed than he was.

As he rounded a corner, a middle-aged woman stomped in front of him, clipboard in hand. She wore a tiger-stripe printed silver dress, and a white leather jacket was draped over her shoulders. She did not put her hands through the arms, and instead chose to wear the leather as if it were a thick cape.

"Hi there! How is everything?" she asked. She spoke loudly despite being inches from Reese's face.

He leaned back. He felt the toilet paper in his hoodie shift, and he staggered as he tried to keep it from slipping out. "Oh. Hello."

"Are you enjoying Store-It today? Is everything working out well?" she flashed all her teeth. Her large cross earrings glinted in the fluorescent lights.

"Y-yeah. Place is great. I store my art here."

"Great!" she drew a ballpoint pen from the clipboard's metal snap. "Would you be interested in filling out this survey? I'm the owner,

Emma Victoria. I'm trying to scoop up opinions where I can, make sure this facility is running at its absolute best."

Emma Victoria shoved the clipboard and pen at Reese in a way that implied he'd need to take both. He stared at the long survey as if it were a dog baring its fangs at him.

"Can I..." he swallowed, "grab this later, if you don't mind?"

"Sure thing!" she smiled. Her heels clacked in the hallway as she walked past him. "Come by the head office anytime between 7 a.m. and 10 p.m. That's when we close."

She slammed the door as she exited.

"...was that a threat?" he whispered.

Reese fumbled his way into his storage unit and emptied his haul into a plastic hamper in the corner. He frowned as he tried to choose which protein bar would be dinner.

Regardless of whether it was a threat or not, Reese suspected the whims of the owner would be much more difficult to keep track of than that of the routines of Store-It's employees. Whether it be by chance or circumstance, Reese had never encountered Emma Victoria before—now that the owner was in play, merely existing on site was a risk, no matter what time it was.

"Maybe she'll forget me, though," he chose a peanut butter bar. "I'm nobody. Other people are here all the time."

You know she won't forget you, he snarled in his mind.

"I don't know what else I can do," Reese let himself fall into his chair. "I could ask Jalen if I could move in with him, but... have we dated long enough? Would he be okay with that?" He put a minimal amount of effort into the lean forward necessary to open his laptops.

Think of how crazy you would've sounded to Jalen if you asked to move in with him the moment you told the truth about Store-It, he berated himself. *That wasn't that long ago. Don't be a freeloader. It's too early. You'd have to relocate all your shit, anyways, and moving is one more thing you can't afford. Even if the stream is doing good, it's not good enough. Not yet. You need to keep growing, still. Keep growing.*

Keep growing.

`Keep growing.`

`Grow.`

`Grow.`

`Grow.`

Reese rubbed the bridge of his nose, sighed, and unwrapped the snack bar. He tried to tell himself a joke, "I've always been this height." He didn't laugh; instead, he put the protein bar in his mouth and stared at the reflection of his slow chew in the laptop's start-up screen.

{33}

{DO SOMETHING CRAZY}

Jalen and Reese, over the course of the next week, had multiple but brief date-night walks in the empty shadows of Harper Park. They wanted to stay connected in a time when both were otherwise burdened: Jalen was burdened with Daniel's death and his in-ring debut at DEF, and Reese was burdened with the increased visibility of *SKELEVENTURE* and the new scrutiny of Store-It's owner. Sweetness became rarer, and took more effort. But the important thing was that sweetness remained! They vented, and stressed, and consoled, and kissed, and parted, reinvigorated, frustrated, back to their inner worlds.

The DEF's next show drew closer, and every action Jalen took—at work, at play, and at home—had a portion of his brain power sectioned off to the map of maneuvers and narrative he and Sean had choreographed. When Jalen plodded up the steps of his apartment, his mind was elsewhere. His mind's eye saw the squared circle, and his position in it. It saw the future of his match, the spots he would work, and the bumps he would take. Jalen tripped over a step on the way up, and the physical disturbance failed to shake him from the lock of his imagination. When he stumbled, so too did his character in the future. It wasn't until he found cardboard boxes at his doorstep that he was finally pulled back to the present.

"Fuck yeah," Jalen scooped them up and unlocked his apartment door.

Jalen kept a secret from Reese; his new character was Sir Mortimer, the skeleton hero of Reese's puppet show *SKELEVENTURE*. Jalen thought the character's cartoonish nature was tailor made for the over-the-top world of wrestling. The DEF needed levity and Jalen thought a neon-coloured, mustached bone-knight was just the sort of goofy hero-gimmick the crowd could get behind. If nothing else, it was the perfect dummy for Sean's Sir Pierre to squash. Jalen didn't mind if the character was a one-off—surely, if nothing else, the surprise on Reese's face would be worth the cost of assembling the outfit alone.

What perfect timing, he thought. He threw the boxes onto his bed and set up Reese's stream on his phone, which had gone live moments prior. He watched his boyfriend play with his virtual puppets, and as he did, he slid into spandex meant to mimic them.

Most of the outfit was a Frankenstein, a repurpose of Halloween costumes Jalen had hunted down online and in thrift shops around the city. The international success of skeleton-themed wrestler La Parka made it quite easy for Jalen to find a similar spandex knock-off. He bought a neon-yellow fabric paint with a glitter finish he intended to go over the "bones" of the suit with—but before he could paint, he needed to test wear the pieces. The body of an athlete tends to workout the proportions of clothes in ways they were not designed for.

"I don't know how much longer I can hold out!" Reese voiced Sir Mortimer's pain as he rag-dolled through an army of jiggly-eyed 3D slime monsters. A donation came in:

CEOofMoney donated $2!
"i beelieve in u mortiman"

"Okay, maybe I *can* do it," Sir Mortimer sheepishly muttered through Reese. He slapped a slime with his polygonal sword.

Jalen pulled the lyrca over his thick calves and quads. As the fabric snapped to his waist, he observed himself in the mirror. With some embarrassment, he considered that he might need to strap down his privates if he didn't want the audience to focus on the wrong bone. He hiked up green-and-purple briefs over the skeleton suit, then elbow pads and laced-up purple boots.

"Oh no, Wimbly's slimes are infused with lightning magic!" Sir Mortimer sparked and convulsed as his sword plunged into the jiggle-monsters.

VideoGameJames donated $1!
"can jello conduct electricity?"

"I am in too much pain for science!" Reese-Mortimer cried out.

From another box, Jalen hooked a harness around his broad shoulders, and attached to the black straps were chunky green shoulder pads. They were polygonal and segmented, as if Jalen's Sir Mortimer had stepped straight out of Reese's computer. The cape attached to the shoulder pads glittered on the inside with disco-era silver, while the outside flowed with royal purple filigree. He practiced ripping the cape off in a single, dramatic motion. It unfurled with ease, and the way the inside caught the light when shed from his form was, in Jalen's eyes, a show-stopper. "Maybe I'll wear it in reverse," he pondered as he waved the fabric under his lamp's bulb.

In the smallest box was the most important piece of his costume, and the only item he had custom made: the mask. The skeleton mask had matching filigree on his cheekbones, horns to mimic the knight helm Reese's model wore, and white-light eyes which softened any fear a neon-skeleton could potentially give a small child. A curly white mustache fringed below the skeleton's nostril holes.

Before he could slip on the mask, though, he realized that he had a problem: his long gray-and-red locs.

LPalmerGames donated $5!
"do something crazy"

{}

Earlier that week, Jalen worked longer hours in the in the DEF with Matteo. So many of these late-night sessions had occurred between the two by this point it had become routine; Jalen leaned against the kitchen counter surrounded by strewn paper and notebooks while Matteo smoked and paced and spun ideas out of his mouth with waving hands.

Matteo, businessman he may be, needed an organized and oppositional voice by his side. Someone who would help him narrow his focus, someone who would say 'no' and explain why. In most circumstances, Matteo hated to hear 'no.' What made it different when it came out of Jalen's mouth was when the flinch of anger welled within Matteo, the expression Jalen had would hit him in a way no one else's could. Jalen's upturned brow, soft and serious, patient and relaxed, was the picture of thoughtfulness. In his hand, his pen hovered over the pages of notes born of Matteo's rambling, organized in a way Matteo himself could never quite muster.

"If you want to grow in this business," Matteo told him, "you have to have control. Control over the smallest part of everything you do—every bump, every mannerism, every breath you take must be controlled for the story of the match. You are nothing in this industry if you can't control yourself."

Every now and then Jalen wondered if he was being taken advantage of. In the gaps of conversation, when Matteo would feed him a nugget of wisdom, he wondered if this, too, was a method of Matteo exerting control over him. In any other situation Jalen might have resented manipulation, but as more nights and responsibilities piled into Jalen's life, he realized the truth about the world, and himself: if you're aware you're being manipulated, you can still use other people's control over you to your advantage. Life is just aggression and concessions organized; the winners are the ones who know how to use which ones, and when.

Jalen nodded and waited for Matteo to take a drag. His boss had a particular timing for when he'd puff his cigarette, and Jalen always waited for it before he grabbed the reins. "That's good advice. But let's get back on topic..."

{}

Jalen drew his fingertips across his long locs in the mirror. Reese's stream glowed in the reflection over his shoulder, and had become nothing more than cartoon background noise. He had spent a large portion of his life growing out his hair, which, when braided, reached down to his upper back. He loved that he still had his hair after all treatment it had received over the years—his father went bald early in life, and in his parents didn't approve of the flashy choice of dying them. At the time he first started to dye his hair, it was an act of rebellion and preening to attract other men. Now that he was a free adult and had a boyfriend, its purpose, beyond aesthetic, was gone.

There was no way his locs would fit in the mask, so he either needed to incorporate them into the outfit itself, or...

"...or I need to take control."

Pirioitieicit donated $!
"bones"

Jalen, lost in thought, missed the descent of Reese's expression in response to the donation. He looked at the mask. Those yellow dots-for-eyes bore back at the wrestler with curiosity.

"Reese never could give you a goal," Jalen whispered, "but *I* can."

"Thanks for the donation," Reese said as the message faded away. He struggled to get back in character.

{34}

{SURVEY}

Reese spent more time in Jolly Molly's than usual.

He entered the cafe around noon and blended into the crowd. He gave a tepid wave to the cafe employees, but otherwise did not interrupt their work flow during the relatively busy hours. Instead, the digital puppeteer buried himself in a corner with his laptop, his eyes heavy from sleepless nights and caffeine. Unimpeded by a cloudless sky, the sun through the glass storefront bore into his skin with heat. Glare found his laptop screen even when he retreated to the shade of a booth.

Any time not spent on the construction of 3D models was used to scour the internet for evidence of 3DBrain, or anything similar to the sightings and symptoms Reese experienced. No alias or information came up beyond Andrew King's arrest years ago. As for his symptoms, there was a range of possibilities according to the internet; they could've been hallucinations, various mental disorders, or a migraine. Each possibility carried its own problematic weight. If it were his mind's decay, he had no health insurance. If it was a migraine, he was disappointed the amount of coffee he normally drank in a day didn't seem to cure it.

Reese's mind was at war with itself. His logical side concluded that this was new paranoia over old experiences, but his emotional side was adamant and loud; *something* was wrong, even if he couldn't pinpoint exactly what it was. The glitches on stream, the donations he received, the way strangers seemed to twist in his peripheral vision, the sudden burst of his audience size was all connected in some imperceptible way he couldn't piece together yet. He went over the connections so many times it became a smear of stress; ever-present, but impossible to grasp.

The worst part of these occurrences is he could think of no way to talk to Jalen, or anyone, about them. How does one say "I'm concerned with how popular I'm getting" without sounding like a jackass? How does one not sound crazy when they try to find meaning in visions?

Jalen slid into the booth.

You can't, Reese concluded, *so I won't.*

"Hey," the wrestler's smile was wide, far wider than normal. He waited for the moment that Reese's eyes were fully on him, and lifted the brim of his cap with his thumb. "What'dya think?"

Reese blinked in surprise. Jalen's beautiful locs were gone, mowed and trimmed into a short, tight fade. The hint of dyed gray and red remained at the tips.

"It looks great, but I'm biased, right?" Reese fiddled his fingers into his belt loops, "I think you'd look good no matter what hair you had."

"Aw," Jalen still wasn't used to the lack of obstruction on his neck. His hair was short and sharp, with a razor's line at his tapered temple. "Well, thanks. I don't remember the last time I had it this short. Felt like it was time for a change."

He neglected to mention how much easier it was to wear a lyrca mask with this new hairstyle.

{}

Night settled onto Dundolk. Reese got out of the ride share, tipped his driver, and plodded towards Store-It. His chin hung to his chest in thought.

He recognized a need within himself to distract his mind from its manic wandering. In such situations, he only had two avenues of output—his boyfriend, and his show. While this is an exact doubling of how many distractions he had before his romance with Jalen, he still felt wanting for options: he had spent his entire morning and afternoon on his craft. It was the night before the big DEF show and, although he didn't know the full truth of Jalen's plans, he knew enough to know this wasn't the night to bother him. With no scripts and with Jalen's understandable unavailability, Reese considered only one other possibility: "I could do an impromptu stream, I suppose."

After all, this the biggest I've ever been, he thought as he punched his key-code into the building. *I'm starting to profit for the first time in a long time. I have to capitalize on it.*

He observed the storage shutters as he passed. At one point in time he would look at their sturdy frames and cool steel and wonder what normal people used them for, what it could possibly be like to live a life where you used a unit because you had too much and not because you had nothing left.

The fact he could walk by these and smile illustrated to himself just how thankful he should be. *Things are going well,* he thought. *If I keep pushing, maybe in a month or two I'll be at a point where I can move out. I'll work tonight, take a break for the DEF show tomorrow, and do a serious finance reevaluation afterwards. Be happy, Reese. It's working out. Finally.*

He turned a corner and stopped himself before he could bump into Emma Victoria.

"Hello!" she beamed. Her pearl earrings bounced as she stomped her beige pumps together with the same snapping strength a Drill Sergeant uses in front of new recruits. She flipped through pages on her clipboard. "Reese, right? Reese Gagnon."

Do you hide behind corners and wait for people to run into you? Fucking hell, Reese thought as he tried to suppress a gasp of fear.

"T-that's me,' he swallowed. "Hello again."

"You didn't get the survey last time," she said as she unhooked a sheet of paper from the clipboard, "so I thought I'd bring it to you."

"Oh. Uh, thanks," he took the paper. It took little study to realize this was not a survey at all—it was a contract, the one he signed when he first moved in to Store-It.

"As you may be aware," Emma clicked her tongue on the roof of her mouth, "it is against the law—more importantly, against the contract you signed—for you to live inside a storage unit. It is *not* an apartment."

Reese could feel the blood drain from his hands. The paper rattled.

"There are resources for the homeless that can be found at the front office," she re-secured the papers on her clipboard and walked past him.

"Please," Reese bit his bottom lip. "I have work. I've never missed a payment. I'm almost back on my feet. Give me a month at most. I'll be out. I promise."

Emma Victoria stopped, thought for a moment, and turned, her blonde bowl cut swayed with her movements. Her smile, pulled taut across her face, was the same one she had used with every sentence she had ever said before, which made it impossible to know when, if ever, she had really smiled at him at all: "You have 24 hours. If you're not out by tomorrow night, I'm calling the police and you're going to jail."

{}

Reese flung himself into the darkest corner of his storage unit and covered his face with his jacket. He sobbed uncontrollably and punched a cloth-stuffed cardboard box near his crumpled body. "This was always going to happen, wasn't it?" snot ran down his nose. "It doesn't matter what I do, does it? I either get other people in trouble, or myself. I'm fucking useless."

Between the heave of his chest and the waves of tears, one part of his mind tried to rationally consider his options, but found only two: Jalen, or hiding.

This exact scenario terrified him. The last thing he wanted to be was a freeloader, and that's what he felt he'd be if he suddenly sprung a request to move into his apartment on his boyfriend. *This situation is of my own making*, he reminded himself. *I can't take advantage of other people. I have to fix this myself.*

"Maybe... I have enough for a hotel night or two..." he choked and reached for one of his laptops. The closest one to his person was the one his father gave him, scuffed and old, held together purely by new parts and a stubborn will. Its load times were quite slow, which gave time for his thoughts to spiral down the anxious drains of his mind. "Maybe I can stay there for a night and find a different storage unit to stay in for a little bit..."

He clicked through websites and hoped this incident at Store-It wouldn't put him on a storage-unit-blacklist, if such a thing existed.

{}

Emma Victoria swung her beige purse across her sand-and-black lace dress and stomped her way to her 2018 Mercedes X350d luxury pick-up truck.

Reese's living situation did not matter to her, in theory. She wouldn't have considered Reese was homeless at all if she had only judged on appearances, as she often did. He looked like one of her children's friends—white, middle-class, and forgettable, the perfect combination of qualities that made Reese faceless and meaningless to her. This all changed when she realized she saw him with such frequency; after all, her only appearances at Store-It were business related. Were *his*?

It was her duty, as owner of the land, to know what happened around her and grant it approval. More than duty, she felt it was her *right,* one earned when she purchased the land. She did quite a good job, she thought. Not everyone is smart enough to marry a real estate agent and illegally broker a deal for much less than the land is worth, then use your mother's inheritance to scoop it up and turn it into a storage unit. Emma Victoria was proud of her work. Passive income was her passion, and no one did it better in Dundolk.

{}

"It's pointless..." Reese's bottom lip quivered as he researched Store-It's competitors. Once he started to factor in the difference in moving costs, equipment, forced downtime for his stream, and the strain of embarrassment for his failure as an adult, he lost hope. "I lose no matter what I do..."

He sucked in a gulp of air and covered his face with both hands. Tears rolled down his palms and forearms and slipped into the cracks of the keyboard keys.

"I deserve this..."

{}

Emma Victoria gabbed the driver-side handle. She felt her phone vibrate in her purse, which gave her pause as she fought the compulsion to fish it out.

Once she became aware of the frequency of Reese's presence on site, she pursued the details of his contract and found a particular oddity. Reese was a paying customer, and while that's great and not a problem in and of itself, the price of his unit *was*. He had locked in on a third party promotion that no longer existed. *How dare you take advantage of me*, she thought when she read the contract. She no longer looked at this paying customer as a customer, but rather, as an obstacle to a higher bidder. A parasite. A leech. Unlike her, he offered no value to the world. If any of her children tried to take advantage of her like this, be it Carter III, Mary-Anne, or Beau-Alexander, why, they might not get a Christmas vehicle at all that year.

The vibration continued. Her obsession won out. She dug her phone out.

{}

"`Okay`," a synth voice pulsed from Reese's speaker. "`I love you.`"

Reese uncovered his face and wondered if the strange sound was an ad from one of the storage unit websites he had opened. Every click on a tab elicited a fuzz from the speakers, as if it came from a mechanical failure within.

"If my laptop fucking dies," he sniffed, "I'm going to lose my shit. I can't handle anything else going wrong. Please tell me this thing isn't dying."

"`Okay.`"

Reese furrowed his brow. Something was a little more direct about *that* one. It was the same line in the same digi-voice, but its tone, its inflection, registered concern, empathy, and contextual awareness.

{}

Emma Victoria flared her nostrils. The notification was from an unknown number. She suddenly remembered a similar sender's text inconvenienced her before. The last time it contacted her, it sent her a blank message; this time, one word:

`bones`

"Screw you," she mumbled as she slammed her thumb into digital keys. "Forget the FTC. I'm going to the police."

She ripped the door of her 2018 Mercedes X350d luxury pick-up truck open and pulled herself in. She didn't know if the police would handle something like this, but she made a reminder to talk to her lawyer about it after dinner. She stabbed her keys into the ignition and fussed with her seatbelt. Normally, this is when she'd be greeted by the smooth voiced sermon of Pastor DJ Billy James LaRae on 610 AM, or one of his many country-gospel vinyl interludes. No such familiarity greeted her; instead, she was met with brittle static, oppressive and accelerating. She fiddled with the dial, and only found the fuzz of distortion, regardless of whether she tuned to AM or FM stations.

Suddenly, a bass voice full of feedback grumbled from behind the truck, its words muffled by the glass. With wide blue eyes, Emma Victoria checked the rearview mirror.

A tall figure stood behind the bed of the pickup, so tall it had to lean its head forward to stare back at Emma in the reflection with white pin-point eyes. Its face came to a point, sharp and curved downwards. This dagger-beak did not remain; in the next moment it was a pile of teeth haphazardly mashed across where a mouth should be, then no features at all, blank in all ways except existence. The creature's body shivered and shook in confusion over its own makeup, discontent with substance and form. It shuffled between shadows, then light, then meat, then sparks. The thumb of its claws popped the knuckles on its talon-fingers idly. The only consistency found in the creature was its eyes and the direction of its movements. It lifted a glitching leg up, which contorted in an electric arc, and pulled the rest of its body up into the bed of the truck. Dark. Light. Spark. Meat. Teeth. Beak. Nothing. Everything. Closer. Convulse. Approach. Groan. Moan. Bones.

Emma Victoria screamed and smashed her foot into the pedal. The creature tumbled out of the bed, knocked off-balance by the sudden acceleration. Wheels kicked rocks in all directions onto Store-It's main road.

"Bones."

The static on the radio cleared and let the creature's voice in. Emma looked down at the digital display of the radio-dial—where the frequency of the radio station should be, was instead a climbing number, far beyond the range of FM.

A claw zapped out of the display and grabbed the wheel. It cupped over Emma's hand and lit the muscles of her fingers and forearms in electric chaos. She felt its power flow through her arm. Smoke billowed from the wheel as the flesh was cooked. The 2018 Mercedes X350d skipped over the sidewalk and slammed into the same light pole the city had replaced from the deer "accident."

As Emma Victoria bled out on the hood of her crumpled truck, her limbs in disarray, her shoulder speared into the splinters of a light pole, her skin full of glass, she spent her last cognitive thoughts remembering which child she left the most money too. She was certain it was Carter III, and that's good, she thought, because Mary-Anne had started to see that Mendez boy with the skateboard and his parents were social workers and there's just no future mingling with a family like that.

As the world faded, the last sensation Emma felt was the bounce of the hood of the car. The creature landed above her and removed her humerus and clavicle with greedy claws, swallowed them in a temporary maw, then chattered and convulsed as if it took bitter medicine.

{35}

{O-K}

The laptop's screen flickered on and off with squares of corruption, then began to shake. It rattled against the makeshift table, the clack of plastic on fake wood rattled and echoed in the metallic storage unit. Reese crawled backwards, his sight frozen on the device. Sweat gushed out of his skin and froze, cold and terrified of leaving the surface.

From the USB ports and speakers and in-between the keys, shadow-filled static rose like smoke. It coalesced into a tall, lurching form, bestial and humanoid at once. It loomed over Reese, its head a misshapen mess of digital noise with skin that shifted between textures. Reese, jaw-agape, tears on his face from a nightmare now replaced, watched as the chaos settled into form. The creature chose its skin.

The shadows melted. Gnarled muscles of dust-color emerged. Tatters of maroon cloth and tassels were tied around its long, scaled neck, scraps of what might have been, at one point in time, beautiful fabric with regal trim. The white lights of its eyes were arrested, transformed into the iris of a new, red sclera prison. When it breathed, its skin seemed to pulse in odd places, as if its muscles were in slow locomotion underneath the surface. Every breath was filled with laboured, vile congestion.

This creature was a bastardization of Reese's vision, an abomination in the vague shape of the vulture-mage villain from *SKELEVENTURE*. Reese wanted to scream, his mouth was open and ready to cry out, but no sound came. He looked upon the beast not as if it brought with it the possibility of death, but that it *was* death, that it was real and imminent, and it chose a form specifically for Reese to understand.

“W-Wimbly...?” Reese struggled to get the creature’s name on his tongue.

“Okay,” it chattered, white matter and foam flicked from its scythe-beak. “Okay. Okay. I love you, okay.”

It popped its knuckles. It was a nonsense reply from a creature that shouldn’t be.

Reese sucked his lips in, spun to his belly, and pushed himself into a manic run towards the shutters. Wimbly’s tree-trunk arm glitched towards him in an electric arc and struck him down. It pinned his stomach to the concrete underneath its knurled claw. Each sword-like digit stabbed into the floor. Reese screamed and pushed and punched at fingers the size of his shoulders. Rubble from the impact of the creature’s claws into concrete pelted Reese’s face, covered it with ash, filled his nostrils. Wimbly’s other arm tore through the air and together the two claws scooped Reese’s body up and pulled him back to its ugsome form. He squirmed and kicked in the monster’s claws.

“What do you want?!” Reese cried.

“Bones,” Wimbly said.

For a moment, Reese’s thrashing stopped. His breathing stopped. His sensation of touch, his awareness of the world around him, all functions of his mentality paused as he focused solely on deciphering the creature’s meaning.

The abomination crawled over to Reese’s computer chair and, with surprising carefulness, placed him in it. Firm enough to hold him in place, gentle enough to protect him from damage. Reese struggled and pumped his legs with all his strength, kicked the mass of pulsing meat in its writhing chest. The ribcage vibrated as if it were gelatin, squished around the sole of Reese’s sneaker, then spat it out. Sparks of electricity gathered around the rubber of his shoe then crackled into nothingness. Reese pushed and cried and fought with the last edges of his strength, but couldn't budge underneath even a single claw. Wimbly, or the creature that wore the tortured approximation of Wimbly's face, brought its scythe beak to Reese's nose. It bumped him with light tenderness. Reese shuddered, confused, terrified.

Wimbly blinked its red-and-white eyes and scanned the small human. It looked at him with undue familiarity.

It opened its beak.

It tilted its head down.

It vomited.

It vomited white matter, chunky, flecked with blood. The vile substance poured like a waterfall, oozed around Reese's frame, and sealed over his lap. The substance hardened, as if it were a soft variation of concrete. Reese wiggled his hips, but could not move.

"What is this?" Reese sobbed as he pulled at the ooze. It gave less than an inch before snapping back into place.

"Bones," Wimbly said.

Reese struggled against the semi-hard shell of bone matter. It had slight pliability from the monster's mysterious digestion, but not enough to tear the material when he dug in with his nails. Wimbly leaned down and vomited on each of the legs of the chair, and secured Reese in place.

"Bones of...*what?*"

Reese scanned his make-shift desk for options. The only thing within arms length was his cell phone. He rotated his chair and grabbed it, but before he could punch in his unlock code, Wimbly snatched it from his hands with pinpoint precision in the tip of its curved beak.

"Bones," Wimbly said. It picked the device with claw tips, blinked at the small black rectangle, then threw the cell phone into its beak. It swallowed.

Reese rubbernecked. He could see the angle of his cellphone move down the abomination's long throat. Wimbly's white pupils grew in surprise as the device plunged into its digestive system. Its body shook with electric fuzz and, for at least one brief moment, struggled to keep its bipedal form. Its limbs became disconnected and shuttered away from its torso before they snapped back into place.

Reese trembled, "What do you want... *from me*?"

Wimbly blinked at Reese. It stared with buried, scattered intellect. Somewhere beyond the cruel light of its eyes, it considered its response. It turned away, slipped a claw-nail underneath the fold of Reese's laptop, picked it up, then gently deposited it onto Reese's desk.

"I love you," Wimbly said. "Okay?"

Without Reese's input, the software for his stream started to open, and the webcam light came to life.

{}

Jalen slipped the Sir Mortimer mask over his head, held up his lycra-covered arm, and flexed his biceps in the mirror. The outfit was complete, and everything fit. "I think, at this moment, I have to be the most buff skeleton on the planet. Right?"

He had returned from his training session with Sean before the next day's show, abuzz in the ways he dreamed of being before a performance. He practiced walking as if he were Sir Mortimer himself, covered in armor, foam sword in hand, powered by righteousness and joyful cheers. This character, by his hand and build and emotive sway, would come to life right in front of his boyfriend's eyes. He let his spandex-fingers glide over his abs, the slippery fabric-on-fabric sensation brought confidence to his mind, and an electric prickle across his skin: *I'm gonna steal this whole damn show*, he thought.

His phone buzzed.

He slid his thumb under the mask and lifted it up above his brow to check the message. It was a go-live notification for the *SKELEVENTURE* stream.

Jalen tilted his head. “He doesn’t normally stream at this time...” he muttered to himself as he flicked through tabs to open up Reese’s stream. If he was unprepared for the go-live, he was doubly so for its contents.

Reese sat in a void of swirling colors. Every model he had ever made was alive around him; they danced and sang and fought and loved, their polygons broke and reformed in a mess of meshes. Slime creatures bounced up and down with googly eyes, then absorbed other figures into their ooze. A Minnow-taur stabbed itself, bled pools of poorly rendered blood, then deflated like a balloon. Sir Mortimer played the drums. Reese thought that if any of these puppets were truly the characters he created, then at least Sir Mortimer would fight back against Wimbly. That if anyone would save him, it would be the hero of his story. But Sir Mortimer was indistinguishable from the creatures around him—he was a passionate concept reduced to nothing more than a puppet mindlessly pulling money in. Every square inch of the screen welcomed in a new figure to lose its cartoon mind to candy-coated madness.

Reese’s mouth moved as if to scream, but it contorted into a wide, unnatural smile, as if his grin were magnified, his jaw stretched beyond human proportions. The sound fished out of his mouth was not his voice. He sang a synthesizer chord, a sustained harmony of beeps and fuzzy static. Reese’s stream was chaos the likes of which Jalen had never seen before, and which he was certain Reese’s setup and computing power was not capable of.

The stream’s chat noticed this, too. Messages flew faster than one could read, exclamations of surprise and laughter filled the column next to the video player. The polygonal monsters of *SKELEVENTURE* seemed to delight in the replies of the chat; they applauded and yelled with speaker-crunching screeches and ate the trees and castle bricks of Reese's carefully constructed fantasy scenery. They vomited it back out into a pixelated mess that was both distorted and detailed, covered in a horrible saliva, and textured in a way that was closer to reality than it had appeared before.

At the top of the screen, Wimbly's floppy model sat. It was king of the chaos, leader of the riots. It waved its hands to the synthetic noise as if it were a beautiful opera, and it was the conductor. But there was no melody, or rhythm, or soul. Just noise, bleeps, boops, static, scratching, wailing sirens and bone-rattling bass. It leapt down and paraded incoming donation messages around the perimeter of the screen, quite proud of the income that rolled in on the back of the show:

{36}

{i love you}

Theodorestache donated $5!
"THIS is exactly why I subscribed lmao"

JudgeOfBreakfest donated $10!
"hi this is my first time here and I'd like to ask: what?"

AnimeMan1777 donated $1!
"this sure is something"

jozzyrulesyo donated $1!
"LOL WHAT IS THIS???"

ArmAllCats donated $25!
"keep it up champ"

ArmandNoScope donated $1!
"do you have song request?"

TPoseGirl donated $6!
"you're an inspiration"

GhoulishGeorge156 donated $5!
"This is really out there, even for you. I'm here for it."

Wimbly4Prez donated $20!
"i'm assuming this is a demo of new software or something. It's great"

BoxBraidGames donated $1!
"chill out lmao"

BunchaNumbersBoi donated $1!
"ah, so this is fear"

Panckes6820 donated $5!
"I really can't believe you just sat down and made a coke-fueled nightmare and made all of us watch it with you. iconic"

Reincarbonated donated $50!
"i've seen the light"

11335566 donated $5!
"praying 4 u"

Ifyouknowyouknow donated $5!
"I'm honestly impressed. How long did it take you to orchestrate this?"

NoNeedfor3D donated $5!
"I see you've finally lost it."

Theinternetnottheband donated $75!
"Remember when this channel was about how to make 3D models? I don't"

MortimersHipBone donated $11!
"skeleton drummer"

thegreatmemachine donated $5!
"DaveedGamez sent me here. I'm cry-laughing"

dadsngamez donated $20!
"king"

TonytheTaco donated $5!
"this made my dad thanks"

herecomestheusername donated $5!
"i don't know wtf I clicked on to get here but I'm glad I did"

TonytheTaco donated $1!
whoops meant 'day' lol"

CODguy0011 donated $1!
"r u gay?"

RedSoxFan89 donated $25!
"so when's the new album?"

CanIGetUhhh donated $5!
"is it just me or is Wimbly's animation more fluid than normal?"

Jalen rubbed his temples as he tried to keep up with the deluge of donations. Reese's new content had brought in more viewers—and opened more pocketbooks—than his normal work had before. The 3D characters led donation messages like livestock, and if Jalen didn't know any better, he could've sworn there was perverse pride on their polygonal faces. The edges of poorly constructed lion maws curved upwards in glee, featureless villagers clapped their paper thin hands, Sir Mortimer took off his skull-head and juggled it along with a donation message.

Reese's pasted on smile battled his furrowed brow. Tear-filled eyes contradicted wide-stretched lips. He was a collage of emotions, a battleground of expressions. In past shows, Reese's acting, even at its most serious, contained the hint of self-awareness; awareness of the camera lens, a subtle restraint and softness unique to him. Here, Jalen was convinced by Reese's manic, twisting face. If this were performance, Jalen had never been so fooled.

But Jalen *lived* in the world of wrestling, a world full of physical theater. He had seen what growth in performance looked like, and knew that such theatrical immersion was rare, at best, and especially with amateurs. Jalen could have been convinced that the actions and effects of the 3D models were the result of new technology Reese had not yet told him about, or some breakthrough in technique. Reese always had his laptop, after all—he was always working on his character's models. But the performance was not Reese's, and Reese had never expressed concern over his presence on camera. Jalen had seen that face up close, and explored it more intimately than anyone. *This* wasn't *him*. Convinced that the duality on his boyfriend's face hid something awful, he texted him:

Everything alright?

He watched Reese's face picture-in-picture, and waited to see if his expression would change, or if the mask would fall. To his surprise, he got an immediate response, despite the fact Reese continued to stare straight ahead into the lens:

" I love_ you"

Jalen's eyes ran back and forth between the text message and the stream. Reese hadn't moved, he hadn't fished out his phone, he hadn't looked away from the camera. He only stared, his eyes coated in fear his mouth seemed to ignore. Wimbly glanced towards the camera. The 3D models hesitated in their chaos for one moment, but resumed their merriment shortly thereafter. Jalen texted:

I'm coming over.

His phone buzzed violently:

"Don/ˇtt"

A ravaged breath ran from Jalen's lungs. He began to dial 911. The phone's dial screen closed after he pressed the '9.' He opened it again, and the phone shut off completely.

"W-what..." Jalen grabbed the side of his head in frustration, "what the fuck?"

Jalen ground the back of his teeth in frustration. He slid the phone into his pocket, grabbed his keys, and fished a baseball bat out of his closet. As he began to sprint out of his apartment, he caught his scandalous reflection: he was still in the Sir Mortimer outfit. With little thought, he threw on an insulated coat and ran out the door.

He threw himself into his Audi and revved the car. The radio clicked on without his input. Jalen's auditory preferences were for podcasts and songs pumped from his phone through an aux cable. He never listened to the radio, so to hear it turn on was already enough to give him brief pause. He looked to the radio's display and watched it speed through different stations. The radio hunted for words:

"Don't," the dial turned wildly. "DON'T!" "don't—" "Don't—" "Don't, please," "don't?" "don't..."

Jalen turned the radio off as he sped towards the gate. It turned itself back on.

"Don't..." the radio hissed before it shut itself off.

Jalen pulled the car up to the electronic gate. The glow of his headlights disappeared on the steel as he drew near enough that he feared bumping the gate if he inched closer. Yet, it still didn't open. He looked down an apartment road and realized the illumination of street lamps was gone. No windows were lit with inner light, nor were there porch lights. The entire apartment complex was suddenly blackened, with the only hint of visibility provided by moonlight. Jalen got out of the car. He realized the hum of electricity was gone from the air. The power in his complex was out. In a panic, he grabbed the community gate and strained against it.

"Come the FUCK on!" he screamed during his exertion. He rattled the gate with anger; Jalen was a strong man, but these bars wouldn't budge for anyone.

He tried to turn his phone on again to see if he could look up how to open an electric gate without power. The phone refused his command. He grabbed the sides of his head and paced up and down the sides of his Audi and, for a moment, considered barreling his car through the wooden fence of the border neighborhood. After some pacing, he decided to investigate the gate. *If the power's off,* he thought, *perhaps there's some mechanism that I can just break to get through.* He discovered a black box on the ground with a cap on it. It wasn't so much hidden as it was obscured by part of a well manicured bush. Jalen removed the cap, and found a keyhole. His apartment key didn't fit, but with brief thought, he realized that didn't matter. He scrambled to his car's glove compartment and began to push aside paperwork and car manuals until he found what he was looking for.

"'*Don't grow your hair out,*' dad said," Jalen snatched a hairpin into his palm. He hopped back to the box and wrangled it into the lock until it was able to turn, then lifted the panel open. He gave the gate a brief push, and felt its lack of resistance. "I would've been stuck here if I listened to you."

Jalen sped down streets with reckless abandon. The city itself seemed to work in concert against him. Traffic lights froze on red, and Jalen recognized they did so with deliberate intention. When he blew past them, they went out all-together, as did the lights along the road. Jalen kept going. The more resistance this force put in his way, the more determined he grew. It almost didn't matter Reese was on the other side; Jalen wanted to overcome the obstacles that clearly targeted him, and him alone.

The radio clicked on and sped through stations:

"What,"

"Would,"

"Your,"

"Father,"

"Think?" the radio taunted him as he peeled down side streets. Jalen slammed the breaks in reply, felt the sweat of fear run down his face. He exhaled hard through pursed lips; there was something about obvious intimidation that had the opposite effect on him.

"So... you can hear me," Jalen kicked the gas pedal in, swerved to avoid a pedestrian on the main road, then turned down a side street towards Store-It.

{37}

{REPEATER}

Store-It's logo was designed and purchased at a remarkably low cost through a third party vendor, far lower than one would pay an artist directly for. What could've been a lucrative contract for the personal touch of a professional turned, instead, into expected pocket change for one of many art-firm-factories that had all but gobbled up the graphic design market.

Jalen walked through the open gate of the unit lot. His hands were firm around the handle of his wooden bat, ready to swing at the slightest shadow. He saw Emma Victoria's body and truck embedded to the splintered power pole, but would never know who she was, or how useless the haggling for Store-It's logo was to her in death. All he knew was she died at the same utility pole that once held the head of a decapitated buck. After what he experienced on his ride through the city, he did not believe these events were unrelated.

The lights were on in the main office. Jalen could see blood on the window, and the hand of a dark-blue-cuffed arm on the ground sticking through the slight open door. It was likely the cuff of a security uniform, he thought. He felt no compulsion to check further: there was no sound, no twitch, no creak of wooden boards or shutter of window blinds. No lives in that room waited for a saviour. Unimpeded, he entered the corridors of units, kept his back to the wall, and looked for hints of where Reese might be.

Jalen's life was carefully constructed by his own rules. When the gleam of a few years of late night weekends and one night stands lost their luster, he knew well enough the mechanisms of reality to restructure it. He made use of Molly to get the jobs he needed, to move into the apartment he wanted, to support himself and effectively cut his ties to his parents. When Molly pursued her cafe, he, of course, encouraged it. He positioned himself to where, if the cafe succeeded, he'd have tenure, and if it failed, he had the safety net of lean living and multiple jobs to fall back on.

His hot breath was visible against the cold air.

He still had other dreams, sure. Jalen wasn't complacent. He took up his role at the DEF to explore what wrestling, the earliest seed from his childhood, could provide for him creatively. Would performance fill the gap in his life? Would script-writing? Booking matches? As long as he could get paid, he could explore himself freely. As long as his safe structure remained, that was all that mattered to him.

He turned a corner, and found a mound of white goo. It was thick, with chunks of hard red-and-gray in its form. Translucent liquid coated and puddled the pile. Were it not for the suggestion of viscera, he might've found the discovery of a material of this color and consistency more amusing.

Reese was far from the first man to look at him with a blush, to look at him with parted lips that failed to speak hidden thoughts. Jalen had seen that expression so many times after he hit is growth spurt, from girls he never desired in high school, to the boring club boys of late night bars, to the self-assured older men of dating apps. Lust was fleeting, Jalen found, both for the ones he chose to lay, and for himself. He didn't *need* sex. He didn't *need* the cafe. He didn't *need* the DEF. What he needed was a part of all of those things, but not exclusive to any of them.

A fluorescent tube began to shudder in the ceiling case above Jalen. Its light flickered, and he noticed the growth of his shadow in its strobe.

Jalen whipped around and hit a home run on the side of Wimbly's head. The wooden bat broke in half. Wimbly's neck tore and bled static. The glitching-beast staggered backwards, its limbs in scattered disarray.

It was only now, in this moment, that Jalen knew what he needed. Jalen needed control.

"What are you?" he asked.

"What are you?" Wimbly returned the question. It brought its claw to its glitching head, hung to the side like a ripped doll, and pushed it back onto its long neck. The vulture-mage's beak clacked as sparks sewed the electric-tear together.

Jalen's brow scrunched inwards. He was offended by such a question from a beast of such impossible composition, "I asked first."

Wimbly's white irises pinned in their red pools. "Bones."

Jalen sucked in a breath. He thought of Emma's body, the white on the concrete, and the strand of material he saw dangle from the creature's beak. He didn't doubt Wimbly ate bones, but based off the phenomenon in front of him, he deduced that this creature was made of some form of electric energy. The mingling of these two matters made little sense to him. It was foolish to try and apply sense to the beast in front of him, he considered, but he tried anyway.

"Maybe your vocabulary sucks, but you're not mindless. You're picking and choosing who to kill. Judging by the truck outside, it doesn't look like you have a problem with killing people in their cars, but you tried to discourage and impede me instead of murdering me."

Jalen pursed his lips, thought for a moment, and took a few steps back down the hall. The creature watched him with twitching pupils from underneath the brim of its mage-hat. It did not pursue Jalen's retreat.

So, Jalen reversed direction and walked towards Wimbly.

"Don't," Wimbly rolled his gnarled, bulky shoulders. He took a step forward in response. The crackle of energy that accompanied the scrape of his talons on the concrete stilted Jalen's next step with hesitation.

"Don't hurt anyone else," Jalen seethed through gritted teeth. "Don't hurt Reese."

"Don't hurt Reese," Wimbly said.

Jalen rose his chin. "Are you repeating what I'm saying?"

Wimbly said nothing. Impatience curled Jalen's fist.

"I'll risk it, you know. I'll risk my life for him."

Wimbly nodded in agreement.

The hum of lights, the quiet tension of muscles, and the scrape of shoe and talon filled the concrete gulf between the two. The abomination's pin-point eyes locked with Jalen's. Jalen considered if the creature had known where he was at all points of the night and didn't choose to appear to him until now, Reese must be near.

"Time to test a theory," he muttered.

Jalen hunched down, exhaled, then pushed forward into a sprint. The air parted for him as he tried to juke and blow past Wimbly. Few men on the planet were as tall, fast, and strong as Jalen was, but Wimbly was no man. The moment Jalen broke past the beast, its gnarled arm stretched, as if bone was not a part of its structure, and its massive, vein-covered claw back-handed him away. Jalen flew several feet and landed on his shoulder. There was a snapping sound that accompanied the thud.

"FUCK," Jalen yelled as he writhed on the floor.

He had taken chops to the chest before; such a thing is part of the job description for a wrestler. Though Wimbly's smack felt more akin to a tackle from a football player, it wasn't the main source of his body's new pain: Jalen had landed awkwardly, and a familiar sensation radiated from his front shoulder blade and down his arm, all the way to the tips of his fingers.

"God, I had to land on *that* shoulder, didn't I?" he worked his way back to his knees and fought back the tears. He knew what happened: he re-tore the same rotator cuff that sidelined him from wrestling in high school.

Wimbly's dark-red coat swirled around its massive body as it turned. "Don't hurt Reese," it croaked, then disappeared into the lights. Jalen stared at the claw marks along the floor. They were the lines that Jalen had to cross if he wanted to save Reese.

{}

Jalen wandered back to the front of the lot. His brain spun as it designed strategies to defeat an enemy beyond his comprehension. His breath was ragged, his left arm had lost all sensation, and he was sure he'd find bruises along his hip and chest if he chose to look underneath the spandex.

Jalen caught a glimpse of himself in the reflection of the main office window, which was still flecked with red blood. He looked at the rib-cage motif of his Sir Mortimer outfit underneath the heavy jacket, and remembered that, so long ago, he expressed his concern over what Sir Mortimer's fate would be in Reese's universe. *Time to find out*, he thought.

He learned from his encounter with Wimbly that injury wasn't off the table. Even if the abomination didn't want to kill him, the numbness through Jalen's arm proved that death could easily find him anyway, whether it was Wimbly's intention or not. He concluded that this wasn't a fight he could win with physical strength.

He hopped up creaking stairs and over the mutilated body that propped the door open. The body in the doorway was partially deflated by its lack of a ribcage. A string of entrails were scattered across the hardwood floor.

"This thing is eating bones for some reason," Jalen tried to keep his stomach from turning. "I guess that's what that... *stuff* was in the hallway after he's eaten it. I don't know if it's better or worse than what I thought it was at first."

The air freshener, on its timed interval, sprayed Summer Joy Cotton Scent™ into the lobby. Jalen jumped in surprise at the sound of its mechanic hiss. The scent failed to cover up the stench of death, but that would not deter it from trying again in 10 minutes.

A middle-aged secretary in a gaudy Christmas sweater sat at the receptionist's desk, her arms removed, her jaw agape. Jalen noticed the glow of the computer monitor reflected on her bloody glasses. Reese's stream played on it, and as Jalen wandered around the counter, he figured the odds of this lady, while she was alive, being one of Reese's fans were slim at best.

"Sorry, mam," Jalen muttered as he pushed the corpse-containing chair away with his foot. He watched the stream's chat: thousands of viewers watched Reese's madness, and the stream of donations went far beyond Jalen's typical weekly salary. The audience was in love with what Jalen thought was certainly Reese's worst nightmare.

Jalen logged in.

The cute, floppy model of Wimbly faced forward, as if he could sense Jalen's presence in the viewing audience.

XCoffeeDropX donated $1!
"Let me talk to him."

The 3D models stopped their rave and parted like the red sea to show Reese's face. The faux-smile plastered on Reese glitched away, and his real terror, and his tear-stained cheeks, shown through.

"J-Jalen?" he sniffled.

Jalen rubbed his forehead. He was a little stunned this worked. "I guess I gotta respect this thing's hustle. It'll do anything for a buck."

XCoffeeDropX donated $1!
"I encountered it and lived. I think it knows who I am. It's smarter than it seems, but it's not quite human, either. What unit are you in?"

The chat room, a lightning rod of scrolling conversation, doubled in speed. They were in awe over the lengths of which Reese had gone for his new performance—he had even created a fake account to incorporate into the act! How innovate and wild! Was this even allowed by the site's terms of service?

"Get out of here!" Reese yelled at the camera. "Call the police! What the fuck is wrong with you? Go!"

XCoffeeDropX donated $1!
"I tried to call them already. It won't let me. But that's fine. I have a fuzzy idea of how Wimbly moves and thinks. Give me your unit number. I'm gonna save you."

Reese sniffled. "Twenty—he's way too strong—eight—please don't do this—R."

XCoffeeDropX donated $1!
"You know what's weird? I'm not scared. I have at least one thing in common with him. Don't worry, Sir Mortimer will win."

Jalen looked past the computer monitor. The doorway's view of the parking lot had been eclipsed by the abomination's frame.

"Bones," Wimbly clacked its beak.

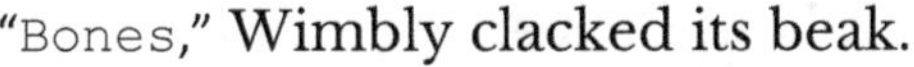

{38}

{BONES}

The screen flickered. Jalen, his body powered by pure adrenaline and the brief memory of the flickering lights in the unit hallway, reacted by flipping the monitor upwards. Two electric arms stretched out of the computer screen as it tumbled off the desk, grasping at a body that wasn't there. Wimbly pulled his arms back from electric portals and peered from the doorway.

"I never saw Daniel's body after he died," Jalen stepped out from behind the desk with a slow, careful pace, "but I do remember complaining to Reese about him. If you're going around killing people to protect him or protect the things he loves, don't you understand you're just putting Reese in more danger?"

"Don't," Wimbly tilted his head.

"What's your *real* goal? You move around in electronics. You're controlling his stream..." Jalen rubbed his chin as he scanned the lobby's options for exits. There weren't many: two closed windows and the door Wimbly stood in front of. "Are you a virus or something?"

"Bones," Wimbly's gnarled arm plunged and vanished into another electric portal. Jalen hit the floor, and felt the parting air of movement above his body. He turned to his back to see Wimbly's arm grope wildly from portal within the Wi-Fi router.

"How long do you want to do this?" Jalen shimmied away from the claw-possessed router. "I know how you move. You know I'm not going to hurt Reese. So all this *really* boils down to is you're trying to keep me from stopping the stream, right?"

Wimbly retracted its arm and chattered. Jalen noticed the tell-tale flickering underneath its pulsing skin.

“Don’t,” Jalen held a hand up. “I won’t stop it. I promise.”

Wimbly blinked and leaned his head to the side and slobbered bone-matter from his beak. The two stared at each other in a moment of mutual observation. After some time, Wimbly turned into an arcing bolt of electricity and slipped inside the automatic air-freshener above the door. The device sprayed liquid laundry-scent into the air, as per schedule.

Jalen rubbed his face. He had told a lie, of course; he was still dead-set on saving Reese. He was lucky Wimbly seemed to have some childlike understanding of language, but beyond playing by the beast’s rules, he couldn’t think of a way to amicably pass it. There was no truce to be had and no way he could fight it head on.

He looked out the window, across the parking lot of empty cars and security golf carts. A dead body was draped over the steering wheel of one of the carts—he had only managed to drive it a few feet before Wimbly caught him.

Jalen took slow, careful steps out of the front lobby and walked toward the golf cart. The wires from the utility pole in the parking lot drifted in the night breeze. Lights that dotted the lobby flickered, and the clink of their tungsten gave way to the demands of a new power. Every direction Jalen turned his sweat-soaked head, he noticed a piece of technology that Wimbly could blink from at a moment’s notice. He could feel the heat of anger crackle in air, only restrained by Jalen’s relationship with Reese, and his promise to a beast.

“I’m going to take a cart back to my truck,” Jalen used a serious, clear voice like an owner does with a misbehaving cat. “Calm down.”

The lights stabilized.

Jalen sighed, and swallowed.

Security golf carts are designed for relatively slow speeds. Most are incapable of breaching 20 miles-per-hour. As such, the slow putter of the machine made it easy for Jalen to steer with one hand, and easier still to slowly adjust the curve of the wheel towards the utility pole. He stopped roughly twenty feet from the pole, then put his hands on the ignition key.

"I changed my mind," he ripped the key out. "I'm *definitely* going to stop the stream."

The security cart rumbled from hood to rear-wheel, as if it threatened to fall apart. The headlights blinked. Jalen flung himself from the driver's seat and watched two gnarled claws punch through the hood. Electric sparks salted the air as Wimbly grasped at the emptiness in the drivers seat. Jalen crawled until he felt his back meet the resistance of the wooden pole. The abomination ripped the hood off the car and pulled its form completely into the real world. Its heavy claws slammed into the concrete, and debris flew.

When Jalen first encountered Wimbly, he thought it was a specter. Though he didn't believe in such things, his mind had to fill in the blank, and the nebulous concept of a ghost was the closest he could rationalize Wimbly to be. Whatever it was, whatever its secrets were, no longer mattered. This foolish gamble, based off of nothing other than his observations in Wimbly's behaviour, was his one shot.

Wimbly's white iris's shrunk as it stomped towards Jalen. It curled its right claw into a massive boulder-like fist and shook with rage. To Jalen's surprise, it stopped and hesitated as it stared at him, eyes twitching as it tried to understand his intentions. It was marred by indecision.

"I'll make sure Reese never streams again," Jalen bit down on his back teeth.

Wimbly's form flickered like a dying bulb. Jalen noticed this—the creature's ever present tell right before it lost control—and rolled to the side as Wimbly swung. It punched the utility pole with such force that it snapped in half. Sparks flew. Wires snapped. The pole crashed over the chain-link fence at the front gate and bent it into the dirt. The lights atop the lobby office, in the hallways of the facility, and all across the parking lot expired, their life-blood cut.

Wimbly's form evanesced. The creature ululated in bass-filled pain as its limbs stuttered and separated. Jalen watched with an expression of bittersweet malaise as Wimbly was reduced to chaotic electric sparks. It arced through the sky, likely towards the nearest active current it could find.

Jalen used his one good arm to push himself to his feet and ran toward the darkness of the storage facility. If this building had a backup generator, then he only had 20 seconds at most to find Reese. He prayed the owners were cheap enough to skimp out on emergency power.

{}

Reese panted and squirmed in his chair. His cherub face was awash in the glow of his battery-powered laptop; it stippled each bead of sweat on his face with a dot of light, and made them indistinguishable from the tear stains down his cheeks. When the power went out, he took only a moment to register its absence; so burdened by the terror of Wimbly, he was consumed by the singular desire to get out of the chair. He was certain the bone-goo had loosened somewhat, as his shakes began to allow the chair to wobble.

When the power went out, so did the life of the stream. The models fell to the floor of the program's window like puppets whose strings were cut. Reese reacted to the sight with a gasp of surprise. The lifeless, inanimate models looked like hope, but it lasted only a moment; he caught a glimpse of movement on the screen.

"Bones," Wimbly growled through the laptop speakers as it pushed the offline corpses off its tiny form. It was the original Wimbly model, cute and soft, no edge to be found on its round body.

"No..." Reese's lungs sucked for air in panic as he rocked the chair again. "No, no, no, no...!"

Wimbly's form began to toughen as it climbed out of the boundaries of the program window. Its proportions lengthened, and the polygons gained organic texture as they stretched. Bloody red veins pumped its muscles to new strength. It flickered, then pushed its electric arm through the laptop screen. It gripped the arm of Reese's chair and began to pull.

"No!" Reese cried. "No! Jalen! Anyone! Please! Help!"

Wimbly pulled itself out of the laptop, sparking, slimy, growling. The screen defied its solid characteristics and parted for the beast like a cheesecloth does for a finger, then settled back to its original flat form. The creature distorted the properties of everything around it, of reality itself. If there was consistency in its existence, Reese couldn't find it, and as it climbed toward Reese, he, as the creator, blamed himself for its impossible nature.

Wimbly towered over him with its doubled height. It straddled him, and bent over to glare down at its creator. The chair creaked. It craned its long neck down, its foul scythe of a beak inches from Reese's face. Reese screamed. He screamed and cried and begged until Wimbly seized the bottom of his face with the palm of its powerful claw. Its thumb curled around his cheek, and the dagger-digits clutched the top of Reese's head. Reese could feel the warmth of the creature's fingers press gently into the roots of his hair, and Reese was sure that if it put even a quarter of the pressure it was capable of into a squeeze, that his skull would crush like an acorn under the sole of a shoe. Wimbly pushed the bottom of his palm with just enough pressure to force

Reese's mouth closed. Then, it opened its beak. Its eyes pinned. It bobbed its long neck, its whole body rocked and wobbled the bone-sealed chair, and then finally, it hacked bone-material onto Reese's lips. Reese screamed again, but was now muted, muffled as the sour, sticky bone-gelatin sealed his mouth shut.

Wimbly rose from the seat, turned its back to Reese, pulled its red cloak taut around its body, and waited.

"Bones..." it seethed.

{}

"Reese? Anyone?" Jalen pulled his face near each unit placard he came across in order to read the numbers. Though the darkness debilitated him, when he considered Wimbly's ability to hide in bulbs and electrical current, he was certain it was safer to be in shadows than in the light. He knocked on units in case there were other survivors, but no matter how far down he traveled in units, the only response was the echo from closed shutters and close quarters.

He turned a corner and pressed his face to the wall. "24-4-R. He has to be in this hallway."

{}

Reese heard a distant voice, and was certain it was Jalen's. He tried to scream out a warning to run, but he could only make sounds of muffled distress. He had no way to tell Jalen that Wimbly had taken up refuge in the battery of his laptop.

Curiously, Wimbly did not, or rather, *could not* walk to the door. It tried to, but as it wandered away from the laptop, its form began to static, glitch, tug as if it were anchored down to the device. It paused, contemplated the problem, and stretched thin across the room; its legs remained near Reese, but its upper body distorted like pulled taffy. It raised its fists high in the air. They clenched and shook as it waited for Jalen to arrive.

After a few minutes, knuckles rapped with light curiosity twice on the steel door. Reese's eyes widened in horror.

"Reese?" Jalen asked from the hallway side of the door.

"Bones."

Wimbly punched the door clean off its hinges. The steel projectile slammed Jalen backwards into the opposite hallway wall. He crumpled underneath the bent frame. Reese could only see his boyfriend's legs underneath the door, and had no way of knowing if Jalen was dead or unconscious. Reese screamed with volume lost in the bone-matter of others sealed around his mouth.

"Bones!" Wimbly cawed. He lurched forward with his talon claws, but fell. His electric jaw hit the floor—his warped form was stretched as far as it would go, anchored by the laptop. It dug its talons into concrete and tried to pull, and the laptop started to edge forward on Reese's desk.

Reese heard the scuff of the shifting laptop on the small table. He leaned forward and stretched his hands out. The corner grazed the tips of his fingers. As Wimbly pulled, its light-form body so thinly stretched across the room that it pixelated, Reese was able to get his fingers to the track-pad of the laptop, and eventually, the keyboard. Wimbly salivated bone and blood out of its panting beak, consumed by the need to eat the structure of the one who betrayed it, who betrayed its creator.

Reese closed the streaming software in hopes it would kill Wimbly, but it had no impact on the vulture-mage's form. He tried to shut off the laptop, but Wimbly's influence forced the mouse away.

"BONES!" it shouted, as if to somehow console Reese, or warn him, or both.

Reese's hand hovered over the keys. *Bones*, he raced his mind in a last ditch effort, *why bones? Why does it want bones?*

Reese looked back to where Jalen laid. He was frustrated, embarrassed at his uselessness, and horrified to see Wimbly's claws barely out of reach of his boyfriend's leg. He noticed Jalen's purple boot twitched with faint life. There was a familiar bone pattern on his thick spandex-clad calf. *Very* familiar.

He keeps saying 'Bones,' but he clearly vomits them, too, Reese blinked tears of realization away and opened the programs he used to make 3D models. He loaded the master file for Wimbly, and the creature's form, in response, wobbled and distorted. Wimbly felt this from deep within itself, as if it were somehow laid bare to the world, exposed, revealed.

"...Bones?" Wimbly whimpered as he turned back around to face Reese.

Reese looked to the creature. They made brief eye contact. The sound and tone Wimbly made was of profound vulnerability, the weakness of a kitten's mew, distorted only by his gravely, electronic voice.

In the program window, Wimbly's model flopped and wobbled like gelatin, a quality it gained from its unfinished nature. In a separate window, Reese opened the file of Sir Mortimer. The abomination crawled back towards the computer with slow curiosity. It didn't caw, it didn't scream, it didn't attack. With quiet reverence, it merely watched its creator at work.

Reese copied Sir Mortimer's rig—his 'bones'—over to Wimbly's model. The fit wasn't quite right; Sir Mortimer's rig, born of different proportions, stretched and distorted the cartoon vulture-mage in odd ways. It would need polish to look right, but, more than anything else, it existed. Wimbly had structure, form, grounding in the virtual world.

Immediately, the abomination became statuesque. It stopped breathing. Its eyes no longer blinked or pinned or contemplated. It became, in that moment, a massive electric doll made of gnarled flesh and strange energy. Reese stuck out a trembling hand and touched Wimbly's knee cap, and the creature did not react. It was stiff to the touch, warm like an oven, and equally as despondent. Now that it obtained the structure it pined for, its sentience seeped away into nothingness.

Reese took a deep breath and experimented: with the mouse, it was able to click on the 3D Wimbly and move its claws. The abomination moved in conjunction, and Reese used its sharp talons to cut an opening in the bone-matter that kept him glued in the chair. Once free, Reese carefully used one of the claw-tips to cut the bone-matter gag off his face, then ran to the door that pinned Jalen. Reese could hear him moan in pain as the two lifted the door.

"Jalen, oh my god," Reese sobbed, "are you okay?"

"No," Jalen groaned, blood flowing from his mouth and cuts on his forehead. "Everything hurts."

Reese bent down and served as a crutch for Jalen to hobble back to his feet. The two stared at Wimbly, whose electric form gave off a soft blue glow. It was the only illuminance in the room or the hallway, aside from Reese's laptop. Bone-material flaked off Reese's cheeks.

"...that thing dead?" Jalen muttered. "What'd you do?"

Reese helped Jalen limp into the rolling chair. He stuttered as he told the truth, because it, like everything else, seemed too preposterous to believe. "I just... gave it what it needed. I put the bones in its model."

Silence fell as the two stared at the architecture of Wimbly's frame.

"So," Jalen wiped blood from his lips onto his shirt, "we should probably figure out a way to... you know. Kill it. Get rid of it. Something."

Reese hesitated. "But... I can control it."

Jalen tilted his head at Reese. "...So?"

"I mean, it's incredible, isn't it?" Reese popped his knuckles against his hip-bone. "Horrifying, but there probably isn't anything else in existence like it. We could use it? Or sell it to... whatever branch of science looks at stuff like this. I don't know. We have this giant, virtual monster, it seems like a waste to get rid of it when there's so much that could be learned from it."

"You have no idea, do you?"

Reese blinked. "About?"

"About how many fucking people are dead because of that thing."

The creator recoiled. "*What*?"

"I think it killed Daniel, and the deer. I know it wiped out all the employees here, because I saw their corpses along the way," Jalen dotted his forehead with the towel. He could feel the heat of his blood against the fiber of the cotton. "We might be the only people alive on site."

Reese looked from Jalen, to Wimbly, then to the floor. He crouched down and covered his face. "Oh my god. This is all my fault."

Jalen sighed through his nostrils.

"This is all my fault," Reese rolled forward into a fetal position. "If I had stayed home... if I had just stayed home and finished Wimbly, none of this would have happened..."

"Hey, don't say that," Jalen muttered.

Reese rose. New tears trickled down his face. He waved his hands wildly and started to pace. "I should... go turn myself in to the police, right? That's the right thing to do. Someone needs to take the blame for this, and I made Wimbly, so..."

"I said SHUT UP!"

Jalen's voice echoed down the hallways and across the steel walls of Reese's unit. Reese's hands fell around his waist.

"Now listen here! I went through *hell* to save you," Jalen chewed on his bottom lip between words. He could feel the blood in his mouth underneath his tongue, metallic and hot. "I didn't risk my goddamn life to watch you throw yours away! Okay? Listen! Listen. You're not responsible for this. This was out of your control. Now here's what we're gonna fuckin' do—"

Jalen tried to stand, but his leg refused his weight. He buckled backwards into the rolling chair, and he would have rolled right out of the room had Reese not caught the armrest and held him in place. He exhaled, and found a calmer voice. "*This* is what we're gonna do. You're gonna go over there and take your laptops and bash them until they can't turn on anymore. Use a hammer, or brick, or whatever we can find. If that kills Wimbly, great. If it doesn't, we know he's locked into the device, so we'll... chuck it in a fire or something. Your phone, too. Anything electronic in here has to go. We can easily start a fire in a dumpster, I'm sure they have one here. After that, you're gonna move the boxes most important to you into my car. You can drive, right? You can drop me off at the hospital and then go back to my place and move your stuff in. We'll figure the rest out later."

Reese trembled as he looked across the room at his laptop.

"A-alright," he sniffled, "I think I have a USB stick or something, let me just back up my work and—"

"No. You're not backing up anything."

Reese turned. "W-what...?"

"You have no idea how this happened, right?" Jalen punched the armrest. "No risks. You don't know what you're dealing with. You can say you have control over this thing, but there's *a landfill* of bodies out there that say otherwise. No, you're gonna break that thing, and you're gonna break any backups you have, too. Get rid of all of it. It's the only safe way."

Reese's head shook involuntarily as he stared at Jalen. This indecision, this refusal to advance forward, angered Jalen.

"What the hell are you waiting for?"

"Jalen, it's..." Reese gripped the hem of his shirt, "you're asking me to get rid of my life's work. This is all I have."

Jalen, in that moment, remembered Matteo's words, and understood them in a new way. When he looked at Reese, he no longer saw the maker, he saw the smoke drift from Matteo's cigarette. He saw not the artist, but himself, the employee, working at a coffee shop to balance his nightly passions. He didn't see his boyfriend, or even a person anymore. He saw debt. He saw the debt Reese had accumulated, and he saw the way that reality bent itself inwards just to collect.

"You can make new shit. If you want to move on, though, then Wimbly, and the stream, and hiding out in a storage unit because you're fucking scared of the world... you have to let go of all of that, first," Jalen said. "I should've been more harsh with you in the park that night. I should've made you move in with me then, or move to a real apartment, or... something. Something! Anything! Anything else than this! You will never, *ever* grow up if you keep hiding away in here. You are more than what you've made, but only if you *want* to be."

Reese looked between Jalen's battered body, and the frozen, electric statue of Wimbly. *This shouldn't be a decision*, Reese harassed himself, *this shouldn't be difficult.*

"Do it," Jalen said.

Reese dragged himself over to the laptop. He knew he didn't have a hammer, so he did the only thing he could think of—he shut the lid and raised it above his head. He stared at the concrete below his feet, and cried as he spiked the past several years of his imagination, and the last gift his father ever gave him, downwards.

The splintering of metal and plastic parts echoed in the dark hallways.

{39}

{PROMOTIONS}

"You put me in a bind, you son of a bitch," Matteo muttered as he tossed a bouquet of flowers on top of Jalen. A bubbly-lettered, pastel card sat in the middle of the yellow-and-white flowers. It was adorned with holographic cartoon cats and read 'Get well soon!'

It was a clear, late morning at Dundolk Hospital. Birds fluttered and sang in the black cherry tree near the window. Warm light streaked in over Jalen's leg casts and shoulder bandages. The sun made it difficult to see the TV, but daytime television didn't interest him anyway—he kept the local news on as background noise, and preferred the warmth across his skin.

"If I don't hear back from some of the calls I made this morning," Matteo said, "I might have to cut an entire match out of the card, or get in the damn ring myself."

"I'd rather take bumps today, I promise," Jalen said as the IV-pump beeped punctuation. "Fewer broken bones."

"What the hell happened?" Matteo reflexively reached for a cigarette, remembered it was against the law to smoke in hospitals, then stuffed his hands back in his polyester pockets.

"I was helping my boyfriend move into my apartment and, well, I fell," Jalen sighed. "And I fell, and I fell, and continued to fall for about four or five years, it felt like. Concrete steps hurt a hell of a lot more than Sean's suplex."

Matteo turned his head. Reese sat in a chair with his forearms on his knees, his blonde hair ruffled from a sleepless night. Matteo noticed that the color was drained from his face—what little he could see of it from its downward tilt, at least.

"Should make you get in the ring, then," Matteo nodded towards him, "for taking out one of my guys. Make Sean toss you around for 10 minutes or so."

"I'd deserve it," Reese mumbled. Matteo furrowed his brow—it wasn't quite the reaction he expected to his joke.

"Well, uh," Matteo tried to recover, "I didn't come here to razz you too hard. Get better soon, man. We're lookin' pretty good for tonight on sales, and that's thanks to your promotional work, as usual. As soon as you're out we can start talking about where to go from there."

"Actually," Jalen tapped the steel bar beside his hospital bed, "after I'm cleared, I'd like to try and get in the ring."

Matteo walked around the bed to get a different view of Jalen's face, just to make sure it was the same person. "*Really*."

"I wasn't kidding when I said I believe in this character," Jalen smiled.

Matteo rubbed his mustache in thought, then nodded. "Alright. We'll talk about it once you're clear. Till then..." he gave a weak salute and left the two alone.

{}

The previous night, Reese helped Jalen limp into the waiting room and stayed with him until he was whisked away for surgery. He drifted in and out of sleep. Then, in the early morning hours, after shaking himself awake, he returned to the car and took out his phone. He may not have had his laptops anymore, but he still had his login credentials and a cell phone camera—enough to record a notice for his channel.

"Hey," Reese drug out on a loose smile on his worn face, "I'm just recording this to say... thanks. Thank you to everyone who watched and supported the stream last night. As you may have noticed, it was quite a different show than normal—I collaborated with a local artist I met as a test for future projects. Clearly, you guys liked it, so thank you for tuning in. This has taken a long time to put together though, so don't expect this sort of thing again anytime soon. We're gonna take what we learned and make something new, so... stay tuned. Peace."

He stopped recording and stared at his digital reflection. His hair had grown back in disarray since his last haircut. Blonde roots were visible on his tuft of green hair. He frowned at the person in his video. On the other side of the screen, Reese saw a miserable person, doughy and tired, a reflection he had not been forced to look at in a long, long time. He replayed the video a few times, growing more disappointed with the person he saw with each watch. After the third play-through ended, he sucked in a lungful of air, then hit upload. It was the last video he'd ever put up on the *SKELEVENTURE* channel.

{}

Neither Jalen, nor Reese, attended the charity show for Daniel.

With Jalen in the hospital and Molly aware of the fact Reese knew how to handle the register, Reese volunteered to substitute for Jalen while he was out. It was the first time he had been hired properly in many years and, though he and Molly never gelled on a personal level, they professionally synced up quite well. Both kept their heads down and did their work. They never talked about anything other than what needed to be done to get through the cafe's open hours, and at this point in their lives, that was all either of them wanted. Reese tried not to stare at Molly's missing finger, and frequently failed.

{}

Dundolk police never found Daniel's killer. They were quickly overwhelmed with new work when Store-It's facilities succumbed to a massive electrical fire. Lost in the flames were several company lives and millions of dollars in customer inventory. Mr. Carter Victoria Jr. declined to comment on the matter to local news outlets.

{}

Jalen was discharged from the hospital a week later. On a crutch, he would do his best to ease back into work life, but never to the same level as before, or in the same capacity. Reese exclusively drove for the two, buying groceries, taking them to work and to the DEF gym.

Reese had imagined that to move in with Jalen would be a celebration, an event, one culminated by a meal at a restaurant, or a party at an arcade, followed by a night of passion. Instead, Reese cooked curry from an online recipe and they watched old wrestling matches together. The curry wasn't spicy enough. They slept facing away from each other. Jalen kept the temperature quite low at night despite the winter season, and Reese wondered if the heater was on at all. He would stare every night at the moon as it hovered over the fence which bordered the apartment property and spent 20-30 minutes shivering before he could finally sleep.

Once Jalen was healed up enough to work full-time again, he took on an assistant manager role at Jolly Molly's, which allowed him direct supervision over the cafe's only subordinate: his boyfriend. Jalen brought Reese to the DEF, too—as Jalen spent more time training and bulking for the express purpose of in-ring work, that left less time for him to function as video editor for the promotion. How convenient it was that his boyfriend knew a thing or two about video editing; with a little training, Reese became his replacement. The two would carpool together to the gym after work at Jolly Molly's, share a light, puckered kiss, then march into DEF with work-focused silence.

{}

Reese bought a small sketchbook and carried it with him everywhere he went. His plan was to use the gaps between his life at Jolly Molly's and the DEF to come up with new ideas for content, new characters, new worlds. He sketched Sir Mortimer and Wimbly a few times, lost his pencil, and never found the will to replace it. The book became a burden he carried with him everywhere he went: always present, always blank. He never bought a new laptop. He did, however, over time, learn how to make quite a few curries.

{}

On a hot night in a packed gym, Jalen introduced his new skeleton-knight character against Sean's Sir Pierre. The knight, now named Horatio, scored considerable offense on DEF's top heel in an 8-minute barnstormer, before he ultimately lost to a low-blow the referee didn't see. Despite the name change, he was the real-life incarnation of Reese's Sir Mortimer. The crowd loved his goofy, dancing persona, his gallantry, his muscular build and surprising acrobatics. Reese saw it all from behind the desk. Though he adjusted cameras, controlled lights, and edited footage, he had no control over the actions of the former Sir Mortimer. Jalen never asked him if he could use the design, and never explained the name change. They never talked about it. Things were fine. They just moved on.

A month after Horatio's debut, Jalen found the strength to ask Matteo for business partnership in the DEF. "I write scripts. I've done promotional work. I'm on the roster. My character's popular. I've recruited staff. I have tenure. And, most importantly, I have a vision."

Matteo was more than happy to strike a deal. Ever since Daniel's death, he refused to be in the building alone. He didn't believe in ghosts, and had no interest in being proven wrong on the subject. The presence he felt, a fusion of his parental and business regrets, hung around the corners of the gym, particularly around the darkened side-exit near storage. He refused to confront it. *Let it be Jalen's problem*, he thought. With control of the budget, Jalen paid, at long last, to have the power in the storage hallway fixed. The lights still flickered occasionally.

Jalen's new power, and income, meant more money for the couple to play with. This didn't change much in Reese's life—independent wrestling, especially one of DEF's size and scope, would never move them out of an apartment. Still, Reese could afford to make larger dishes. Sometimes he and Jalen would go out to see a movie, or have dinner. But they'd never return to Harper Park. Jalen was never up for Pizzapolis, or *Gradius*. If he was anywhere, doing anything, he was usually at the DEF, and there, usually in the gym.

The largest change that Reese noticed under Jalen's management was the outcome of Horatio's matches. The skeleton-knight, who had been battered by Fang Wylin's backhands and knee-strikes for roughly twelve minutes, surprised all in attendance when he, while face down on the mat in a familiar setup for Fang's camel clutch submission, twisted with a second wind, hooked Fang's leg, rolled him up to his broad shoulders, and secured a surprise pin-fall for a victory that popped the room, children and adults alike, with cheers and applause. The predetermined outcome was even hidden from Reese, who sat stone face behind a computer screen.

Horatio ran across the ring and pantomimed excitement and surprise underneath the skeletal mask. He hopped up onto the second turnbuckle and held his hands up in the glow of victory. Blue spotlights rained down on his shoulders. He looked down with his painted yellow eyes, cartoon dots of curiosity, to stare into a camera and give a thumbs up.

Reese was not far beyond that lens. Seated behind a computer screen, he had a clear view of Horatio. He looked up and met eyes with the creature who wore painted, inspired skin. Reese studied the vague shape of his hero; his eyes lazed along the curves of painted-on bones around massive pecs and biceps and traps and calves and quads. Horatio-Jalen was man, and skeleton, and hero, and boyfriend, and boss all at once, and Reese conceded to this because what else could he have done? Who else was he? He was a man behind a desk, in the background, out of sight, hidden in the credits, and lost in the shuffle, safe, silent. Despite the halo of light, and the children's cheers, and the adults' applause, and the echoes of joy in the room, and the comfort of his life, and the security of his jobs, and the pat of Matteo's calloused hand on his shoulder in congratulation for another successful show, the muscles in Reese Gagnon's face did not twitch. He didn't applaud or rise from his chair. He did not cheer, and made no change in his demeanor or expression, for he felt nothing at all.

How could he?

It was just another normal day at work.

{}

`Save complete.`

ABOUT THE AUTHOR

Millard Crow is an author, journalist, and artist.
He has never been attacked by a vulture, and would like to keep it that way.
You can find out more about him at crowspaceboy.com

▲

OTHER WORKS BY MILLARD CROW:

THE NEXT GREAT DEITY

(The Next Great Deity #1)

THE ANGELS ARE VOYEURS

(The Next Great Deity #2-coming soon!)

ACKNOWLEDGEMENTS

If you discovered a critique of capitalist, competitive societies in this novel, it will be because of the influence of the work of Michael Brooks in my life. Michael passed away in July while I was compiling the final work-document of this book for print. He will never see this. I've never met him, and now, as I am writing this, I know I never will. He was a hero to me for his clear, passionate, and empathetic worldview in a time where the world is none of those things. I am heartbroken and, in this moment, find great difficulty in continuing on in a dimmer world. Luckily, if Michael taught me anything, it's that if something is difficult, that's all the more reason to face it head-on. So, onward I type.

"Be ruthless with systems. Be kind with people," he said. Clearly, I agree with him.

Thank you Michael for all that you have done, and all that you've inspired in others.

Thank you to all my friends who helped make this possible.

Thank you to everyone that has enabled me this far. I will go further, still.

And finally but most importantly, thank you for reading.

{}